UNTIL YOU

UNTIL
BOOK 1

BRIAR PRESCOTT

Copyright © 2023 by Briar Prescott

All rights reserved.

No part of this book may be reproduced in any form or by any electronic or mechanical means, including information storage and retrieval systems, without written permission from the author, except for the use of brief quotations in a book review.

This is a work of fiction. Any resemblance to persons, living or dead, or business establishments, events or locations, is coincidental.

All trademarks are the property of their respective owners.

Cover artist: Cormar Covers

Editing: Kate Wood

Proofreading: Heather Caryn

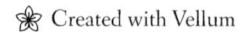

❀ Created with Vellum

*To Alexandra, Michelle, Kristy, Kuba, and Valentina.
Without you, this book would not exist.*

ABOUT THIS BOOK

I'm the first one to tell you I have issues. Trust issues. Family issues. Probably a few others I haven't discovered yet. Which is why I prefer to keep my life as simple and uncomplicated as possible.

Until him.

Blake McAdams barrels into my life and refuses to leave. He's relentlessly optimistic, incredibly smart, annoyingly persistent, and... wants to be friends? Because... he thinks I'm interesting?

Yeah, I'll pass. Thanks.

Only, somehow, we end up doing just that.

And then that friendship evolves into something more, and suddenly, I find myself navigating completely foreign territory: a relationship.

But Blake has his own issues, and once the truth comes out, my simple and uncomplicated life? Turns into anything but.

Before

ONE

Every life has a before and an after.

An invisible line that divides a life into two halves: the before and the after.

Catalysts vary. Small, big, seemingly insignificant at first, invisible, cataclysmic—all of them life-changing in the end.

It can be anything. Getting a new job. Moving to another state. Another country. Having a baby. The guy that smiles at you in line at the bank turns out to be your soulmate. Or you might simply be in the wrong place at the wrong time. The mole hidden in your hair turns out to be cancerous. You step onto the street at the wrong time, get hit by a car, and walking will suddenly turn into something other people do, but you can't anymore.

Maybe there's a path mapped out for all of us, and we follow it, crossing off life events one after another until our road ends.

A dead-end street on the map of life.

Maybe it's random.

One of those mysteries of life.

Unexpected.

Unpredictable.

Unexplainable.

Whatever it is, however it plays out, some moments leave a permanent mark and change you forever.

For better or worse?

Time will tell.

One day.

When you look back.

My line was drawn when I was seventeen.

I didn't see it back then. The line is invisible while it's being drafted. It's only in hindsight that you can detect it, locate it, dissect it.

Later, you can break it apart. Disassemble it into smaller pieces. Analyze and scrutinize. Take it apart like a puzzle and put it back together. Try to make sense of it if you're brave enough. Ignore it if you're not.

The first dot in my line was my name. Spoken in a hushed voice in the dead of night, stopping me in the hallway, one foot in the air, frozen to the spot.

"What about Jude?" Mom whispered.

Eavesdroppers never hear any good of themselves.

Sound advice. I ignored it. I'd always been too curious for my own good.

I slowly put my foot down, avoiding the creaky floorboard on my left that'd gotten me in trouble before, and took two steps back until I was right next to my parents' bedroom door.

Mom sighed—a long, tremulous exhale that seemed to sweep out from the crack in the door. Goosebumps dotted my forearms, and the back of my neck tingled uncomfortably. Call it a hunch, but I had a bad feeling about this.

"We promised Jude we wouldn't move again."

There it is.

My shoulders slumped, and I closed my eyes. Silent curses gathered on the tip of my tongue. My nails dug into my palms.

Fucking, fucking, fuck! They were really going to do this to me again?

"I know," Dad said.

"We. Promised."

"I know," Dad repeated, patient as ever. He was the rock of the family. Always calm and steady, like one of those lighthouses that stood on a stone platform just off the coast. Battered by murderous waves for a hundred years or so, it showed no signs of crumbling. That was how I'd always thought of my dad. Infinite calm in every storm. A guiding light. Whatever problem I had, whatever trouble I got into, he was always there, ready to point me in the right direction to untangle the mess.

The bed creaked, sheets rustled, and I took a step back, calculating the distance between me and the stairs. If either of them came out, could I make it into my room in time?

And then what? Pretend I know nothing and act surprised when they break the news?

No. Not happening. Let them find me. Let them catch me. They'd promised me. *They'd promised!* Promised we'd stay. Just this once.

I liked Portland. Maine was cool, unlike some other places we'd lived in over the years. I wanted to finish high school here. I'd spent my whole life being the new kid, and I was so sick of it. I finally had friends. I was doing well at school. I didn't want to leave it all behind again.

And for what?

The three of us? We weren't important people. Dad worked in a warehouse, and Mom was an office manager. I went to high school. There was nothing extraordinary about any of us. We'd never once moved for a career opportunity or to be closer to family. We went because… To be honest, I didn't really know why we kept uprooting our lives all the time.

Mom and Dad were restless souls. Ever since I could remember, we'd always been after the next adventure. Every year or so, we'd pack all our belongings, stuff them in the back of our car, and go. It'd be another pointless city in a chain of many, and even before we'd arrived, I'd have one foot out the door because I knew we wouldn't stay. We never did. Once a city started feeling familiar, it was time to hit the road.

I had no idea what they were searching for. Or if they were searching for anything at all. Maybe it was just a serious case of wanderlust. Whatever it was, the outcome was always the same.

We left.

And I was tired.

"He's going to be so mad at us," Mom said.

Those mom-senses were doing their job tonight, seeing as "he" was getting pretty pissed right behind their door.

"I know." Dad sighed. "He'll come around. Jude's a good kid. Besides, it's high time for a new adventure."

There was a long pause. So long I almost gave up listening, ready to sneak away, go out to a party, and drink until I forgot the looming moving day, but then Mom spoke again. "We did good, didn't we?"

"Yeah, we did good. I see you in him, you know? Everything I love about you is in Jude, too. Kind. Compassionate. Smart as hell. Our kid's the full package."

"Our kid," Mom repeated, and I could hear the smile in her voice.

My head dropped forward, and the breath I'd been holding escaped silently from between my lips. Anger melted like a snowball in a desert. Not that I'd ever been one to hold a grudge for long. I may not have wanted to like them right then, but I'd always been aware that in the parental lottery, I'd won the jackpot. What Mom and Dad had... It was the kind of devoted, once-in-a-lifetime, I'd-do-anything-for-you type of love that wasn't supposed to exist in real life, but somehow, they'd found it with each other. And they loved me with the same heart-stopping force. I'd never had any doubts about that. Couldn't even if I'd wanted to, because they made sure I knew.

We had a great life. Even if it involved adjusting to new towns, new homes, and new lives a little more frequently than I would've preferred. At least we were in it together. I'd never once had to play the if-Mom-and-Dad-divorced-who-would-I-live-with game in my head. We were a team. A united front.

My shoulders slumped. Mom and Dad were the kind of parents who believed in being there. For every competition, recital, play, game, and whatever else I participated in. They always showed up. Usually with posters and other embarrassing and over-the-top paraphernalia, but I secretly loved that they did it. Even if it meant piano teachers in several states had had to hold parent-teacher conferences to discuss appropriate recital behavior. I didn't have any siblings or extended family, so the three of us were all we had in the world. No grandmothers or grandfathers, aunts or uncles, nephews, nieces, or cousins. Not that I'd ever felt the absence of a bevy of relatives. It was difficult to miss something you'd never had.

I swallowed a sigh and closed my eyes. Deep breaths. It was going to be okay. What was one more move? A year from now, I was going to be in college anyway, so if moving was what Mom and Dad needed to be happy... I would deal. I'd had plenty of practice, after all.

"He's the best thing we ever did," Mom whispered.

"Yes, he is."

"Right?" she continued. "He is."

I frowned and leaned closer to the door. It was technically a nice sentiment, if only it hadn't been delivered in a tone of a person trying very hard to convince themselves they were right.

"Abby..." Dad said.

"She's still out there," Mom cut him off. Her voice had gone so soft I had to really strain to hear her. "She got her life together, by the looks of it. She's married. Did you know that?"

The silence stretched on for a long time before Dad said, "Good for her," in a measured voice. "I'm glad she's well. It doesn't mean anything. You're not supposed to look her up."

"I know, but aren't you the least bit curious?"

"No. It's in the past. Where it belongs."

Mom sighed. "Grant..."

"Can we drop it?" Dad said.

Another stretch of silence. Were they done talking? Now? Really?

"Jude will be done with high school. He's got all these dreams and plans," Mom said. "He's been talking about Berklee..."

"You say that like it's a bad thing. He'll do what all people do at eighteen. Fly the nest. Find himself. Grab life with both hands and enjoy the ride. Means we've done our job right. We've always known he would go, and if he's talking about Berklee, more power to him. The boy's talented as hell. He better do something with it."

"Grant," Mom repeated.

"Abby. Drop it. We've gone over this hundreds of times. It's fine."

My heartbeat was thudding in my ears, hammering loudly, drowning out sounds.

"I shouldn't have snapped," Dad murmured after a second.

"It doesn't matter," Mom said. "I shouldn't have brought it up. I know how you get."

"And I know how you get. Heck, *you* know how you get, so why do you keep doing this to yourself?"

"I know. Just…"

"Jude deserves a great life. He's a good kid. He's well-adjusted. He's happy. He's *our* kid. That's all that matters."

"I know. Ignore me. I'm being silly. It's the middle of the night. You know it's not my best time of the day."

"You go full-on reverse-Pollyanna. Believe me, I know."

Mom laughed softly and murmured, "Smartass."

"Yes, but I'm your smartass."

"Yes, you are."

I backed away because I had *not* signed up for all the kissing noises that followed.

My plan to sneak out and go to the party disappeared under the noise in my brain. Back in my room, I lay down on the bed and stared at the ceiling, seeing nothing. The pieces of the conversation I'd just overheard flew around in my head, arranging themselves this way and that while a sick feeling twisted my stomach into knots I couldn't untangle.

None of it made sense.

Or maybe I just didn't want it to make sense.

TWO

"Here's the deal. If you're adopted—and I'm not saying that you are, but if you *are*—you have two options." Stephen shot but missed.

I caught the ball when it bounced off the backboard and dribbled past him.

"Yeah? And what are those?" I huffed, threw the ball, and watched it sail through the net without touching the hoop.

"You can either ignore it and wait until your folks bring it up themselves, or you can confront them."

I caught the ball and tossed it to Steph. "I can't ask them," I grunted and wiped the hem of my shirt over my face.

"Because?"

"They clearly don't want him to know, genius." Blair yawned. She was lying on the grass next to Steph's driveway, half-asleep, half-alert. Ready to insert her thoughts if we happened to say something that interested her.

"So? It's not just about them," Steph countered. He gripped the ball in his right hand and pointed it toward me. "You have the right to know."

I dragged my palms over my face and rubbed the bridge of

my nose. A headache had been brewing at the back of my neck for the better part of a week. Thoughts circled and crashed, got up and made extra rounds, until it felt like my head was going to burst open. I'd gone over everything I'd heard when I was standing behind that door too many times to count, hoping and wishing I'd misinterpreted something, but after a week I still hadn't found a way to twist the truth into something more palatable.

It was highly, highly likely Mom and Dad weren't my biological parents.

And if that was the case... Who was I? Did it matter that Mom, Dad, and I didn't share DNA? Logically, no. But then again, yes, it kinda felt like it really did. But it also didn't, because no matter what, they were still Mom and Dad. I still loved them. It didn't matter that somewhere out there was a stranger who'd given birth to me. Only it did.

Should I let it go? Should I ask questions? Would they ever tell me if I didn't? Could I just... not say anything?

What'd happen if I did?

There was a whole landscape of unknowns in front of me, and I didn't know where to start exploring. Or if I even *wanted* to explore.

I squeezed my eyes shut and thumped my fist against my forehead. I'd been doing that a lot lately. Trying to knock my thoughts out of my head. It wasn't going well.

I might not have known what I wanted to do, but there was one thing I knew I didn't want to happen.

"Don't want to hurt them," I muttered.

"But you're curious." Steph came and stood next to me, nudging me with his shoulder until I looked at him. "You don't have to feel bad about it. I'd want to know if I were you."

It wasn't that I'd thought Steph or Blair would judge me, but it was still nice to know it was normal to feel this way. That

I wasn't being ungrateful or selfish for wanting to know the truth.

"Yeah, I'm curious." It's as good a word as any to describe the mess inside my head. *Curious*. It felt good to put a name to the feeling.

Blair pushed herself up on her elbows, long legs crossed casually, dark ponytail a tousled mess, and peered at me over the frames of her sunglasses. "You know, there are other ways to find lost family. You don't have to go straight to your parents."

"Ask a genie?"

"Order a DNA kit," Blair said like the reasonable person she was. With Blair, there was always an easy answer, and she could never quite understand how other people failed to see the obvious. "Send your sample in, and they'll see if they have matches for you on their database. See what happens with that and go from there."

And there it was. The easy answer. One that sounded simple. Doable.

I let out a breath—the one I'd been holding on and off for the past seven days—and my shoulders relaxed a bit as I nodded. That sounded like a plan, and the best part was, I didn't have to go to Mom and Dad right away. Anything that helped me postpone *that* conversation was a winner in my book, especially when I wasn't even sure if I was maybe just overreacting.

I nodded, and the knot in my stomach eased up a bit. "Okay, that's good. Because maybe I'm reading too much into it. It could just be a misunderstanding for all I know. This way I don't have to make it weird."

Stephen grinned. "Problem solved. Come on. Enough with the moping. You're bumming me out."

Blair rolled her eyes. "Well, God knows we can't have that."

"Time to get your ass kicked," Steph announced and tossed me the ball.

THREE

It was the last month of life as I knew it.

All my memories from that August had a dream-like quality to them. Bits and pieces stood out, while everything else melted into the background, getting hazier and hazier and then disappearing altogether.

A colorful box arrived in the mail—Steph's house, because my parents couldn't accidentally find out what I was up to.

The instructions were simple enough. Swipe a cotton swab on the inside of your cheek. Put the swab in a vial. Cap on. Into the envelope. Rinse and repeat.

Three weeks of waiting.

Sweaty palms and heart palpitations.

Nerves. Fear.

Then...

A match.

A name.

An email address.

Nausea, and then a strange calm.

Here's the proof you were after. In black and white. You're adopted.

Sitting up all night, working myself into a nervous mess, trying to write an email to a stranger. This woman I didn't even know. Wasn't sure if *she* even wanted to know about *me*.

After all, once upon a time, she'd given me away.

"Don't be a coward." Blair's words of wisdom when she clicked send for me.

An email in my inbox.

Staring at the unread email for hours before giving up because I was too nervous to open it.

Steph to the rescue.

His eyes moving over the words, his lips flattening into a thin line. The ever-present smile on his face slowly morphing into a tight frown when he exchanged glances with Blair.

Anxious looks sent my way, Steph's mouth opening and closing with no sounds coming out until I couldn't take it anymore. Grabbing the laptop to read the email myself.

Shaky hands and a shaky heart.

And words.

So many words.

Words that didn't make any sense.

Words that started wiggling and swimming around on the page the more I stared at them.

Because this was stupid.

Ridiculous.

Impossible.

Somebody had a sick sense of humor.

Somewhere, somebody had made a mistake, and those words on the screen? They were lies.

Lies.

Lies.

Lies.

Snapping the laptop shut so hard I broke the screen.

Ignore.

A week of my inbox filling with emails.
Delete.
Delete.
Delete.
Trying to act normal.
Mom and Dad sending me worried looks at the dinner table.
Their anxious eyes taking in the forced smile that had taken up permanent residence on my face.
Calmly listening to the news that we were moving. Michigan, this time.
Relief.
Suitcases in the trunk of the car. A few books and Dad's fern. We traveled light. Always had.
Almost done.
Almost gone.
The piercing sound of the doorbell echoed through the empty rooms that morning.
And then...
My life as I knew it?
Over.
Every life has a before and an after.
An invisible line that divides a life into two halves.
The before.
And the after.

After

FOUR

THERE'S ALWAYS one asshole at every costume party who doesn't dress up for the occasion. And then when somebody asks them who they're dressed as, they do that thing where they say they're dressed as 'a guy at a party,' or 'Jim from *The Office*.' Assholes that figure low effort is too much work, so they aim for no effort.

"Who are you supposed to be?" the half-naked sailor with the most obscene six-pack I've ever witnessed in my life yells over the loud beat of the music. He says something else, but I don't pay attention. I'm too busy appreciating his abs. You could grate cheese on those bad boys. And because that's not enough, said six-pack is framed by two perfectly symmetrical V-cuts.

I've seen my fair share of those over the years, so I feel like I'm qualified to say that these are top tier V-cuts. The top-shelf variety abdominal muscles, if you will. Right here. In front of my very own eyes. Attached to a sailor in glittery blue hot pants. Those things, by the way, would not fare well in a storm. Then again, they're so tight they could almost certainly double as a Speedo, so in case of a shipwreck, wet clothes wouldn't drag this dude down to a watery death. And he could use the little neck scarf-thingy that's currently tied into a jaunty little bow at his throat to strangle bloodthirsty sharks.

"I'm Peter Parker," I yell over the music.

He nods and points his thumb toward his chest. An impressive move considering he's also holding a glass in his hand while he does it and somehow doesn't spill a drop.

"Sean," he shouts. Or, at least, I'm pretty sure that's what he said. It's loud in here, and my ears are already ringing.

"Jude," I yell back.

The frown that mars his very handsome features is almost too adorable for somebody who looks like he could bench press a horse. "You just said your name was Peter."

Oh.

"No, that was a... I'm dressed as Peter Parker," I explain.

Yes, yes, I'm the no-effort asshole.

The sailor's frown deepens. "Peter Parker? That someone famous?"

"He's Spiderman." Amazingly enough, I manage to come off as both lazy and stupid, but Sean must have low standards because he stays put. I don't criticize. Low standards are my jam. My own are so close to the floor limbo dancers could use them for practice.

"Spiderman has that blue-and-red bodysuit," Sean informs me, sounding very much like one of those overachievers who put actual thought into their costume. And I resent that because I, too, put a lot of thought into this particular costume. Namely when I was racking my brain outside, trying to figure out how I could explain my obvious lack of costume in the least douchey way possible.

"I'm not, though. Spiderman," I say in response to Sean's befuddled expression.

"You just said you *were* Spiderman."

"No. I said I was Peter Parker. He transforms into Spiderman."

"You gonna do a costume change?" Sean asks with raised brows.

In an unexpected turn of events, it now seems *I'm* the overachiever in the costume department. It's in Sean's head only, but I'll take it.

"We'll see where the night takes us," I say. I'm not planning to come clean. I told the previous guy who asked about my costume that I was dressed as a nudist on strike, so it's hardly a matter of principle. If Sean here wants to operate under the impression that I'll pull on a red and blue unitard as the night progresses, I'll gladly let him.

"That's hot," Sean's lazy grin turns appreciative. He leans closer until his mouth is right by my ear. "You've got a nice ass. I'd like to get in there."

Ah, romance. You're not dead after all.

Sean takes another drink from the glass in his hand before he tips his head toward the bathrooms and raises a brow. "How about it?"

There are three possible right answers to that question: yes, sure, or let's go. Any one of them would've done the job. I dragged my nice ass out tonight to get laid, and by God, laid I am gonna get. Why the hell my brain malfunctions in the stupidest way possible and makes my mouth blurt out a "Maybe later" is anybody's guess.

I watch sailor Sean shrug and saunter away to bigger and better things before I sigh, turn around, and flag down the bartender. Try to flag down the bartender. By my fifth attempt, I'm feeling sufficiently invisible in this sea of bare-chested cowboys, bare-chested pirates, bare-chested devils, and bare-chested gladiators—there's a running theme to this party—but since my own chest is safely tucked away beneath a clearly offensive layer of fabric, I'm effectively invisible. Invisible enough to reach over the side of the bar and blindly grab the first bottle I can get my hands on. Nobody notices. It's nice to know my efforts to fly under the radar haven't been in vain.

Deep down, I like to think I'm a decent person, so I also drop some cash where the bottle was before I take off.

I walk and inspect my loot. It's never good to linger at the scene of the crime. And would you look at that? Seems karma caught up extra fast today, because I just majorly overpaid for a bottle of fucking gin. A drink that tastes like potpourri in liquid form on a good day and a shot of straight-up Lysol on all the other ones. Good choice, Jude. You sure know how to pick 'em. But it's what I've got now, so it'll have to do. It's not the first time I've settled, and it won't be the last.

I push through a sea of gyrating bodies. Or, to put it more accurately, I stumble, fumble, and try not to fall on my face as people push me left and right like I'm a rag doll. Even Moses with all his sea-parting abilities would've taken one look at this mass of humanity and gone, "Fuck it. Back to Egypt we go. I'll take my chances with the pharaoh."

For every two steps forward, I'm pushed back one, so I'm effectively moving at the pace of an injured snail.

"Really?" I mutter when, just as I'm about to escape the throng of bodies, a bare-chested fireman stomps on my foot with his combat boot for good measure.

"Watch it!" I shout after him and then promptly clamp my mouth shut.

I'm not sure what's wrong with me tonight. I should be out there, rubbing my ass against someone's crotch, making questionable decisions. Instead, I'm dodging half-naked bodies like I'm afraid sweat turns into acid with skin-to-skin contact.

I should really take Sean up on his offer and turn this night around, but when I look around, I don't see him anywhere, and it seems like too much effort to go and look for him.

Instead, I cradle my bottle of gin more firmly in the crook of my elbow and gently carry it out of the room like I'm handling a newborn. This gin is my one-night stand now, and the two of us are gonna have some fun.

I take a cursory glance around before I slip through the door that leads to the roof, purposefully ignoring the large Do Not Enter sign.

A minute later, I prop the metal door that leads to the roof open with a brick and wander outside. I put the gin on the ledge, my palms on either side of the bottle, and peer over the edge. The street is filled with cars. Nothing new to see there, so I unscrew the cap of the gin and take a big swig to get this party started. And promptly follow that by gagging. It's worse than I remembered.

I put the cap back on as quickly as I can—lest the evil spirits that make the contents of this bottle taste so vile escape—before I lift the bottle up in front of my face. "I'm afraid this is going to remain a one-sip stand. No offense."

That was a short-lived love affair, even by my standards.

I should head home and get some sleep. This isn't my day, so I should just cut my losses and call it a night, but it's blissfully peaceful up here, so I stay put for a moment longer. Gusts of wind ruffle my hair, but it isn't too cold. The few stars that might've been visible otherwise are hidden by a thick layer of clouds.

The air has the feel of an impending storm to it. An electric current that makes the hairs on my forearms stand up from both the static and the anticipation.

I absently toy with my watch. It's an old habit that refuses to die, even though it should. One of these days, I'll pick my way through the strap and then I'll lose the watch, and that's the last thing I want.

The nagging restlessness that's been making itself at home in the bottom of my chest for the better part of the last decade slowly settles and leaves me be for the moment. I make a conscious effort to relax and empty my head of all thoughts. I even throw in some deep breaths Blair swears by to really get this relaxation business on the road.

And then that vehicle crashes.

Somewhere below, a door slams and footsteps bang up the stairs. Everything clenches back up again. From relaxation city to tension town in less than a second. It's a personal best.

Resigned to my fate, I slowly turn around, just in time to see a man stomp out onto my rooftop.

"Seriously, what kind of stupid fucking asshole—"

That's how far he gets before he looks up, stops short, and clamps his mouth shut. He also throws in some blinking and wide-eyed looks while he's taking me in. For the longest time, he just stares. And not in an oh-shit-I-just-insulted-a-complete-stranger way. It's dumb, but it almost feels like he didn't expect to find me here. Me, specifically. Not some random asshole. Me. That must've been some potent gin because the only way that makes sense is if I'm drunk.

My new companion breaks the silence.

"Hi?" the guy says, his brow furrowed, looking to the left and right of me like he's searching for something.

"Hi," I reply, which brings his gaze back to me.

He looks confused.

"I'm the stupid fucking asshole," I say, in case he hasn't put two and two together yet.

"Oh." The man lifts his hand and slides his palm over the top of his head, messing up his hair and making his biceps flex while he's at it. He's not even showing off, which makes it that much better. Accidentally hot is always preferable to purposefully hot.

"Sorry. That was..." He seems lost for words for a second.

"It's fine," I interrupt. "It was an asshole move. And you don't have to worry about how to tell me to leave. I've been in this situation before, so I know the drill."

Both of his eyebrows hike higher. So much for making a good first impression. Interestingly enough, he doesn't ask me to get the hell out of here. Instead, he nods toward the doorway.

"There are currents of cold air downstairs if you leave this door open. Pisses people off. But there's a simple solution."

"I wouldn't—"

But he's already nudging the brick I used to prop the door open with his toe.

"There's no handle on this side," I rush out... Just as the door shuts with a resounding click.

The guy whips his head toward the door. For a moment, he's completely still. Then he blinks. First at the door and then at me.

"Well, shit," he eventually says. "Guess *I'm* the stupid fucking asshole."

"Welcome to the club. First time?" I ask. He looks so completely bewildered at the turn of events that I can't help but chuckle.

"Being a stupid fucking asshole? Not really." There's a quickly diminishing embarrassed awkwardness about him that only makes him that much more attractive.

It's an impressive feat seeing as he's already ridiculously handsome.

"I'm doing a favor for a buddy of mine. He needed a barback, and I happened to be in the wrong place at the wrong time, so I ended up employed for the night. Never been here before," he explains.

"For future reference, then," I say.

"Duly noted. I don't suppose you have a crowbar on you for times like these?"

I pat myself down before I shake my head. "Sorry."

"Well, he's not going to ask me to come back after tonight, that's for sure." He takes one more look at the door, but he doesn't seem too worried about losing his job.

He doesn't say anything else, and neither do I.

I'm not sure what his excuse is, but *I* have no time to talk because I'm busy looking. Yeah, I'm staring. Unabashedly. I've always enjoyed looking at beautiful people, and this guy definitely qualifies. The man has a face that would make *People* execs go, "Chris Evans who?"

It's dark up on the roof, but what I see of him, I like. His dark blond hair and the regal looking narrow nose. The soft, almost delicate bow of his lips and the tall, wiry frame. Dark eyes. Brown. Or maybe green. It's difficult to say right now, but I'm open to further investigation.

Too bad he didn't get the dress code memo, so instead of a bare chest, he's sporting a long-sleeved T-shirt and black jeans.

While I'm busy blatantly checking him out, his eyes run up and down me too. It's hard to say whether he's returning the favor or trying to gauge if I pose a threat to his wellbeing. I turn my eyes away first to signal I'm fairly normal and can uncomfortably avoid eye contact with a stranger with the best of them.

After a minute, the guy saunters over and settles in next to me. His elbow grazes mine. Purposefully. I look down and then up. Meet his gaze. He smiles, all relaxed and friendly.

My pulse kicks up a notch, which is frankly a bit unexpected and a lot unwelcome. I look away.

I have sleeping around down to a science. I have a type—easy—and I know how to pick him out from a crowd. I'm a simple guy with simple tastes: I want to be fucked and leave after. No pulse kicking or heart jumping required.

Although, I do kind of wonder what kind of impression I've made.

For a while now, it's been a firm belief of mine that I am a better-on-paper person. As in, I look good on paper. As in, I'm a textbook example of that dating profile you read and think to yourself 'this one sounds almost promising,' so in the end, you swipe right because hope springs eternal, and you're desperate to strike gold.

I look sort of unassuming. I'm not exactly the reincarnation of the hunchback of Notre Dame, but I'm not so incredibly hot that you'd dropkick an octogenarian out of the way to get to me either. I'm your run-of-the-mill average guy. Average brown hair. Average blue eyes. Average features. Average build. Basically, I'm the kind of person who'd be a bitch to identify in a police lineup. Not that I'm planning to rob anybody. But if I did… Well, all I'm saying is good luck with that police sketch.

I'm also rather unremarkable in other aspects of my life, and that's how I like it. A simple life is my ticket to getting this thing over with as unscathed as possible.

"What's your name?" I ask my new cellmate, breaking the silence.

"Why?"

He's got a very nice voice. Strong, sure, and slightly scratchy. Another point in his favor. He's absolutely welcome to say dirty things to me in that voice all night long. If he's interested, that is. It's difficult to say what he's thinking. If he finds me as fascinating as I find him.

"Call it curiosity, but I'd like to know if your name is as hot as the rest of you."

I swear, he blushes.

It's adorable.

"Smooth," he says once he's gathered himself a bit. I've always appreciated a straightforward approach. Why waste time beating around the bush?

"Blake," he adds, putting a name to the face.

I might be pushing my luck, but I take it as my cue to let my gaze wander over him once more. A small smile tilts his lips. Honestly, this all bodes well for me.

"What's the verdict?" he asks once I'm done.

"It suits you perfectly."

"Thanks," he says and raises his brows, looking at me expectantly.

"Jude."

He angles his hand toward me, and we shake.

"Nice to meet you, Jude."

Yeah, definitely a very nice voice. And a confident handshake. And the sexy half-smile doesn't hurt the overall package either.

"So, Jude," he says, and I have to take a moment to really appreciate the way my name sounds on his lips. "What brings you up here tonight?"

"Taking a breather." I glance toward the now-locked door. "An extended one."

His smile transforms from flirty into something almost bashful.

"I really didn't mean to do that. And while we're on the subject, I didn't mean to call you a stupid fucking idiot either," he says.

"Asshole."

He blinks. "Anybody ever tell you you're terrible at accepting apologies? You should be more like, 'water under the bridge, super cool stranger.'"

"I meant you called me an asshole earlier, not an idiot... super cool stranger."

That endearing streak of self-consciousness from before is back in full force. "Well, shit."

I wave him off. "It's fine. I didn't want to be down there anyway, so you did me a favor."

"In that case, you're welcome." He tilts his head to the side. "Guess you owe me one, then."

I laugh out loud. "That spiraled quickly. Anybody ever tell you you're greedy?"

He squints as he pretends to think about it for a second. "It comes up every now and then."

"Oh good. You already know. I'd hate to be the bearer of bad news."

His laugh sends a spark down my spine. A gust of wind blows through his hair, and a strand falls in front of his eye. Blake's lips seem to be tilted in a permanent smile, and going by my first impression, he's the embodiment of everything I like in a man: easygoing, uncomplicated, and interested.

Now that we've moved past the whole stupid asshole thing, the sheepishness is gone, replaced by the kind of quiet confidence that makes it very clear that this man is comfortable in his own skin. It's the kind of confidence I thoroughly value because it most likely extends to confidence in other areas.

And here I'd thought this party was going to be a complete bust. Seems I was wrong.

"So... you do this often? Wander around on roofs?" Blake asks.

"Rarely." I rest my chin on the palm of my hand and look at the sky. Those clouds are starting to look more and more threatening with each passing second, slowly rolling over us in thick layers of dark gray and black. "I've been trying to do this thing where I follow rules instead of breaking them, and roofs are generally off-limits, so..." I shrug one shoulder.

"But you made an exception tonight?"

"I'm just going to have to trust you not to rat me out."

He chuckles and shakes his head. "Another favor. Don't worry, I'm just going to add it to the tally."

"I appreciate it. They're not going to miss you downstairs?"

"Maybe. Not before they run out of beer, though. Until then? I don't think anybody will even notice I'm not there."

"I find that very hard to believe," I say.

He starts to laugh at that. "You're good. Not too brazen. Not too aloof. Not trying to play it cool, but still somehow coming off as cool. Impressive."

"I do try."

"Straightforward, too," he adds.

"It's a character flaw."

"Is it? I like it."

Something jumps in the bottom of my stomach. It's nice to be liked, even if the person doing the liking is temporary.

"You don't think it's a good thing?" he asks after a second.

"It makes me a loose cannon." I turn my head toward him only to find him still looking at me.

Brown. His eyes are definitely dark brown. Slightly tilted up at the corners.

"A loose cannon?"

"I say stupid shit that gets me in trouble."

"Like?"

I quirk my brow. "That's a lot of questions. It's starting to feel like you're trying to get to know me, and if that's the case, I should warn you, I don't really do that."

"Sounds like a challenge."

"Not really. Besides, I've heard it's a two-way street, so if that's what we're doing I'd have to start asking questions, too."

"I'm an open book, so we can take turns."

I pretend to think about it for a second, even if it's just for show. Temptation seduces, and I'm easy. "I don't know... Are you interesting enough to make it worth my while, Blake?"

In response, he tilts his head and smiles. "Why don't you find out, Jude?"

This has trouble written all over it. He's interesting all right. Fascinating. And that's a problem, because right now he also seems to be a genuinely nice person. *Seems.* That's the important part to note. History has proven time and time again that I'm a terrible judge of character, so I don't really trust my own assessment. But I'm also stupidly curious.

"Nothing?" Blake asks.

"You're impressively impatient. Give me a second, I'm trying to eliminate the boring crap before I get started."

His mouth falls open in pretend shock. "The boring crap?"

"Things I don't care about. The unimportant stuff. Hopes, dreams, goals... I want dirt."

"I'm a bit scared now."

"Backing out already?"

"Approaching with caution," he says. "And trying to figure out how to handle the more incriminating details while I'm at it."

"A lot of skeletons in your closet?" I ask.

"Difficult to get the door shut by now."

"Excellent news."

"For you, maybe." He seems to contemplate it for a moment before he says, "Go ahead. Surprise me."

Now *that* feels like a challenge. One I don't live up to.

"What do you do for a living?" I ask.

His lips twitch, and he shakes his head. "And the fireworks go out with a barely audible hiss. Hard-hitting journalism right off the bat. Really digging deep for that dirt, are you?"

I turn to lean one elbow on the ledge and face him. "Already something to hide? Seriously?"

"I'm thinking strategically. If I veto, will you assume I'm a spy or something interesting like that?"

"Sure," I say. "A spy. Or maybe something like an internet troll or a lobbyist. Something embarrassing you don't want to admit out loud. Could go either way, I suppose." I look down to where his hands are resting on the ledge and make a thoughtful face. "You have very long fingers." His eyes snap down to said fingers, looking at them like he's seeing them for the first time.

"Perfect for a keyboard warrior," I add thoughtfully.

He laughs out loud. "Good to know I have options. You weren't too far off. I actually do work in IT."

"And here I was leaning toward a secret agent."

"Ah, shoot." The corners of his mouth tilt up. There seems to be a permanent spark of laughter in his eyes. How is it even possible to be so... happy? Not that I begrudge the man his obvious optimism, but I'm beginning to think I should ask him to teach me how to live like that. It seems nice. I wonder what it feels like not to expect the worst from people right off the bat?

"What do you do?" Blake asks.

"I work at a sandwich shop." And as a delivery rider. There's an occasional stint as a server at parties. And I have a night gig at the Barclays Center changeover crew. There are a few other things I squeeze in there from time to time. Basically, if it pays, I do it. New York is expensive, and those lawyer fees are no joke.

"Do you like it?" Blake asks.

I shrug. "It pays the bills and keeps me busy."

This time he waits patiently while I figure out my next question. Too bad everything in my head is either something very basic or way too dirty to ask a stranger. Finally, I go with, "Best memory?"

"And here I thought you didn't care about sentimental crap like that. Don't worry, though. I've got a good one," he says.

There's a dreamy look in his eyes, like he's reliving the good old days. "We built a homemade bike ramp with some of the kids on my street, and then I volunteered to test it out first because I was the new kid, so I needed to impress people."

"And did you?"

"Oh yeah. We were a bunch of kids building a ramp, so it wasn't the most stable thing out there. Then again, what it lacked in sturdiness, it made up for in height. Also, I may have exaggerated my BMX skills a tiny bit. I lost the bike midair and landed on my right foot. The bone snapped like a twig, and then it came right through the skin. I impressed everyone who managed not to puke. Or cry. Or faint. For the record, I did none of those. I'm hardcore like that. And I was in shock. But mostly the hardcore thing. It was an awesome day. I got to touch my own bone," he says, like that's the greatest achievement ever.

"That's your best memory?" I ask. "A gory injury?"

"A gory injury that made me infamous in Spokane Valley. You can't put a price on the kind of street cred it got me."

I laugh at the pride in his voice. "Is that where you're from?"

"No, but I lived there for a while. This is flat-out cheating now, by the way. You've had two questions in a row. It was my turn."

"Sorry."

"You should be." He considers me for a little bit. "Do you have any hidden talents?"

"Yes."

"Which are?"

"That's another question."

"It's an extension of the previous question. It doesn't count as a new one. Nice try, though."

"It was worth a shot." I hesitate for a moment. It's not like I have that many to choose from. Still feels weirdly personal to say it out loud. Most of my interactions on nights like these are limited to the logistics of fucking.

"I play the piano," I say.

Blake raises his brows. "Really?"

"Why do you sound so surprised?"

"Not surprised, exactly. Are you good?"

"Extremely talented," I say off-handedly.

He squints his eyes. "I don't know you well enough to figure out if you're telling the truth."

"Guess you're just going to have to believe me. Or not. Your choice."

"Or you could prove it to me."

"Sure. Produce a piano, and I'll go right ahead."

He grins, but not in an oh-my-bad way. More like an I'm-determined-now way.

"I'm gonna get you to play for me," he says.

"You're welcome to try."

"It's happening."

"Guess we'll see," I say. Well, why not? Let's pretend we'll ever see each other again after tonight. I can't exactly put my finger on why, but I'm in no hurry to finish this conversation, even if it means revealing personal information.

"Your turn," Blake says.

This time, I have the question ready. "What's your best quality?"

A frown of concentration appears between his eyebrows as he mulls it over like it's the most important question ever asked. Like his answer really matters.

He hesitates for another second before he says, "I'm loyal. You?"

It's so much easier to be critical of yourself than to be kind and see the good, but I make a concentrated effort to do just that. It's also somehow easier to be honest with a stranger I'll likely never see again after tonight.

"I give a fuck," I say.

Blake's thumb moves over his fingers, touching the tips of each one, his eyes following his thumb. "That's a good answer." He glances toward me. "What's your worst quality?"

Can't say I have to think about it for too long. "I'm extremely cynical. You?"

It takes a long time for him to answer that one. His eyes stay locked somewhere on the skyline when he eventually says. "I'm loyal."

I'm fucking curious about that answer. Who wouldn't be?

But...

That'd mean veering toward serious, and that's not my preferred direction. It's too close to personal, and that's territory I rarely venture into even if it's just me, let alone with another person.

"Weirdest fear?" I ask, blocking that path.

Blake's gaze snaps to mine. He looks at me curiously for a moment.

"Waking up one day and finding I'm the only living person left in the world," he says.

Well, he got the weird part down. "How would that even happen?"

"A meteor hits the Earth. I'm a heavy sleeper, so it's entirely possible I wouldn't hear a thing. Then I step outside for my morning jog and find the world burning to the ground. Or aliens come and kidnap everybody, but they deem me too much of a loser to take with them."

"Both sound like a solid possibility," I say, doing my best to keep a straight face.

"You laugh now, but once it happens, you'll feel bad you did."

"I'll think of you when I'm being whisked away from Earth on that alien spaceship for cool people."

"Will you also send thoughts and prayers while you're busy being useless?" he asks. "Or, here's an idea, you could stop the ship and tell them they left somebody behind."

I scrunch up my nose and nod slowly. "Yeah, about that... No offense, but I don't want to be known as the guy who brought the loser with him to an interstellar trip."

He clutches his chest and staggers backward. "Ouch. Stabbed right in the heart."

"For what it's worth, I don't think you have to worry too much about any of that happening. The probability is ridiculously low."

"Not *that* low. I bet there are plenty of asteroids ready to go rogue."

"No, I meant the probability that you're the one lucky survivor. It's infinitely more likely you'll die with the rest of us."

"What a relief. And you're still laughing. Nice. Come on then, what're you afraid of?"

"Moths. Creepy little fuckers."

"They're actually very important as links in the food chain and as pollinators. Not to mention, they're beautiful, and completely harmless," Blake says like some kind of moth-loving freak.

I send him a dirty look. "What's with the moth propaganda? No. They're erratic, hairy, winged psychopaths whose sole mission in life is to fly into your face and traumatize you for years to come."

He presses his lips together and gives an exaggerated shake of his head. "Ah. You're one of *those* people."

"Those people?" I ask.

"You know, the ones who care about looks. I bet you have nothing against butterflies, do you?"

"Ah," I shoot back mockingly. "You're one of *those* people."

His lips twitch. "Those people?"

"A judger. You take one tiny comment and draw huge conclusions based on it."

His mouth falls open. "Do not."

"If you look in the rearview mirror, I think you can still see exhibit A waving at you."

Blake chuckles and shakes his head. "I think it's your turn now."

My turn?

"Out of questions already?" Blake asks while I'm still busy trying to catch up with the program. "Does that mean I win?"

"This isn't a competition."

"Spoken like a true loser, but okay," he says, lips twitching.

Fuck that. I might not be ultra-competitive, but backing down from a blatant challenge like that? No.

I send him my most innocent smile. "Biggest turn on?"

He stills for a moment before his chest rises with the slow breath he draws in.

I half expect him to laugh it off or turn the answer into a joke.

He doesn't.

"I..." He hesitates for a moment, but when I quirk my brow at him, he rises to the challenge. "I like to be surprised. Intrigued," he says. "When people aren't what I expect them to be." His voice drops an octave. Goes even quieter. Turns more intimate. The edge of it scrapes over my nerve endings.

I clear my throat.

"Interesting," I say, trying to sound unaffected. Not sure I'm succeeding. "Your turn."

A devious look appears in his eyes. Hot, hot, hot.

"Weirdest place you've had sex?" he challenges.

My mouth clamps shut, and Blake raises his brows. "Really?" he says, and eagerly leans closer as if he's afraid he'd miss something otherwise. "That bad? I'm all ears."

"It's not..." I huff out a breath. "In a church bathroom."

His grin takes up his whole face now. "I had high expectations, and you surpassed them. Bravo."

"Thank you," I say dryly. "Your approval means a lot. What's yours?"

"Locker room," he says.

I motion for him to continue. "I'm listening."

"It's a pretty straightforward story. I had sex in a locker room."

"So hot. With all those raunchy details, it's like listening to porn," I say.

He laughs again and looks down, shaking his head before he turns his head and meets my eyes.

"You're something else, Jude."

"Stormy nights on rooftops give me mystique. Trust me, in daylight, I'm as average as they come."

His smile shifts. Turns into something knowing. More.

"Liar," he says softly.

I'm not going to stand here and claim it doesn't feel nice to be somebody... somebody else. Just for this one fleeting moment in time.

Wind sweeps over the rooftop. Pushes us closer. I lean forward. Into the depths of these whiskey eyes and that warm body.

"Tell me something," I say, my face inches from his.

"Like?"

"Something I don't know yet."

He considers me for a moment.

"I..." he says slowly.

Want to take you downstairs and fuck you. Want to take you back to my place and fuck you. Want to fuck you right here.

"Can't sleep with you."

Seeing as my options were so much better, it takes my brain a moment to switch back to reality.

Well, this is disappointing. I could've sworn he was into me, but it seems I was wrong.

"Can't?" I ask. Let's add a little masochism into this thing, shall we?

He looks down, jaw tightening. "Won't."

"Straight?" I ask.

He shakes his head.

"In a relationship?"

Another shake.

By now the reason seems kind of obvious. "Not your type?"

He swallows hard. The head might stay still this time around, but it's not hard to fill in the silence.

Nice. Talk about barking up the wrong tree.

"I—" Blake starts.

That's when the door of the roof bangs open. A man peers out, his scowl visible even across the rooftop. Blake tenses.

"Seriously? Again? This place is off-limits. There's a sign." The guy speaks so fast all the words blend into one.

Seriouslyagainthisplaceisofflimitsthere'sasign.

"Sorry," I say quickly. "Sorry. It's my fault."

There's no reason for both Blake and I to get into trouble for this. And I'm just a guest. I don't work here or anything. Plus, I suppose you could argue that without me coming up here in the first place, none of us would be here.

The guy rolls his eyes before he slides the brick back into place where it was holding the door open and disappears downstairs. Blake's eyes remain on the doorway for a moment before he sighs.

He closes his eyes and shakes his head for a moment before he turns to look at me. "Duty calls."

He looks disappointed, and I don't understand why.

I straighten up.

Blake lingers.

He looks like he's about to say something, even opens his mouth, but then he snaps it shut, and presses it into a firm line. Like he's making sure nothing escapes by accident.

It's like he feels bad for not wanting me, even though he really shouldn't. If I'm not his type, then I'm not his type. It happens. It's a shame I'm not, but what can you do?

"Thanks for the company," I say. There's a finality in those words. We both hear it.

Blake nods and a small smile tilts the corners of his lips up. "You're welcome. We'll add that to the running tally of favors you owe me."

I laugh and head to the doorway. I wasn't lying before. I am extremely cynical, so I usually expect the worst from people. But tonight I want to hold on to the feeling that there are good people out there for a change. The genuinely nice ones who'll live happy, uncomplicated lives because that's what nice people deserve.

The trek down the staircase goes by silently, with Blake a few feet behind me. I'm just about to clear the last step when Blake walks into me from behind. I lurch forward, but instead of faceplanting on the ground, fingers wrap around my wrist and Blake pulls me backward. We stumble a bit, but eventually regain our balance, so we're standing toe to toe, chest to chest, face to face. I inhale and let his scent fill my nostrils. A tease for later.

"Sorry! Sorry," Blake says. "Wasn't watching where I was going." The guy looks really flustered. He even pats me down to see if I have any injuries, even though I didn't come close to falling.

"It's fine," I say, taking a step back. "Just knock one favor off, and we'll call it even."

He laughs.

Still way too likable.

Damnit.

I take a step back.

"It was nice to meet you, Blake," I say.

"Likewise, Jude."

I nod.

He nods.

And then I get the fuck out of there.

FIVE

I TAKE A CAB HOME. My whole street seems to be asleep. All my neighbors' windows are dark and still. I trudge up the stairs and drop my keys and wallet into the wire basket hanging by the door while I toe off my sneakers. Then I shrug out of my jacket and hang it up before I head to the living room-slash-kitchen-slash-bedroom.

The apartment is quiet, like it always is. I lean my shoulder against the doorjamb and look around.

Being alone hasn't bothered me in a long, long time. I prefer it, to be honest. But sometimes, late at night, aloneness morphs into loneliness. Soul-scratching, painful loneliness—that squatter in the back of my brain I just don't seem to be able to evict for good.

Instead of nipping that shit in the bud and going to bed, I wait. A masochist in the middle of the night. What's the point of hiding if you do it from your own feelings? You can't outrun your own mind. Loneliness, like all the monsters in the closet, has to be faced and felt and dealt with.

I'm ready for it.

Only tonight there's nothing. My body is abuzz with

pleasant feelings, so there's no room for anything else. I had fun with a nice guy.

I sit down on the couch just for a second.

Next thing I know, I wake up with a jerk and a crick in my neck. I'm not sure how long I was out, but it's still dark outside, so the only reasonable thing to do is to crawl into bed and stay there for the next few hours. Sounds like a plan.

I get up and pull my T-shirt off.

Stop. Not just stop. Freeze.

Something's wrong.

It takes me a moment. It's late, and I'm a pendulum swinging between awake and asleep.

My stomach lurches uncomfortably, then hollows as I stare at my wrist. My very naked wrist. I blink and stare some more before I dive for my T-shirt.

It's fine. It's fine. Completely fine. The watch just got stuck in the fabric. It's somewhere in here. It must be. It has to be.

My fingers squeeze every inch of fabric between them before I throw the T-shirt on the ground again and rush to the hallway to do the same with my jacket. I stuff my hands through the sleeves. I shake the jacket. I even check the pockets in case I have a fairy godmother somewhere, and she sees my desperation and decides to step in.

Still nothing.

I go through the pockets of my jeans and even stuff my hands inside the sneakers I was wearing earlier, because why not go full-on insane? I was already teetering on the edge anyway.

Nothing.

Shit. Shit. Shit!

I tear my front door open and trek down the stairs, carefully scouring the floor every step of the way. The hallway lights are on a timer, so every two minutes, I have to flick the switch and turn them back on. By the time I make it up the stairs to my apartment again, my heartbeat is just desperation and adrenaline and nothing else.

The watch could be anywhere. On the street. In the cab. At the bar. On the roof. The chances of me finding it are slim to none. Somebody will have picked it up by now. It's a vintage Patek Philippe. Stupidly expensive, so that thing was gone even before it hit the ground somewhere. Wherever that somewhere is.

I let out a mirthless snort of laughter. A nameless, faceless somebody is going to have a good day, at least. The fact that the watch is worth an obscene amount of money is of very little importance to me, though.

It's Dad's watch.

I can't lose it. I just can't.

I breathe, and I breathe, and I breathe, trying to come to terms with this monumental fuckup.

Why did I have to wear the watch? I could've just kept it at home. Why risk losing it like an idiot?

Of course, Dad would hate it if I hid the watch in a drawer somewhere. He always had that watch on his wrist, because *what's the point of having things when you don't use them, son?*

I take another deep breath and force myself to chill the fuck out.

I can't give up so easily. I might be chasing wind on a field here, but whatever. I trudge back upstairs, pull on my jeans, grab my jacket, and head outside. It takes me twenty minutes to find a Lyft and then another twenty to get back to the bar. The place is dead, but when I try the door, it's still unlocked. I take the elevator up. Inside, a tired-looking man is mopping the floor.

"Dude, we're closed," he says when he sees me. "Try again tomorrow."

"I'm not here to party. Do you happen to have some sort of lost and found, by any chance?"

He stares at me like he's having a difficult time comprehending what I'm saying, but then he nods and motions for me to follow.

He pulls out a large cardboard box and slams it on the bar, tired and careless. "What're you looking for?" he asks and yawns widely before he starts rummaging around.

"A watch," I say and peer into the box. There's all sorts of crap in there. A lone shoe. More than a few phones. Jewelry. Your usual selection of underwear.

"This one?" the guy asks and puts a watch on the counter.

I shake my head.

He goes back to looking, unearthing more crap until he finally shakes his head. "Sorry. No more watches."

My earlier hope morphs into a lump in my throat.

I nod. "Thanks anyway." I make a last-ditch effort. "My phone number is on the back of the strap. If anybody finds it..."

"We'll call," he assures me. I'm not sure he means it, even though he really does look like he's feeling sorry for me.

I tap my fist on the bar twice before I give the man a final nod and get out of there.

There goes my last hope.

SIX

I SPEND my Sunday feeling sorry for myself. Really, pathetically sorry. Binge watching TV type of sorry. People deal with loss in different ways. I eat pizza in my sweatpants and watch aliens land in LA. Then I watch aliens land in LA in another movie. I'm right in the middle of watching aliens land in LA for the third time when my phone rings. I glance at the display, hoping to see an unknown number because that might mean somebody found my watch.

Instead, it's Blair.

I do my best to ignore her, but in a battle of stubbornness, she always wins. I tried to ditch her once upon a time, and look how that turned out.

The phone just keeps going until I sigh, pause the movie, and answer.

"What?"

"Well, that's a nice greeting," Blair says.

I drag my palm down my face and sit up. "I didn't mean to snap."

"Cool. You're not getting off that easily. An in-person apology

might get you off the hook, though. Dinner in thirty. We're going to La Casa. You're paying."

"Pass," I say.

"You don't get a pass. I'm pregnant."

"That's not my fault. Pass."

"And yet, if you want little Mercury Starcruiser to know his uncle, you'll get your ass to that restaurant, or I swear to God, you're dead to me."

I groan. "Go annoy your wife. Why even get married if you still need me to do stuff with you? Be like a normal newlywed and forget you have friends. Grow apart from me, woman!"

"You should really make more of an effort to keep me around. If you push me away, who's going to find your corpse when you kick the bucket? Besides, Nora's still at work, so chop-chop. We need to hurry before she gets back."

"I keep telling you I'm not gonna help you cheat on Nora."

"Yes, because as we all know, it's my dream in life to cheat on my wife with a gay dude. Get a grip and get a move on. I'm hungry. I'll see you in thirty." With those words, she hangs up.

I look toward the TV longingly before I curse and get up.

I fight through traffic to the restaurant Blair picked out and lock my bike to a signpost before I head inside.

The place is packed, so naturally I create chaos in my wake while I try to squeeze through the maze of tables and chairs blocking my path. I mutter apologies the whole way to the table where Blair and Nora are watching my march of doom. Nora is put together as always in one of her designer dresses and shoes with heels so high I'm not sure how anybody's supposed to walk in them. Her auburn hair is pinned up into a neat bun at the back of her neck, and she's wearing honest-to-God pearls like she's expecting the king to make an appearance. Her wife is lounging next to her in yoga pants and a loose sweater that hangs off one of her shoulders, her chin-length hair a mix of black, blue, and pink. Even slouching, Blair still manages to look graceful.

The two of them are polar opposites, but somehow they just fit.

"Lovely. The traveling circus we ordered has finally arrived." Nora arches her brow. "How hard is it to just be on time?"

I send her a toothy grin. "So hard." I grab the menu from the table. "Sorry. I was trying to find an excuse not to come here, and—" I make a strategic pause, squint my eyes, and lean toward Nora. "You've got a little something…" I gesture toward the collar of her dress.

Her head snaps down, inspecting the immaculate forest-green fabric. "Where?"

I point my finger toward her neck. "Right there. Next to the collar."

She almost dislocates her neck trying to angle her head in the right direction. "Where?" she asks. There's a hint of panic in her voice at the thought of looking less than put together.

I should really be a good person and cut it out.

"A little more to the back," I say. She obediently strains her neck even more.

"Right there," I say. "Just behind the shoulder. A little bit more." I wonder if I can make her rotate her head 360 degrees? Might as well find out. "You almost have it," I say with an encouraging nod. "Just a little bit to the left. A bit more. It's right there."

Blair sighs and shakes her head. "He's messing with you, babe." She puts her palm on Nora's cheek and gently pushes her head back straight.

I glare at her. "Traitor."

"I hate you," Nora says, sounding like a teenager. I bring it out in her. I really think it does her some good.

I snicker until Nora kicks me in the shin. I flip her off. She looks around to make sure nobody notices and returns the favor.

"Can you two behave?" Blair admonishes.

"You're the one who dragged me out. Also, why am I here if Nora's with you? You said she was at work."

Nora beams and kisses Blair on the cheek. "I came home early. Talk about lucky."

"Lucky," Blair echoes.

Nora doesn't seem to notice the slight edge to her wife's voice, but I do. I raise my brows at Blair.

"Later," she mouths.

"How's life?" I ask Nora as I reach out and steal a crab cake from her plate. She gives me an annoyed look.

"Busy, but it's going to be worth it because once this case wraps up and Nicolas is born, I'm going to take some time off. It'll be great."

"Yup," Blair says with a nod. "As soon as little Jaxxen Blaze is born."

Nora frowns. "I thought we agreed that the next one gets the stripper name and the first one will be classy?"

"We did, but I got to thinking last night when I couldn't sleep," Blair says. "It's already a lot of pressure to be the first-born, so I think we should make it clear to him we had low expectations from the start. That way there'll be no extra stress for the kid because he knows we love him even if he ends up becoming a stripper. We'll put the pressure on the second one."

Nora takes a moment to think about it, then nods. "You know, in a strange way, that makes sense."

I steal another crab cake. It's a fancy restaurant, so they don't serve proper-sized crab cakes, instead opting for a bunch of bite-sized ones. No wonder I have to go back for more. I've eaten junk food all day, and these are excellent crab cakes. I'm already eyeing Nora's food again, prepared to strike.

"If I see that hand near my plate, I'll chop it off," Nora says, eyes still on Blair.

"Tough words from somebody who faints at the sight of blood," I say.

"I do not faint! I might get a little lightheaded, but that's the extent of it," Nora protests, finally tearing her gaze away from Blair. "It's a completely acceptable reaction. Blood is supposed to remain inside the body, not outside of it. We're not meant to see it."

I reach out again and steal another crab cake. Nora tries to stab me with a fork, but I'm too quick for her. I throw the crab cake in the air and catch it in my mouth.

Nora's frown deepens and she pulls the plate toward herself, hiding it behind her arm like a pirate protecting her treasure. If she pulls it any farther, she'll end up wearing her appetizer.

"We're in a nice restaurant," she growls. "Stop acting like an animal."

I just send her another grin and make a real production out of chewing loudly and with my mouth open while Nora looks at the ceiling and mutters something. Based on the direction she aims the words, I'm thinking it's prayers and not curses, so that's good news. She clearly seems to think there's still hope for me, which is nice.

Blair shakes her head and folds her hands over her swollen belly. "Maybe you two can cut it out for a little bit," she suggests. "I'm not dressed for a food fight."

"I would never," Nora protests.

"I was there last Christmas." Blair sends her a knowing look.

"He started it!" Nora says indignantly, pointing her finger at me.

Blair just raises a brow at that.

We high-five, and Nora tries to glare while fighting a smile. "Why are you always on his side?" she complains.

Blair shrugs. "We're friends."

"And that's the deepest bond in the world," I say solemnly, like the paragon of virtue I am.

"I'm your wife," Nora says.

"I know. I was at the wedding," Blair says, picking up a crab cake of her own from Nora's plate and stuffing it into her mouth.

Nora narrows her eyes at Blair.

"It's for the baby," Blair says through the mouthful, blinking innocently while rubbing her belly so hard it looks like she's expecting a genie to pop out.

Those are the magic words. Nora, a firm believer that food is not supposed to be shared unless you're lost in a cave and starving to death, immediately pushes the plate toward Blair like she's afraid the baby's going to perish if she doesn't get some sea food into her wife ASAP.

Blair reaches out her hand, leans forward, and lets out a breath. Like normal people sometimes do when they reach for food. But Nora whips her head toward Blair, eyes wide with alarm.

"What's wrong?"

"Nothing," Blair says quickly. Then she pauses. And very deliberately starts rubbing her belly again. "I'm fine. A tiny bit lightheaded for a second, but I'm fine."

Nora is up out of her seat in a snap. "I'll go see what's taking so long with the food." She points at me. "Pour her some water, please. Does it feel like you're about to faint? Heartburn? Any pain anywhere at all? Do you want some juice? I'll get you some juice." The clatter of her heels is like a war cry as she heads toward the bar area.

As soon as Nora is out of hearing range, Blair straightens up and leans toward me. Her voice goes low and urgent, like she's afraid we'll run out of time. "You have got to take her out."

I raise my brows. "I'm sorry, what?"

"Nora. Take. Her. Out. I cannot deal with her anymore. I'm serious, you need to take care of this for me. I'm begging you!"

I narrow my eyes because I don't think she's saying what I think she's saying. My eyes move to Nora, who's by the counter, looking like she's giving the hostess an earful. I turn back to Blair. Then again, she might be saying exactly what I think she's saying.

"Just to clarify, when you say take her out, you mean..." I pull my forefinger over my throat and raise my brows at her. "I'm not saying no, but you're going to have to back me up when they ask for my alibi."

She gives an impatient huff and glances over her shoulder to where Nora is still talking to the hostess. "Idiot. I mean, take her out. To a bar, to a bowling alley, to a freaking spa day. I don't care where, just get her out of the house for a few hours. And just to clarify, by 'a few hours,' I mean a minimum of five hours, and when you bring her back, she better be so drunk she falls into bed and doesn't wake up until the morning. And once that morning comes, I want her hungover. So hungover she'll only be able to sleep or quietly stare into space while contemplating the meaning of life. Got it?"

"Uh... sure?" I say slowly. "What's this about?"

Blair takes a deep breath and forces a pleasant smile onto her face. "I'm just worried about her. She has a stressful job, and then she comes home and takes care of me the rest of the time, but when is Nora-time on that schedule? It's just that the unfairness of it all really just... grinds my gears." She presses her lips together, clenches her fingers into a fist, and shakes it at the ceiling. There's also some sort of growl included into this package of crazy. Blair used to be a ballerina. Get her in a pair of pointe shoes, and she can convey every emotion in the book flawlessly. Speaking parts really aren't her forte, though.

"Nice try," I say.

Blair chews on her bottom lip so hard I'm starting to fear she's going to draw blood.

"Fine," she grits out. "Fine. That woman? My wife?" She says 'my wife' the same way one would say 'Satan.' "She's driving me insane. I need a few hours to myself! Ever since we found out about the baby, she's gone crazy. It's been six fucking months!" She takes a deep breath. "You know why Nora and I fit so well?"

"Love and mutual respect?" I venture a guess.

She rolls her eyes and waves her hand impatiently. "Sure, yeah, that too. But..."

"But?"

"But it's also because Nora gets me. She gets that I need my alone time too. You know how there are these couples who call to tell each other what they had for lunch or just to say I love you? Those who're, like... when one of them is out of town for two days, the other is miserable and puts her shirt on a body pillow, so she'll feel closer to her and can smell her while she's sleeping?"

"There are people who do that?" I gotta be honest, I'm genuinely mystified. "Why?"

"Aww. There's the cynical asshole we all know and barely tolerate. Yes, there are people like that. They're everywhere. It's an infestation. But we're not one of those couples! I mean, if it's your thing, more power to you, but it's not for me. I love Nora. I love her so much I occasionally even tell her I do, but I can't have her in my face all the time. And she gets it. She doesn't want to be that couple either. Only now we *are* one of those couples because of the baby."

"You poor thing. Having somebody who cares about your life is the worst."

"Die," Blair says shortly. "I'm surrounded by people at work, all day every day. Then I come home, and there's Nora. Because now she doesn't stay late at the office anymore. No, she brings work home. And she doesn't go out to drinks with her coworkers. She stopped going to the gym. And sure, do I like to watch her do yoga every morning? Yeah. A lot. But it also means I haven't gotten a single moment to myself. And maybe it wouldn't be that terrible, but she worries like she's trying to turn it into a separate career. Every sound I make has her on high alert. 'Are you okay, baby? Does anything feel wrong, honey? Was that a normal sigh, sweetie?' Gah!"

I study her silently for a bit while she frowns and glowers.

"You know it's because of the miscarriages," I say gently.

Her head drops back, and she groans. "I know," she says impatiently. "I know," she repeats more calmly. "I get it. She's worried about me, and she's scared shitless, and I'm a terrible person, but I just need an evening without anybody hovering and freaking out about every sound I make. I'm six months pregnant, and the miracle of life is uncomfortable and exhausting. Of course I'm going to be miserable when there's a fifty-fifty chance I'll end the day hugging the toilet!"

"Okay. Just an idea. Have you talked to her about all of this?" I ask.

She sighs and seems to deflate a bit. "Yeah, but then she just worries silently. And I get that she can't help it. She'll worry, and that's okay, but for just one night, maybe she could worry while she's somewhere else? Besides, *she* needs it as much as I do. If she keeps it up, she'll end up having a heart attack. Call me overly emotional, but I'd like a wife who's alive."

I chuckle and shake my head. "So that's what this dinner is really about, huh? I feel used."

"Well, no. Definitely not about that. I just... wanted to see you. Because I missed you. And I wanted to tell you I think you're really smart. And incredibly handsome. And so kind and understanding. Selfless. Did I mention pretty? Because you are. Soooo pretty. And you're the best friend anybody could ever have."

"Wow. You really are desperate."

She puts her thumb and forefinger together. "Just a little bit."

I laugh and shake my head. "How about Friday? That work for you? Can you handle five more days?"

All the tension leaves her body like a demon has called it quits on a possession, and she slumps back in obvious relief.

"Thank you. I love you. And, hey, you really are pretty, so I didn't even have to lie about that one."

I snort. "Only about the kind, smart, selfless part?"

"I had a feeling I was laying it on a bit too thick to be believable." We both smile, and Blair says, "I meant the best friend part. No exaggerations or lies about that."

"Right back at you," I say.

We're having a moment. It's kind of sweet. Until Blair starts blinking rapidly and wiping at her eyes.

"Damn hormones," she says angrily, dashing her sleeve across her eyes.

"Sure, blame the hormones, you crybaby," I say. She flips me off just as Nora comes back to the table. She looks between me and Blair, who's still holding her middle finger in the air.

"I'm not even going to ask," she says and smoothly folds Blair's finger down.

"Smart move," I say. "Did you get the food sorted out?"

Nora nods distractedly, eyes still on Blair. "Are you sure you feel okay? You look a bit pale."

"Speaking of food," I jump in loudly when Blair's hands ball into fists and she starts breathing like she's in a Lamaze class. Nora sends me a funny look, but I ignore it. "We should go out. You and me. How about Friday?"

"Sure. I'll have to check my schedule, but I think we're free, right?" She raises her brows at Blair.

"I've got a work thing," Blair says immediately.

"What work thing?" Nora seems genuinely surprised about this fake work engagement.

"A new client at the studio," Blair says smoothly.

"Oh. It wasn't on the calendar."

Nora's whole life is on her calendar. She's a busy woman. Nora is one of those genius kids who managed to live up to her potential and not burn out by the age of twelve. She's incredibly smart, and while I won't ever say it to her face, she's pretty damn badass in her quest to help countries and individual people reclaim stolen artwork and antiquities displayed in all the most prestigious museums of the world. Her expertise and first love is cultural property law, and it's a testament to her skill that she has plenty of enemies in museum circles.

"Totally slipped my mind," Blair says. "But this works out kind of perfectly. I'll be out late anyway, so you two can go have a nice dinner in the meantime. Maybe grab some drinks at a bar. Hang out. Drink. Do some bonding. While drinking. Just throwing ideas out there."

"I should probably come and help you, though," Nora says with a frown. "Your equipment is kind of heavy."

"That'd be great, but you can't."

"Because?" Nora asks.

"I'm taking pictures for some couple's OnlyFans. You have

to pay to see the goods, babe. They're not gonna want to show them to you for free."

"Fine," Nora says with a sigh. "But the moment you feel anything unusual, you call off the shoot, okay?"

"That's decided, then," Blair says with a decisive nod. "Too bad I'm going to miss it, but I'm sure you two will have a great time together. At the bar. Fun!"

Nora looks at me. "Guess I'll see you on Friday, then?"

"Sounds like a plan."

The rest of the meal goes by quickly. Blair is definitely more relaxed with the Nora-free evening looming on the horizon. I even forget my own bad mood while we're chatting and eating.

"Want to share a ride?" Nora asks once we're outside the restaurant.

"No, I'm good. I've got my own wheels," I say as I unlock my bike.

Blair wraps her arm around Nora's waist and leans her head on Nora's shoulder. They say their goodbyes and walk away. I'm just about to throw my leg over my bike and take off when I hear the muffled sound of my phone from my backpack. I dig it out and frown at the unknown number.

"Hello?" I say.

"Hi."

Silence.

Then, *"Jude?"*

I frown and look around as if expecting to see somebody talking to me. I'm stupid like that sometimes. "Yeah, that's me," I say after the brain activity has returned to normal.

"It's Blake."

I stop wrestling with my bike and look around again. It's nice to know I'm consistent in my idiocy.

"We met last night? At the party?" Blake continues, clearly

taking my silence as confusion. *"The roof?"* he adds, as if it's really possible to forget him that easily.

"No, no, I remember," I say quickly. "Hi."

He laughs, and it sounds just as good as it did when we met. *"Hi,"* he says back.

"Hi," I repeat because it seems like I should say something and nothing else comes to mind. Why is he calling?

I know I said he was too nice for my tastes, but if he's changed his mind and wants to finish what we started on Saturday, then I'm taking him up on that offer, no questions asked.

"Listen," he says, *"I think I may have found your watch? Or, I found a watch at the party, with your name on the strap. And clearly your phone number, so yeah, I'm pretty sure it might be yours?"*

My heart stops and then starts working overtime, and my hands start shaking with sheer relief. "My watch?" I repeat. "You found it? This isn't a joke? You have it?"

"Well, I didn't just randomly guess your phone number," he says. *"Plus, it'd be a pretty terrible joke. I'd like to think I can do better."*

I let out my first proper breath in more than twenty-four hours. "Shit," I say on a massive exhale. "That's... Thank you. Really. You have no idea what this means to me."

"You don't have to thank me. It's no problem."

"It's a huge deal for me. Just take my word for it. Where are you? I can come pick it up right now. Or whenever is good for you. Just tell me a time and a place, and I'll be there."

"I'm driving back to the city, but I'll be pretty late. If you're free tomorrow, we can meet up. Grab a bite to eat while we're at it?"

He sounds hopeful, which makes me force down a perplexed *why?* and instead go with, "Yeah, yeah. Of course. My treat."

"One o'clock? Unless you have something planned."

I go through my schedule in my head. I don't think there's anything there, but even if there is, I'll call in sick if I have to. "One o'clock is fine."

"There's a place near South Street Seaport. Do you like seafood?"

"Sure. I'm not picky. I eat everything."

"In that case, I'll text you the address, and then I'll see you there. Tomorrow."

"Tomorrow," I confirm.

There's a pause, but my fingers refuse to cooperate and end the call.

"Night, Jude," Blake says after I've just been listening to him breathing for a little while. Like normal people do.

"Night, Blake," I say.

I toss the phone back into my backpack, grab my bike and throw my leg over it.

In an interesting turn of events, it seems I'm going to see Blake again. Can't say I understand why he wants to have lunch, but I can do lunch if it means I get my watch back, which is all that matters.

SEVEN

I storm past people like I'm an Olympic sprinter going for the gold. It's a new sport called 'how many pedestrians can I hit in twenty minutes.' Not to brag, but I'm headed for the world record. If only because the sport hasn't really taken off yet, so there's not much competition. That just means I'm a pioneer. The first world record holder. It's got a nice ring to it.

"Hey!" a woman yells after me when she narrowly escapes being mowed down.

"Sorry," I shout back. What's with all the people? Lost tourists? Is somebody giving out free Taylor Swift tickets? Who knows, but there's a shit-ton of people rudely blocking my way. Which wouldn't be an issue if some asshole hadn't stolen my freaking bike. I liked that bike. It was my lucky bike. I'd had it for two years! It's the longest I've gone without some dickbag stealing my bike. I suppose my luck had to run out sometime. It always does. I didn't even bother reporting it. What'd be the point?

Monday. Still out there trying to prove why it's the worst.

"Hi!" I say way too loudly once I storm into the restaurant, making the waitress jump. I wince and lower my voice to an appropriate volume. "Sorry."

"Unfortunately we don't have any free tables," she says, and boy does she not look sorry at all. It's almost like they're trying to keep their standards in place and aren't interested in sweaty, yelling clients.

"It's fine," I say breezily. "I'm meeting somebody." I turn to look around. It doesn't take me long to locate Blake. Let's be real, the guy stands out.

I carefully make my way toward him. A slow smile spreads over his face, and my stupid stomach gives a jolt. Blake smiles with his whole body. It's not just tilting the corners of his lips for him. It encompasses his whole being. I bet even his soul is smiling.

"And here I thought you were going to stand me up," he says once I reach his table.

"I just enjoy being fashionably late. Helps establish my superiority."

His smile widens. "Ah. I was wondering what your secret was."

"Use that knowledge wisely. With great power comes great responsibility."

Yeah. I just said that. Fuck me. With how many Spiderman references I've been using these past few days, you'd think I was a fan. I'm not. I've only seen one movie, more than a decade ago, and I kind of fell asleep halfway through, so why that's my pop culture reference of choice lately is anybody's guess.

Blake laughs again before he puts his hand in his pocket and pulls out my watch. He hands it to me, and I immediately put it back on my wrist before I inspect it.

The strap seems completely fine. I figured it must've broken or there'd be a problem with the clasp, but everything seems as good as new.

I'll be more careful in the future. My shoulders relax once the watch is back on my wrist. When I lift my eyes, I meet Blake's gaze. A frown mixes with curiosity on his face, creating a peculiar expression.

"It's my dad's. He gave it to me for my sixteenth birthday. Sort of a family heirloom," I explain as I lift my wrist. "It's stupid, but I'm a bit attached to it."

He tilts his head to the side. "Not stupid at all. Why do you say that?"

"I... Well, I don't really know. I don't think you should be this attached to material things, I guess?"

"Maybe not all the things you own. That'd border on hoarder territory, but I don't think there's anything wrong with keepsakes. Shows you have people in your life you love."

"That's a nice way to put it." I look down at the watch and slide my fingertips over the face. "Anyway, I owe you lunch."

"You do. I was just trying to figure out what the most expensive thing on the menu is."

I nod. "Good to know. Dine and dash it is."

Somebody clears their throat behind me.

"That was a joke," I say.

The waitress from before glares at me. I pull out my wallet and open it before I very purposefully flash some cash at her. "Should I maybe pay you right now?"

"You haven't ordered yet," she says.

"We're obviously getting off on the right foot, you and me, aren't we?" I say.

She gives me absolutely nothing. Not even a raised eyebrow.

Blake's lips twitch, but he valiantly fights the laugh, and we give the waitress our orders.

She nods, takes the menus, and walks away, but I can feel eyes on me long after she's gone.

I turn back toward Blake, and then I don't really know what

to say next. I don't do this part. Usually I just sleep with people and then get on with my day, but now I'm here with somebody who's made it very clear sex is not on the table, so I'm a fish out of water.

"So," I say.

"So," Blake replies. He looks amused.

"So," I say again, because apparently I just really want to underline that I'm not a great conversationalist. "You found my watch. I still can't believe I just lost it like that. Where was it?"

"Lying by that staircase that led to the roof. It took me a bit of time to call you. I didn't look at the back, so I didn't know it was yours at first. And then when I finally figured it out, it was already late, so I thought it'd be rude to wake you. And then I was out of town, so I only managed to call you last night. Sorry."

"Sorry for what?" I ask. "I'm the dumbass who lost it. You don't have to apologize for that."

"Force of habit," he says with a grin.

Part of me had hoped I was wearing booze goggles Saturday and that's why I'd found Blake so attractive. Seems I can't blame that one sip of gin, but there's still a chance it's just my brain viewing him as some sort of challenge. A moment of, *ooh a shiny new toy! We haven't slept with that one yet!* It happens every now and then, so it very well might be that Blake is just shinier than some other toys I've played with.

Fingers crossed he'll say or do something that'll just obliterate my interest.

"How was the rest of your weekend?" Blake asks, a teasing spark in his eyes. "Get stuck on any other roofs? Sneak into places you weren't supposed to be?"

"It's nice how we're just conveniently ignoring that you're the one who locked us out in the first place."

"So glad we're on the same page about that."

"You'll be happy to hear I've been a law-abiding citizen since then."

"And in your case that means...?"

"Watched shitty sci-fi movies and ate pizza. Like people do."

He sends me an amused look. "A fan?"

"What's with the tone? Bad sci-fi is the absolute highest form of entertainment."

He purses his lips and cocks his head. "Is it?"

I narrow my eyes and try to process the skeptical tone of voice. "You don't think so?" I raise my hand when he opens his mouth. "No, it's fine. I guess nobody's perfect. Although this is a pretty serious flaw, so you should give me a moment to try and come to terms with it."

"I guess I've never really seen any terrible sci-fi movies."

"You just keep getting less and less attractive. Bad sci-fi movies are a comedic goldmine that you can tap into for eternity. Especially if it's a franchise. Number one is bad. Two is worse. Number three is where it usually gets outright brilliant."

Blake laughs. "I'm starting to think there's a gap in my education. Somebody should really help me fix that. Maybe somebody who appreciates questionable cinema?"

Once again, I'm forced to swallow down a confused *why*? But I nod, and say, "Sure" anyway. It's not like we're going to do it, so I can be polite.

"Cool." For some reason, he looks super pumped about this platonic movie date we're never going to have.

"What about you?" I ask. "Good Sunday? Go somewhere interesting?"

"It was okay," he says. "I was meeting a client and was really late getting back to town."

"You said you work in IT?"

"Yup. Computers," he says.

"I mean, if you tried, I'm sure you could be even more vague."

He chuckles. "Cybersecurity. I do pentesting."

I raise my brows and just look at him until he quirks his brow right back at me and asks, "What?"

"You're a nerd," I say.

"I'm a highly sought-after professional," he protests in a very dignified tone.

"A big ol' nerd," I repeat with a smirk.

"People pay me loads of money for what I do."

"They should. I mean, the things you have to do day in and day out." I lean forward and hold his gaze. "Penetrating defenses. Hardening. Testing the back door. Going as deep as you can until you're as far inside as possible. Takes a real man to do the job properly."

He barks out a laugh and shakes his head. "It's impressive you managed to make it sound *that* dirty."

"To be fair, the source material did most of the heavy lifting. How did you get into pentesting?"

He scratches the back of his head and refuses to meet my gaze. "Uh... I sort of hacked this company when I was fourteen and got caught," he says. "It unraveled from there."

Well, fuck. This is definitely not the way to de-intrigue a person. He's an IT nerd. He should be boring. It's in the goddamn job description.

"Which company?"

He hesitates for a bit before he says, "Helios."

"You hacked Helios?" I repeat because I'm pretty sure he's pulling my chain. "The space company, Helios? We'll-put-man-back-on-the-moon-this-decade Helios? That one?"

"To be fair, they weren't that big of a deal a decade ago, and their security systems left a lot to be desired back then," he says. "I guess I got curious. Plus, I was fourteen, so I wasn't exactly good at thinking ahead. Throw in an over-inflated ego and a fair bit of distain for rules, and you've got a perfect storm. And a lot of trouble."

"What kind of trouble?"

"Legal," he says.

"The fine kind of legal?"

"The juvie kind of legal."

It's interesting. Here we are. Two relative strangers. Two different worlds and two different life experiences that somehow brush in the most unexpected places.

Blake lifts one brow at me as if in challenge. *I showed you my cards. What are you going to do with them?*

He's completely still, eyeing me carefully. I don't know what he expects me to do here. Run for the hills because a mistake he made a decade ago?

"So what you're saying is you're insanely smart," I say.

He blinks. "That's what you're getting out of this? No offense, but your deduction skills could use a bit of work."

"I'm sure you're right. Did you go to college?"

He looks stumped. There's a curve in the road, and he didn't expect the change of direction. The confusion is sort of amusing.

"Yes, I went to college," he says carefully.

"Where?"

"Stanford."

I let out a low whistle. It's a good thing I'm not interested in him, because he's way out of my league. It's not a self-confidence issue. I don't think I'm exactly dumb, and what I lack in book smarts I make up for in practical life skills. It's more of a common sense issue. A birds-of-a-feather-flock-together issue.

The waitress comes over with our food. She slides the plates toward us and sends me another suspicious look. She'd probably lock the doors if it wasn't a fire safety violation.

Joke's on her. She's not the first person I've alienated with my questionable sense of humor, and she most likely won't be the last, so I resist waving cash at her again and pick up my fork instead.

"Have you always lived in New York?" Blake asks as he digs into his food.

I shake my head and spear a shrimp with my fork. "No."

Blake sends me a curious look. I suppose not elaborating on that seems weird.

"We moved around a lot," I say, stabbing another shrimp to keep myself busy and not think about what I'm saying too much. It's been a while since I've let anybody ask me these basic get-to-know-you questions, and I'm a bit rusty. "I've lived all over."

"Like?"

I wave my fork around in a circular motion. "Chicago. Austin. Columbus. Louisville. Denver. Atlanta. Miami. There are a few more," I say breezily. "My parents loved moving around. Some people are like that. Itchy feet." I hope that's enough, and I don't have to explain why.

"Do you have itchy feet, too?"

I have to think about that one for a bit. "I like to know that if I wanted to go right now, I could. That I don't have anything that ties me to one place for good. I might not necessarily want to move right this second, but I like to know that if I felt like it, I could pack my bag and go."

He nods slowly. "And how long have you been in New York?"

"A few years."

"Do you have family here?"

I hesitate for a moment before I nod. "I have a… Blair and Nora."

"Sisters?" Blake asks.

"Of sorts."

I feel like I'm under a microscope with all that intense attention aimed at me.

"You're close?"

"I like them more often than I dislike them," I say.

He laughs, and it suddenly hits me why it's so easy to talk to Blake: he gets my jokes. Correction, he gets *when* I'm joking. I can't even begin to count how many people I've accidentally offended over the years by saying things that *I* meant as a joke, but other people took personally. I can't blame them. Half the stuff that comes out of my mouth should never have passed quality control.

I look up and then I stare. He's sawing his knife through the spaghetti.

Blake looks up at me. "What?"

I aim my gaze pointedly at his plate. "What are you doing?"

He looks down at the pasta, then up at me. "Cutting the spaghetti," he says.

I raise my brows. "Because?"

"Because I'm planning to eat it?"

"Most people just twirl the pasta around their fork."

He squints his eyes at me. "Is this the part where you tell me about your Italian grandmother, who'd spear and twirl my entrails on a fork for disrespecting the food of her ancestors like that? Because I'll have you and your nonna know, you can't eat spaghetti without cutting it. It's all different lengths, so inevitably something will tangle off the fork, and I'll just end up slurping them until there's sauce everywhere. Makes people stare."

I listen to the speech before I reach my fork to his plate, twirl a ball of spaghetti on it and bring it to my mouth. I might not know a lot of things, but I'm fairly handy with utensils. I can even rock chopsticks like a pro. Spaghetti on a fork? Easy-peasy.

Blake sends me a sour look. "Nobody likes a showoff."

The way his eyes are stuck on my mouth as I chew? Yeah, I don't believe him. Let's see if I'm right.

"*You* do," I say smugly.

He makes a valiant effort to scowl. "I really don't."

"You find me so hot right now."

His lips twitch. "Less and less with every passing second."

"Irresistible."

"Damn, you're cocky," he says, but then he's laughing again.

I waggle my brows. "And it turns you on."

He can't even hide his amusement anymore.

"You want to climb me like a tree," I continue.

Blake smirks and shakes his head. "Still not gonna sleep with you."

I shrug. "Worth a shot. If you're not interested in sleeping with me, why exactly are we here?"

He blinks in surprise. "You really are straightforward."

"To be fair, I did warn you."

"You did," he acknowledges. He leans back and shrugs one shoulder. "I find you very interesting. And I'd like to get to know you better."

Well, this is awkward. How do I put this nicely?

"Thanks? But I have zero interest in dating you. Or anybody. It's not personal. All evidence points to the fact that you're a very nice person."

"No, I'm not asking you to date me. This is not what's happening here. I'm not really the dating type."

My brow furrows in total confusion. "Then what?"

"I figured we could hang out," he says. He laughs at whatever he sees on my face. "It's a thing, you know? People do that. You're interesting," he repeats, like he's trying to hammer the fact home. Or flatter me. I'd be lying if I said it wasn't working. It is. At least a little bit. Not enough, though.

Contrary to popular belief, I don't actually actively want to be a dick. It just always works out that way in the end.

And now he's looking at me all handsome and friendly and goddamn nice. And he's probably expecting me to be equally friendly and nice and well-adjusted and normal and—

I panic. Sort of. It's not pretty.

"I already have friends."

"And you're not allowed to add more to the existing friend pool?" he asks.

"The pool's plenty big as it is," I say. And there goes my plan to not be a dick.

"Fair enough," he says easily. "If you change your mind, though..."

"Sure. And hey, if you decide you want to sleep with me after all, let me know."

"Can't really be friends if we fuck, can we?" he asks with a smirk.

"You sure? We should test that theory out. You're a nerd. You should get a kick out of research."

"I'm pretty sure a lot of people have already conducted that research, and it hasn't worked out for them."

"I wouldn't have pegged you for a pessimist."

He laughs. "I just have different goals than a quick fuck. I can get that anywhere."

I push my empty plate away and lean my arms on the table, leaning forward. "What if I'm not just a quick fuck? What if I'm the kind of fuck that does things other fucks won't do?"

He blinks slowly, and something in his gaze changes. Just for a tiny moment, but it's there. The definite spark of interest. But then he takes a very measured breath, eyes wandering up and down my body for a moment before he snaps his gaze away. His hand squeezes his fork into a death grip before he slowly puts it down and extends his fingers on top of the table.

I don't get it. He clearly wants to, so I'm not sure what his deal is... but it's not my place to push him.

Although he's clearly operating under the impression that I'm going to try something, because after taking a quick glance at his phone, he gets up rather abruptly.

"I have to get going. I've got work to do."

"Okay," I say slowly. I suppose we don't have much else to discuss, seeing that we both have very different goals for what we hope will be the outcome of this lunch.

He pats down the pockets of his jeans until he finds some cash and throws some bills on the table.

"Put those away," I say. "I said lunch was on me, didn't I? You did get that the dine and dash thing was a joke, right?"

"Yeah, no. I got it." He leaves the money where it is, pulls his jacket on, and then he just stands by the table for a few moments.

"We should do this again," he says.

"Sure?" I say slowly.

He gives a curt nod, and in a few seconds he's out the door so quickly that I'm tempted to check if, unbeknownst to me, the place has caught on fire.

Well, that was interesting.

Twenty bucks says I'll never see him again.

EIGHT

I'M gonna have to give myself some credit. When I promise something, I deliver.

Maybe a bit too well at times, but that's not really important. What matters is that I told Blair I'd get her wife drunk, and I did. Did it to the point where Nora is now hogging the stage at a karaoke bar, determined to perform every Nickelback song known to mankind. She's already done four in a row.

She's currently waving her phone around, asking people to, "Look at this photograph." She's very loud, but surprisingly in tune. Well, not surprisingly. It's Nora. She does everything well, so naturally she also has a very nice voice. And the crowd is eating it up, cheering her on and singing along. The dance moves are a bit questionable, but considering how many shots of tequila are swimming around in her bloodstream, it's a miracle she's even upright.

Do I feel bad that I'm filming this whole thing and am definitely going to use the footage for blackmail later? Or endless jokes? Or both? Most likely both. Admittedly, I did for a moment there, but then Nora pointed at me and yelled, "And what the hell is on Judy's head?" and my conscience skittered back into the black hole where it usually resides.

Also, Blair will kill me if I tell her this story and don't deliver the goods. I'm not afraid of much, but the wrath of a pregnant Blair is in the top three of things that make me slightly apprehensive.

The song ends and Nora lifts both her hands in the air. The one holding the microphone and the one holding the bottle of beer.

"Whoo! Thank you, New York! I love you!" she yells at the top of her lungs. And then she does a mic drop before she skips off the stage. She's surprisingly steady on her feet, even if she's clearly drunk off her ass. She drags her fingers through her hair and sits down.

I aim my phone at her face.

"If it isn't our very own rockstar. Say something nice to your wife."

"My wife," Nora says, and her features soften, her mouth curving into a sickeningly dreamy smile. "You know, the first time I saw Blair... You know what I said?"

"We've all heard the story. She tore you a new one when you stole her parking spot and you said, and I quote, 'You're kind of a bitch.' And then you two lived happily ever after."

Nora beckons me closer and lifts her hand up to the side of his mouth. "Noooo," she says. "That's the official version. The first time I saw Blair, I said, 'That's my future wife.' And then the bitch thing after. She didn't hear the future wife part." She lets out a very un-Nora-like giggle and lifts her forefinger to her mouth. "Shh! She'd never let me live it down if she knew I said something so sappy."

"Your secret's safe with me," I assure her.

"I know," Nora says. "You're a good guy, you know? And I'm saying it as somebody who didn't like you at first, but I forgive you." She stabs her index finger into my chest and repeats, "I forgive you because you're a good guy."

"Well, thanks," I say. "You're not too bad yourself."

"No, really." Nora wraps her hand behind my neck and pulls me closer until our foreheads are touching. The tequila fumes are so potent I can feel myself getting drunk just breathing them in. "Even if you are sarcastic and emotionally damaged and don't trust anybody... Underneath, you're still a good guy."

She smacks a kiss on my cheek and lets go of me.

"I'm not emotionally damaged. And I trust plenty of people," I protest, unreasonably hurt by the blunt statement. Drunk people, like small children, lack filter. Sometimes the results are not pleasant.

"Name one," Nora challenges.

She's looking all smug, so I feel like this is a trap, but I proceed anyway.

"Blair," I say.

Nora quirks her brow and gives a derisive snort. "Right. When you fell off that stupid bike of yours and twisted your ankle so badly you couldn't walk for a week, remind me, did you call Blair and tell her about it? Ask for help? Or did she find you camping out on your bathroom floor when she randomly dropped by your place three days after it happened?"

I want to say something. Make that moment make sense. No, I hadn't called. I'd considered it for a moment, but in the end, I just... didn't.

"And don't even get me started on Stephen. You two are supposed to be friends, but you never talk about anything that truly matters. He's fucked up. You're fucked up. The depth is there, but you only skim the surface. You have no idea what's really going on with him and vice versa."

She flings those words at me so easily, and no matter how hard I try to argue, I come up empty.

I don't *not* trust Blair and Steph. But...

You can't trust people because they can and will let you down. Even those people you think are incapable of betrayal will still detonate a nuclear bomb in the middle of your life and turn everything you thought was real into smoke and ashes.

"Truth hurts," Nora says wisely and burps.

"Like you're any better," I say.

"Oh?" She quirks a brow and starts ticking on her fingers. "My dad. My mom. Blair's parents. Quinn. Avery. He's my hairdresser. My hair is actually bright orange, but he makes it pretty, and nobody knows I'm a carrot. And he's never said a word about it to anybody." She giggles again. I make a mental note of the hair-thing. For the future. You never know when a gem like that might come in handy.

"And those are just the ones I trust completely," Nora continues. "There are also a bunch of people on the lower levels of trust. There are four, in case you're wondering. Those are the ones where I maybe wouldn't trust them with my life, but I'd trust them enough to ask them to be my getaway driver because I know they wouldn't rat me out to the cops. Whereas you sort of have Blair and Stephen, but you're not even a hundred percent in when it comes to those two. It's kind of sad if you think about it. They're your best friends, man."

"What's your point?" I ask.

She sends me an unexpectedly sober look. "Sometimes I worry about you."

"Why? I'm fine."

"I want you to be happy."

"I am."

She has the audacity to laugh out loud at that. "No, no, no. You, my darling," she says, pointing the neck of her beer bottle in my direction, "are completely, one hundred percent fucked up."

"Thank you," I say dryly.

Nora takes a long drink and sends me an equally lengthy, level look.

"Come on. It's not like it's a surprise to you, is it? You're so afraid people will screw you over that you avoid anything more serious than being somebody's passing acquaintance. Once the girl at Starbucks started spelling your name correctly you were all, 'Well, this is getting awfully serious,' and started going to a different coffee shop!"

I decide not to address that one. "Screwed-up people can't be happy? Is that your point?"

"Not the way you do it. You're keeping everybody at arm's length, even though you don't really want to. That whole every-man-is-an-island nonsense you've got going on? It's bullshit."

"No, it's not."

"Bull. Shit," she repeats sternly. "The Jude Blair and Stephen talk about from when you were younger sounds like a whole different person."

"This might come as a surprise to you, but people change when they grow up."

"Personality develops by the time you're seven," Nora informs me.

"According to what? Popular science?" I scoff.

"Newest research," she counters. "I can see right through you, you know? You're lonely."

"Is this the part where you tell me all I need is love?"

"Aww, babe, I'm the furthest thing from Cupid."

"Then what's the point of this conversation, exactly?"

"The point is you need to let people in," she says.

"I let people in on a regular basis."

"No, you don't," she argues.

"I absolutely do. I just expect them to leave once they pull out."

She rolls her eyes. "I'm not talking about your ass. The inside I'm talking about is metaphorical. I get it. Trust is a difficult thing, and I get why you're like that after that whole thing with your parents, I just think you deserve better. You deserve more out of life. And the only way you can get it is if you take the plunge again and give people a chance. You can't just write off everyone from the sta—"

My fingernails are pressed so deep into the soft part of my palm that the skin has turned numb. It stings like a bitch when I pry my hands open and push myself to my feet.

"Where're you going?" Nora calls.

"To get a drink!" I snap over my shoulder. I don't need to sit here and listen to this. She's wrong. I'm fine. We'll leave it at that.

She jumps up and barrels past me. "Ooh! Tequila shots!"

"Great idea," I say and stalk to the bar.

Quinn pushes a wad of something white toward me as soon as I open the door of his car.

I blink blearily and make a grab for it. And miss. I squint. Should I aim for the Quinn on the left or Quinn on the right? That is the question.

"I'm rethinking a lot of my life choices," Quinn says, getting out of the car as Nora is leaning against the side of it, fondling the window. He gently maneuvers her out of the way and opens the door before he helps her inside. He fastens her seatbelt and makes sure she stays upright before he shuts the door.

I get inside as well, and it only takes me three tries to put the seatbelt on.

Quinn gets inside and yawns before he rubs the heels of his palms over his eyes. "All right. Everybody ready to go?" he asks and glances into the rearview mirror.

"Yeah!" Nora says. "You know what we should totally do?"

"I'm afraid to ask," Quinn says.

"Afterparty! Ooh!" Nora says loudly. "Let's call Steph. Yeah, yeah. Tell him to fly here. He's the best! We'll make a weekend out of this."

"We're not calling any more people at this time of night," Quinn says loudly while Nora's trying to wrestle her phone out of her purse.

She leans forward and pouts. "Why not? Ooh! Let's go to a vineyard! I've always wanted to do that."

She lifts her phone up, squinting at it.

"Do you know their number?"

"Yes. Just give me your phone and I'll call a vineyard for you."

She slaps the phone in Quinn's palm, and he drops it in the map pocket.

Nora frowns and throws herself against the seat. "You're no fun."

Quinn closes his eyes and counts to ten under his breath before he throws that something white from earlier into my lap.

"What's that?" I ask.

"Plastic bags. You feel like puking, you do it into one of these. Got it?"

I salute him. "Loud and clear. Unnecessary, though. I don't puke. I just pass out."

Quinn throws another glance in the mirror at a now-snoring Nora. "You two have got something in common, then."

"Mhmm," I mumble and lean my forehead against the cool glass as Quinn maneuvers his fancy car out of the parking spot. "Thanks for coming to get us," I say with a yawn.

"It's what I'm here for."

"To cart your drunk best friend around town at"—I check the clock on the dash—"four a.m.? Kind of screwed you over with that call, didn't we?" Another yawn cracks my jaw. "I'd feel bad, but honestly, it's a lesson to turn your phone off when you go to bed."

"It's fine," Quinn says.

"Four a.m. is fine?" I look toward the backseat and then at Quinn.

"I was going to be up in an hour anyway."

I make a face. "Why? It's Saturday."

He throws me an amused look. "Didn't your mother ever tell you the early bird catches the worm?"

"No. She was normal."

He falls silent while navigating us through the dark city streets toward Brooklyn.

"Aren't you going to be dead on your feet tomorrow?" I ask.

"I'm willing to wager I'll be in much better shape than you two," Quinn says. "You'll need to give me some directions now. I don't know where you live."

I direct him to my building, and he parks at the curb directly in front of the door. Nora mutters something and peers at me out of one eye.

"I don't feel too hot," she says.

Quinn snaps his head toward her. "Get it together, this is a no-vomit zone."

Nora clamps her mouth shut and sways a bit.

"Fantastic," Quinn mutters.

"Relax. I'll get her upstairs, and she can sleep it off at my place," I say, getting out of the car.

Quinn doesn't even pretend he's going to argue about who gets to take care of Nora. He just helps her out the door, too. She wobbles a bit in her high heels. First time I've ever seen her do that. Quinn looks at her for a second, sighs, then picks her up in fireman's carry. She giggles and starts swaying her arms left and right. We trudge up the stairs and once inside my apartment, I point Quinn to the bedroom. He puts Nora into bed and pulls the covers over her. She doesn't even stir.

I stumble back to the living room and faceplant on the couch.

"I'm heading out," Quinn says from the doorway. "Will you two be okay?"

"Thanks," I mutter into the couch cushion. My arm flops over the side, fingers grazing the floorboards.

I'm almost asleep when I remember Blair. Shit. Should probably text her about Nora. I flop on my back and dig my phone out of my pocket, squinting at the bright light. Eyes half-closed, I shoot off a quick text and drop the phone somewhere on the floor.

That's my last memory of the night before I pass out.

NINE

I WAKE up to the sound of a gunshot. Or at least that's what I think it is.

I sit up so quickly my head starts to spin from the sudden movement. And then the pain arrives. A bright, hot flash of agony hits my temples before it spreads through the rest of my head.

"Holy fuck," I gasp. My fingertips dig into the sides of my head. I'm not sure what my goal is. I'm either trying to contain the pain or trying to squeeze my head until it explodes and the torture ends. One or the other.

I look up just as Blair marches into the room. She looks furious as she strides toward me. Once she's in front of me, she slams her fists onto her hips and stares at me, nostrils flaring. This goes on for a few seconds before she puts her thumb and forefinger between her lips and whistles. It's one of those extremely high, loud, ear-splitting whistles that effectively makes me want to die. I let out a very undignified whimper.

"What the fuck is your fucking problem?" I look up once the worst stabs of pain slowly start to ebb.

"Serves you right." She bends down, picks something up,

and slams it on the coffee table. I stare at my phone and then at Blair.

"Would it have killed you to text me about this little sleepover you and Nora are having?"

I squint my eyes at her. Brain activity is at the lowest level it's ever been. The lights are on, but the residents are still drunk, passed out in the backyard.

"What?" I eventually ask.

She huffs and motions toward the bedroom. "I woke up today, and imagine my surprise when I found my wife still missing. And you won't even answer your phone, you stupid jerk!"

I slowly pick up the phone, all the while eyeing Blair carefully in case she decides to attack. Once she starts pacing, I glance at the phone.

"It's on silent mode," I say. "Shit. Sorry."

"Not good enough. Was it really so hard to send me a text?"

Something tickles in my brain. An indignant need to argue the unfair accusation.

"I did send you a text," I say.

"No, you didn't."

"I absolutely did!" I slide my thumb over the screen and go to messages. Things are still a bit fuzzy, but I swear I fiddled with my phone at some point, and it wasn't to find porn.

"Shit," I say when I stare at the last message I sent. Well, this is just great.

"What?" Blair demands.

I stare at the screen. The good news is I was right. I *did* send a text. The bad news is that instead of Blair, I sent it to somebody else. And as it is, Blair just happens to be right next to Blake in my list of contacts.

Which means that at exactly—I glance at the phone—4:21 a.m., Blake got a text from me that said: *mission accomplished got her drunk and took her to bed.*

"Fucking shit," I say and stuff my face into my pillow. With any luck, I'll suffocate. It's a good plan. For exactly three point five seconds before Blair pulls the pillow away.

"Excuse me," she snaps. "But I'm not done yelling at you."

"Go ahead. You've got until asphyxiation takes me out, so I'd hurry if I were you."

Blair crosses her arms over her chest and frowns. "Try and look livelier. You're taking all the joy out of yelling."

"My bad," I mutter. "Wouldn't want to ruin this experience for you."

Blair frowns and pulls my phone out of my hand. She slides her thumb over the screen and gives me a blessed few seconds of silence while she reads.

"Who's Blake?" she asks.

"He's... some guy I met at a party."

Blair snaps her head toward me, Nora temporarily forgotten. "You met somebody at a party?" She's looking very interested in that particular turn of events. "And you got his number?"

"Uh-huh," I mutter.

She's still staring.

"What?" I ask.

She sends me a very pointed look. "You got somebody's number? *You?*"

Nora chooses that moment to stumble into the room. She looks like she just dug herself out of her own grave as she flops down on the couch next to me. She sends me a disgusted look while she starts rubbing her temples, very slowly and very carefully, as if even the smallest of movements hurts.

"Good morning." I nudge her with my shoulder until she looks like she's about to puke. "Had a good night?"

Nora winces when her body jostles. She looks at Blair and

then nods toward her right arm. "Can you do me a favor, babe? Cut off my hand and slap Jude with it?"

"How's your head?" Blair asks. She sounds way more sympathetic than she did with me. "I'll get you coffee." She heads to the kitchen nook.

Nora and I spend the ten minutes Blair is busy in the kitchen staring into nothing. Once she's back, she pushes the biggest mug of something that looks like straight-up tar in front of Nora. Nothing for me. Figures. I don't even feel bad when I swipe the mug.

"Bless you," I say.

"Did you two have a fun night?" Blair asks.

"I'm never drinking again," Nora says weakly. "Ever. I'm a dignified, sophisticated woman. This is *not* dignified. Or sophisticated." She turns her head toward me and narrows her eyes. "Oh, and look who's here," she says. "The architect of my misery."

"I didn't force you to become the main sponsor of Jose Cuervo. You volunteered." I mean, I encouraged the first few shots, but I don't think this is the right time for confessions.

"You proposed the idea of going out. It makes you the instigator. They've jailed people for less."

"There, there. What matters is you two had fun," Blair says diplomatically. She sits down next to Nora, who leans her head on Blair's shoulder and closes her eyes.

I'm drinking Nora's coffee and staring into space when Blair breaks the silence.

"So who is he? This Blake of yours."

Oh good. We're back on that.

I roll my eyes. "He's not *my* anything. He's a random guy I met when I was at a party. We got to talking. That's it."

She seems to ponder it for a moment.

"What's he like?" she asks.

Funny as hell, sexy as fuck, and sadly, not interested.
"He's... nice."
Nora peers at me from the corner of her eye. "Who's nice?"
"Jude's new boyfriend," Blair says.
"Next time I see your mom, I'll tell her you two are planning to name your baby after her. She'll be so happy," I say. "I'm sure sophisticated, confident people like you two will have a kid who'll be able to pull off Bertha."

Blair tips an imaginary hat toward me. "Well played, sir."

There's a moment of silence, but as soon as I think she's dropped it, Blair says, "Seriously, though. Nice is good. Very good." She purses her lips.

She's done now.

No, she's not.

"Hot?" Blair asks.

"Sure," I say.

She exchanges glances with Nora.

"Good in bed?" Nora lifts her brow.

"Now there's a pointless question to ask. It's not like anybody's going to say, 'Oh, you know me, below average stamina and a small dick. Lower your expectations accordingly.'"

They both whip their heads toward me, eyes going comically large. "You haven't slept with him?"

"No, we're saving ourselves for the wedding night," I say. "It's supposed to make it extra special."

They exchange glances again. This time with extra eyebrow action thrown in. It's like watching people communicate in a foreign language. They're clearly talking to each other, but I have no clue what's being said. Well, not *no* clue. It's about me, for sure. And I can take a stab at the general subject area.

It goes on for the longest time before Blair opens her mouth.

"Oh my God. You like him."

"I—" I start to argue, but denying takes too much energy, and my reserves have been drowned in tequila.

They're clutching each other's hands now, lips pressed together, identical I'm-holding-in-an-excited-scream expressions on their faces.

It's getting weird.

"That's great," Nora says with remarkable composure, considering what she told me last night about me being a distrustful, pessimistic sociopath. They're like two moms whose prayers have finally been answered because their loser son has finally made a friend, so they're trying to be supportive while not being overly enthusiastic in case this whole thing goes to shit.

"Are you going to call him?" Blair asks.

"No," I scoff.

"Why not?"

"Because," I say maturely.

"Because what?" Blair asks with annoying persistence.

"No point. He wants to be friends."

"Okay, then be friends," Nora says and looks at Blair. "He does know he doesn't have to sleep with everything that moves, does he?"

"I wouldn't be too sure about that," Blair replies before she turns toward me. "Here's a novel idea. Do it."

"I don't want to."

"Ah," Blair says with annoying smugness. "I get it. You don't know how."

"I don't know how what?" I ask.

"You don't know how to make friends."

"I'm friends with you, aren't I?" I counter. "For some reason."

"Please, that was all me. *You* don't know how."

"I do know. I just don't want to." I sound like a five-year-old.

"Prove it." Blair glances at her nails, a mildly bored look on her face.

I know what she's doing. I absolutely know. That doesn't mean I don't silently take the bait anyway.

"I don't feel too good," Nora says, interrupting the staredown before I can say anything I'll later regret. Divine intervention is real.

Blair immediately forgets me, squeezes Nora's knee, and gets up, extending her arm to Nora. "Come on. Let's get you home and to bed."

"I love you," Nora says, and Blair, who's generally vehemently against any kind of PDA, verbal or otherwise, lets it go this once.

They both say their goodbyes and get going, and once the front door shuts behind them, I drag my ass to bed.

By the time the sun is starting to set I'm ready to pick up my phone and face the music, so I go back to my messages, sigh, and start to type.

Despite all evidence pointing to the contrary, I'm not actually a deranged pervert.

When no reply comes, I hide the phone under one of the cushions and go take a shower. Once I'm back, I approach the couch with the same amount of wariness I'd display if I found a skunk in my trash can. I fish the phone out, put it on the coffee table in front of me, and eye it for a few minutes until I'm forced to roll my eyes at my own dramatic behavior. I swipe my thumb over the screen.

You're not? That's disappointing.

The easygoing, friendly Blake from the roof? It seems he's back. Only I'm not sure what to do with him now. I'll explain the text, I suppose, but what then? I have no clue. Maybe Blair was right, and I really have lost the ability to not sleep with people.

The thing is, sex is easy. You just need another willing body and you're golden. Relationships, on the other hand, are where it gets complicated. And I don't do complicated. Even thinking about it makes it feel like something disgusting is crawling around inside me, and I need to vomit it out.

I concentrate on the phone again.

I went out with a friend and things got a bit out of hand, so she stayed at my place. The text was meant for her wife.

I nearly jump out of my skin when my phone starts ringing. Who the fuck calls people? What kind of weird social experiment is this? I'm not even sure what compels me to pick up, but pick up I do.

"Hi," I say. I might not like the lurch of excitement in my stomach, but it's there anyway.

"So you're a sloppy drunk, huh?" Blake asks, the laughter in his voice coming through loud and clear.

"What gave you that idea? I'm extremely classy while drunk. Obviously."

"It sounds like you had fun, at least."

"I did. Could've done without the hangover, but I guess you can't have it all."

He laughs. *"How bad is it?"*

"Let's put it this way, I now know how vampires feel in the sunlight."

He makes a sound that's a mix of laughter and sympathy. *"You should eat some fruit. Bananas, watermelon, blueberries. They help."*

"Do you think I can substitute mayonnaise and some questionable Mexican food? Cause that's about all I have in the fridge right now."

"*Depends.*"

"On?"

"*Whether or not you've developed a fondness for vomiting and want to do it some more.*"

"I'll have you know my hangovers come sans vomit."

"*You gonna risk breaking the streak by adding Mexican food?*"

"Good point. Fasting until Monday it is."

He laughs, something rustles, and after a beat of silence...

"*You know, this is one of those times when it really pays to have friends who just happen to be free to stop by and drop off some stuff for you. Friends who just happen to live above a corner store that sells all the staples.*"

"Oh," I say slowly once my brain catches up to the obvious. "This is sort of like blackmail."

He chuckles. "*And you like it.*"

"Not really," I say. "Don't get me wrong, I respect the hell out of it, but I definitely don't like it."

"*Did I lose some more hotness points?*" he asks.

"On the contrary, sadly. If anything, devious blackmail just makes people hotter."

"*In that case, we should definitely hang out. I'm sure I'll say something stupid, and that'll undo the damage.*"

"Doubtful."

"*But you're tempted.*"

"No."

"*You keep telling yourself that,*" Blake says. "*I assume you're texting me your address right now?*"

"My fingers are so still they might as well be frozen."

"*Sure they are. I'll see you in a bit.*" He hangs up, leaving me staring at my phone.

I'm not gonna lie, there's a moment of pure panic where I contemplate tossing my phone and moving to another state, because Blair is absolutely right. I don't know how to do this. I don't know how to trust people. I don't know how I'm supposed to hand over the keys to all the places I've locked up inside me. *Here. Take them. Do what you will. I know you won't screw me over. Because you're a safe place.*

I just don't.

But.

The thought is small—minuscule, tiny, practically imperceptible—but it's there.

But is that the kind of person I want to be? In the long run? Is it? Because if it is… it's going to be a long, lonely journey.

The logical course of action is to delete Blake's number and forget about him.

The logical course of action.

The sane course of action.

The safe course of action.

I text him the address.

I hesitate before I throw the door open.

"Hi," I say to a smiling Blake.

He wordlessly hands me a paper bag, and I peer inside. Blueberries, strawberries, raspberries. A few bananas and kiwis. A mango and a slice of watermelon. There's more. It's a very healthy bag.

"You get that I'm hungover, not dying of scurvy?" I take the bag and motion him inside.

He's in my hallway. Eyes moving over the small space. Smile still firmly in place.

"Thanks," I add, lest I sound like a dick after he went to all this trouble.

"I wasn't sure how dire the situation was, so I figured better safe than sorry," Blake says, and takes off his sneakers.

He pulls off his hoodie and stands there in a pair of black sweats and a white T-shirt. The lingering remnants of the hangover headache grow fainter as adrenaline takes over. Because he looks good. So. Fucking. Good.

Blake plops down on the couch and stretches out his legs. He looks around, curious gaze taking in everything. It's sparse. I have very few personal belongings, and the place has a sterile, hotel room air about it I've never bothered to combat. I mean, it's a place where I go to sleep, so what's the difference? I'll move on in a few months.

Although, I have to say I lucked out this time. One of Blair's friends went on tour for eight months, so he rented this place to me for a ridiculously low price. Say what you will, but there are definite perks to living alone and not sharing everything with ten strangers.

Blake gets up from the couch in all his graceful, long-limbed glory, clearly too curious to sit still. I know I'm supposed to be all about platonic friendship here, but some people are just nice to look at and impossible not to appreciate.

He stalks over to the few personal items I have lying around, zeroing in on the photos. Me and Blair at Stephen's first gig in some random bar. Blair and Nora's wedding. Me and Steph with our backs to the camera in the Grand Canyon when the three of us took a road trip on Blair's eighteenth birthday.

Blake tilts his head to the side when he gets to the final photo and stares at it for the longest time.

My feet carry me to Blake's side.

A woman with long, dark hair and a dark-haired man wearing sunglasses, with freckles dotting his face, are both kissing the cheeks of a grinning, equally dark-haired kid. In the background, the waves of the Pacific are lapping at the shore, the sand so light in the sunshine it's practically white.

Blake glances at me.

"Where was this taken?"

"San Diego."

I was seven.

I liked it there.

"Your parents?" Blake asks.

"Yup."

He looks at me and then back at the photo. Me again.

"You kind of look like them."

I stare at the little boy and the man and woman on the beach. The wide smiles and tanned faces. Dimples and toothy smiles. Grains of sand stuck to skin freshly coated with sunscreen. Boardshorts and sticky ice cream palms. Happiness. Belonging.

"Yeah," I eventually say. Because I do. I have my mom's dark hair, and my dad's blue eyes. Her sense of humor and his wry outlook on life. I get my disgustingly inconvenient streak of empathy from her and my stubbornness from him. I'm so much like them, and at the same time not at all.

I can feel Blake's eyes on the side of my face. "Are you close?"

I turn away from the photo. How do I answer that?

"Relatively."

"Do they live in New York, too?" he asks.

This is why I stay away from people. People want you to talk. And share. They want to get to know you.

Every word he says, once it reaches my ear canals, transforms into an interrogation. Might as well shine a spotlight on me. *Tell me about your parents. Address. Full names. Birth dates. Education. Jobs. Criminal history.*

"My dad's upstate. My mom's dead. Do you want something to drink? Or some fruit? I have a lot."

"I could go for some fruit," Blake says. At least he knows how to take a hint and stop asking questions, so there's that. If we can shut down all personal questions, this friendship might not be doomed after all.

I take the cutting board and lay out all the fruit. "I feel like I should do something that resembles cooking with these," I say thoughtfully. "Do you like your fruit with mayonnaise?"

"I'd rather go without if at all possible."

I shrug. "Not an adventurous eater, huh?"

"More like I have fully functional taste buds."

I rummage around in the bag and pull out what seems the most appetizing in my current state.

"Can I help?" Blake asks.

"I thought you'd never ask and was honestly getting slightly concerned you were impolite underneath this golden boy exterior."

"Thank God we avoided that."

"I'll say. I guess let's cut these up."

He stands next to me and starts doing just that. Our elbows and sides touch while we work. It's kind of nice, actually. Never done this before, but yeah, it's kind of nice. My track record with cooking is adequate at best, but there aren't a lot of ways to screw up cut-up pieces of fruit, so the result isn't inedible.

I grab two forks from the drawer and hand him one. "Want a bowl of your own?"

"This is fine," he says, and we head for the couch. I put my feet on the coffee table, and we eat. Turns out I'm actually hungry now that I'm not actively wishing for death any longer.

"You know what this could use?" Blake asks when we're about halfway done.

"Pizza?" As nice and healthy as this is, there's only so much flavored water I can take.

"Yup. I mean, this is good, but it's a bit..."

"Bland?" I offer.

"Fruity."

I snort and get up to grab my phone. "What do you want on your pizza?"

"Cheese."

"I think that's a given."

"I have no other requests."

"Double cheese. Got it," I say.

"See if you can get them to do triple cheese, and I'll be your humble servant forever."

"All of that for one pizza? You're a cheap date."

He waggles his brows, and I turn away because I shouldn't like having him in my space this much.

The pizza arrives twenty minutes later, and we camp out on the floor in front of the couch with the pizza box between us.

"Who are the other people in the photos?" Blake asks, munching down on a slice. His eyes are on the shelf again. He's been doing that a lot over the last half an hour. Looking.

"The one with the dark hair is Blair. The redhead is her wife, Nora. The guy is Steph."

"And Steph is...?" Blake asks.

"I met him and Blair in high school when I was living in Maine. Blair lived next door to me and took me under her wing, and Steph and I were both playing in the school band and hit it off."

"And you're all still friends? That's kind of sweet."

"What can I say? I'm a sweet person."

"I'm starting to believe you. And now you all live in New York?"

"Blair and Nora do. Steph is in LA."

He looks at me thoughtfully for a moment. "You said you

play the piano," he says.

"Yup."

"Not planning to become a musician?"

"No."

"Why not?"

"I don't want to play professionally. Being on stage in front of hundreds, if not thousands of people? No. Pass."

"Stage fright?" he asks.

"Nope. Just like my privacy too much."

"Okay, yeah. I get that."

"Thought you would."

He grins and cocks his head. "Do I look like somebody who's especially pro-privacy?" he asks.

"Aren't you a white hat? I figured you jerk off to data privacy laws when you can't sleep at night."

His eyes are shining as he nods. "Those do get me going. Quote me some SHIELD act, and I'm all hot and bothered. Integrity of private information. Data security program. Ooh, yeah, baby. Talk dirty to me."

His voice does very interesting things to me. The way he closes his eyes while he pretends to moan? Yeah, that's even more interesting.

I swallow down the interest and look away. "You're a strange man."

"You said you were into me, so what does that say about you?"

"That I should enunciate more clearly. I said I wanted to *get into your pants*. That comes down purely to your looks. I have no standards other than that. You can be a complete dick, and I'd still do you as long as you're hot. I'll even pretend to agree with you as long as it gets me what I want."

He looks thoughtful. "Interesting. What if I was a climate change denier?"

I shrug. "After me, the flood."

"A megachurch pastor?"

"Praise be."

"A flat-earther?"

"I'd walk to the edge of the world with you. Or to the nearest flat surface, at least."

He chuckles and takes another slice of pizza. "Liar."

"You keep saying that."

"You keep lying," he says through a mouthful of pizza.

"And yet, you don't seem that put off by it."

He sends me a look I can't decipher out of the corner of his eye. "We're all liars," he says. "Seems hypocritical for me to mind."

I consider that for a second.

"I'm not," I say.

He raises his brows at me.

"I don't lie." I refuse to elaborate, though. Not the place and time for that, even if the way he looks at me makes it seem like he can see right through me. It's absurd, of course, and I'm projecting. But the feeling remains.

Blake's phone starts to ring, and he glances at it, frowns, and silences it without answering. I take the empty pizza box to the kitchen, and when I come back, we settle in on the couch.

"What's next on the agenda?" Blake asks.

I shrug. "Strip poker?"

"I suck at poker. I'll be naked in under a minute."

"I'll get the deck," I say and start to get up.

He laughs. Like he does. Always. So. Fucking. Happy. And I want to keep him laughing because for some unfathomable reason, his laughs make me lighter.

"Strip Go Fish?" I ask, and Blake snorts out another laugh, so I keep suggesting games to get naked to, and he keeps laughing, and it's the best I've felt in a long, long while.

TEN

I spend my Sunday carting food to the many, many New Yorkers who don't feel like going outside and follow that up with a shift at the Barclays. Once Monday arrives, it's back to the sandwich shop. Rinse and repeat, week after week.

I have a routine, and it hardly ever changes. I work every day except the two Sundays a month I go to see Dad. All those other days, I like to keep myself busy. Leaves me less time to think, plus I need the money. I'm the perfect person for keeping the gig economy alive. Temporary positions and short-term commitments. Nothing too permanent. I've been at the sandwich shop for three months, which makes it my longest temp job by far. Generally I prefer to have the freedom to come and go as I please, but the owners, a nice married couple, are dealing with some shit, and need the help, so here I am. It's a simple existence. A simple life.

Or it was.

There's an intruder. A very chatty intruder at that. One I don't know what to do with.

It starts with a text.

Have a good one.

Totally out of the blue a day after the hangover incident. It's not exactly a sext, which is my preferred means of communication, so I almost don't reply. I think after Saturday there's plenty of evidence I *can* not sleep with people, so technically I could draw a line under that experiment and call it done.

But I reply anyway.

You too.

Another day arrives, and with it another message.

I'm eating a hot dog, and there's a dog next to me eating a hot dog.

There's a selfie attached. A grinning Blake on a park bench in all his blond, golden glory, smiling brightly like the sun, holding a hot dog. True to his word, there's a shaggy dog wolfing down his own hot dog next to him.

You have a dog? I ask because I'm suddenly curious.

If I can outrun the guy who came with him, I do. Fingers crossed.

I laugh and get on with my day. The good mood lingers.

The next afternoon, I get the next message.

Check out this cloud. It's exactly like Mushroom from Super Mario.

No matter how much I squint, I can't see it, so I send back a photo of a random cloud and say it's the exact shape of a cloud. The reply is short and sweet.

You suck at this game.

In the five days that follow my inbox suffers an avalanche of random texts and messages that, for some inexplicable reason, make me smile a lot more than normal.

On Friday, Blake calls, and we grab sandwiches and eat them on a park bench before I head to work to set up for a concert.

Two days later, we hang out at a bar and play pool. There's a lot of shit-talking and not much else. We drink. I proposition him in a halfhearted way just in case he's changed his mind. He grins and shoots me down. I go to my apartment, and he goes to his. And... I don't thoroughly hate that the night ends in two different places and not with me underneath him.

He's out of town for the next few days, so it's back to text messages for a while.

On Thursday, he sends me an airport selfie to say he's back and starving and would somebody please feed him. I feel a tiny bit regretful when I have to inform him that somebody won't be me because I'm working. He goes by himself and spends the next hour and a half texting me photos of his food, and I kind of, maybe, a bit would like to hang out with him instead of working.

That's a first.

I turn off my phone for the rest of the day because it's clearly radiating terrible ideas, and they're infiltrating my brain.

But when Blake calls the next day, I pick up, and let him drag me to a Rangers game.

My inbox fills with more photos of clouds and food, shots of sunsets and pigeons, people sitting in cafés. Street art, jokes, memes, thoughts, observations.

And I don't know how to stop liking it.

I try, and I fail.

So when it's suddenly been two days of radio silence, I notice.

I'm not sure if I should really be so aware of how quiet my phone is. It doesn't help that the waitstaff gig I had lined up falls through, courtesy of a strategically executed salmonella outbreak, so I have a sudden free evening on my hands.

And that's how, against my better judgment at eleven o'clock at night, I finally give up, take my phone out, and call.

He picks up on the tenth ring.

"Hey." He sounds distracted and weirdly muffled.

"Hey," I say. "You sort of disappeared on me." *How clingy of* me. "Just checking in to see if you're still alive." *Better, but only marginally.*

There's the sound of keyboard clicking before he says. *"I'm finishing up this thing..."* his voice fades away to the soundtrack of clack-clack-clack. *"Why aren't you at work? I'm pretty sure you said something about bartending?"*

"That was yesterday."

I can easily picture the frown on his face. The way his brow crinkles and he squints slightly when he's concentrating on something.

"No. You definitely said Saturday."

"Which was yesterday," I say. It's difficult to say if this is cute or alarming. "You okay? You haven't been hit to the head with an axe or anything like that?"

The click-clack pauses. *"Who the hell would hit me with an axe?"*

"A jealous ex-lover. An angry current lover after life insurance money. Evil stepbrother."

"I didn't realize I was living in a soap opera."

"People never do until they're six feet under."

"You can breathe easy. I'm still in one piece and above ground."

I do kind of breathe easy because the usual humor is back in his voice now. But it doesn't change that he's somehow managed to misplace a whole day. The click-clack returns with a vengeance.

"What are you doing?" I ask.

"Working," he says. *"Shit!"*

I jump at the sudden exclamation.

"What?"

There's a long pause before he says, *"Huh. It really is Sunday."*

"Have you slept at all?"

He hums like he's deep in thought. *"Maybe. I think."*

"Okay. I say this with all the friendliness in the world. What the hell is wrong with you? Go the fuck to bed."

"That's the plan. Right after I've finished this. I need another hour at the most. And then I'll go and find something to eat and call it a night."

"I have a follow-up question now. When was the last time you ate?"

There's another lengthy silence while Blake does some mental calculations. Then I hear something crinkling.

"Based on the amount of granola bar wrappers I'd say I've definitely eaten something in the last forty-eight hours."

"Good for you. Ask me nicely, and I'll come bring you real food."

"You won't do it out of the goodness of your heart?" The smile in his voice carries all the way over from his place to mine.

"I can try, but I can't guarantee there'll be enough goodness to actually make it out the door."

After some more waiting and some more clacking, Blake speaks again, *"I'll probably fall asleep on you, but will you please bring me something to eat?"*

"Fine," I say with a dramatic sigh. "Since you asked so nicely. What are you in the mood for?"

"Anything that's not granola related will do."

"And?" I ask.

"And... Uh... To be honest, I don't really know what you want to hear. Please wasn't nice enough? You want compliments? I can do that. You're super hot. Awesome ass. Best eyes I've ever seen on a person," he rattles off and lets out a loud breath. *"My brain isn't really equipped for hints today, so if this is the kind of nice you need to get your awesome ass to my place, you're gonna have to spell it out for me loud and clear. Preferably with very short words. Four letters max."*

"As nice as it is to hear your thoughts about my ass, I meant do you want anything to drink, too?"

"*Oh. Well. Awkward. Something with lots of caffeine in it? One of those energy drinks with a name that makes it sound like you'll be drinking drugs. Liquid Shot of Caffeine. Energy Straight to the Vein. Max Hypershot of Lightning. Find me one of those, will you?*"

I give an evil laugh and shake my head even though he can't see me. "Water. Got it."

"*Why even ask me if you're not going to do what I say?*"

"Mostly for fun. I enjoy causing disappointment. I'll see you in thirty."

"*With water,*" he grumbles.

I'm still laughing at the put-out tone when I hang up.

"You look like shit," I say the moment I lay eyes on Blake.

He blinks and starts sheepishly combing his fingers through his messy hair, which only makes it stand up even more. If I had to venture a guess, I'd say he's fallen asleep behind his desk several times over the course of the last few days.

His T-shirt is rumpled, and the round glasses with thin golden frames are a tiny bit crooked. Those are new. Nothing about this should look attractive, but somehow it still is. Probably because he's so unapologetically himself, and that seems to really do it for me.

"I should warn you, I haven't showered, so it'd probably be better if you stayed at least five feet away until further notice." He yawns and takes the bag of takeout I'm holding out.

"This is great stuff," I say when I've taken off my shoes. "I can feel your hotness level dropping by the second, so by the time we get to the living room, I'll probably have no problem not sleeping with you. Thanks for taking care of that for me."

"I live to serve. What'd you bring me?" he asks and yawns again.

"Stuff. Did you finish working?"

"Almost. Just have to read through my…" He frowns and squints for a bit like he's trying to remember the right word. "Report," he finally says. He doesn't move, just stands there like he's so tired he's forgotten how, so eventually I put my hands on his shoulders, turn him in the right direction, and start walking, pushing him as I go. Shower or no shower, he still smells good.

His apartment is as small as mine, but it's almost the polar opposite in terms of coziness. I keep my place bare. I don't have much stuff, and except for the few photos, the little I have is not on display. Blake's place is filled with knickknacks, and seemingly a completely random assortment of them. Old, dog-eared paperbacks, a chipped mug filled with pens, rocks, and seashells, a single marble on a glass plate, keychains, fridge magnets, and all sorts of other things decorate most available surfaces. It's not messy, though. More like controlled chaos. Like all those seemingly random items are somehow important to him.

The bed is separated from the living room by a partition wall. The solid dark brown wood has cuts in it creating a pattern of leaves. It's all very clean and neat, except for the desk Blake has set up against the wall opposite the bed. That area is a mess, with screens, a laptop, and a bunch of shit I can't even begin to identify. Papers are strewn all over the place, mixed together with granola bar wrappers and water bottles to create one big mess.

"I should clean up a bit," Blake says and starts to head that way, but I grab his arm and stop him mid-stride.

"I'm not your mother. I'm here to feed you and to get you into bed, not make you clean up after yourself."

"Will you tuck me in, at least?" He grins, but he also manages to look kind of hopeful, so I don't have the heart to tease him about it.

"Let's start with feeding you." I take the bag back from him and go to the breakfast nook. I unpack the food while Blake goes to the bathroom. I hear him turn on the shower, and I ignore the thought of a naked Blake on the other side of the wall.

He comes out of the bathroom, hair wet, wearing only a pair of shorts.

"You're staring," he says as he plops down on one of the chairs.

"Yup." I take one of the spring rolls and bite into it before gesturing toward his upper body. "I thought you wanted me to stare. Otherwise, what's the point of going without a shirt?"

He looks down at himself as if he hadn't even realized he's not wearing one. "I don't like it when my shirt sticks to damp skin."

"And I approve. One hundred percent. If you have any objections to pants and damp skin, feel free to rectify that, too." I wave toward the food. "I should've probably asked about allergies and things. Do you have any? Because with my luck there are definitely peanuts in there somewhere."

"We're good. Ah, food." He sighs happily. "Hot, delicious food that didn't come in a wrapper. If I cry a little, ignore it."

I laugh and watch him devour everything he can get his hands on for the next fifteen minutes, before he leans back and lets out a satisfied sigh.

"That was the best thing I've ever eaten."

"If you don't eat or sleep for two days straight, how do you even function?" I ask.

He takes the last spring roll and chews thoughtfully. "You just have to get over the low point where you really want to go to sleep. Once you're past that and reach the overtired state, you're golden. By then, food doesn't matter much either. I should've finished this project during the week, but I got caught up in another project and kind of dropped the ball on this one."

I shake my head and straighten myself. "In that case, I better let you get to bed. Sounds like you deserve it."

"Do you…" He hesitates for a second. "Do you think you could do me a favor and stay for a bit?"

"Because you want me to watch you sleep? I try not to judge, but that's weird."

"More like make sure I stay awake while I finish reading my report. You can slap me when I nod off."

"Kinky," I say, and nod. "I'm in."

He laughs and it turns into another huge yawn that makes his eyes water. He rubs his palms over his face and blinks. The guy looks like he's going to fall asleep standing up.

"Will you keep your shirt off, so I have some eye candy while you do your thing?" I ask.

He gives a tired chuckle. "Sure. I can let you objectify me for the greater good."

"I know it's hard, but some of us have to do the heavy lifting," I say.

"I'm not sure I'd call keeping my shirt off hard work."

"Neither would I," I scoff. "I was talking about me. Eyeball strain is a real danger. You, on the other hand, are basically doing paperwork, which, you know… cool. But not really comparable to the sacrifices some of us are making."

"It's so nice to be appreciated."

"You're welcome. Go on. Grab your stuff, and let's do this."

A few minutes later, we settle in on the couch. Him with his laptop, and me with a remote and the TV to give an air of propriety to all the ogling I plan to do.

Or I would do if he weren't so damn squirmy. He's fidgeting so much I'm starting to feel like a pervert after a little while.

I give up. "You know the shirtless thing was sort of a joke. You *can* put one on, and I promise you I'll still slap you."

He lifts his eyes from his laptop. "What?"

"You're squirming like a virgin on prom night."

He looks down at himself and frowns. "No, it's not that. I've just been sitting for so long it's hard to find a comfortable position. My ass is completely numb by now."

"You know there's an easy fix to that, right?"

"Chop off my ass cheeks?"

"That's your easy solution?"

"In my defense, I'm very tired," he says, and to his credit, he looks suitably pathetic as he makes the claim.

"Well, we've now conclusively proven why people shouldn't make life-changing decisions when sleep deprived. I was thinking more along the lines of lying down on your bed," I say.

I'm starting to feel really sorry for him because the guy looks like deciphering that simple suggestion takes everything out of him. "Yeah, that does sound better," he finally says.

So we migrate to the bed. A half hour passes with Blake slowly going through his report and me scrolling on my phone, sending an occasional look in his direction to check if he's still awake.

Every time I look at him, he's slid further down the headboard until he's flat on his back, holding the laptop above his face, and moving his arms left and right.

"What are you doing?" I ask.

"My eyeballs don't seem to want to move anymore," he mumbles.

"But the arms still have staying power?"

"I'd have asked you to do it for me, but I didn't think you would."

I put my phone away. This is getting ridiculous. Entertaining, but ridiculous.

"Do you absolutely have to finish it tonight?" I ask once I really do feel sufficiently sorry for him, because it's starting to look like he's about to drop the laptop on his face.

"Deadline," he mutters, and keeps waving the screen in front of his eyes ever so slowly.

I pluck the laptop from between his fingers. He's still keeping his arms extended as if his brain hasn't quite managed to send the request to lower them. So I do it for him and push them down.

"I need to finish it," he mumbles.

"Yeah, yeah." I put the laptop in my lap. There's about twenty pages left.

"Stop me if you hear something you don't like," I say and start to read out loud. "Aside from XSS, the issue lets attackers perform scriptless attacks despite having the

CSP in place. This could result..."

It takes me twenty minutes to slog through what Blake's written, because honestly, this isn't exactly riveting reading. I fix a few spelling mistakes along the way, and Blake stops me a few times to correct something or other or add more boring computer mumbo-jumbo. Most of it goes right over my head.

Once I'm done, I hold the laptop out for Blake so he can send his report.

"Thanks," Blake mutters and closes the lid. "It's a good thing you're not a hacker, because you absolutely shouldn't have read any of that."

"You should definitely hope I'm not," I agree. His eyes fall closed, and he mumbles something I don't understand before he turns over on his stomach. I get up and switch off the lights in the rest of the apartment before I sneak back into his bedroom. He's breathing softly, face in the crook of his elbow.

I stand by the bed and watch him, and for once, I don't concentrate solely on how hot he is or what a shame it is he's friend-zoned me. Well, to be precise, I do look. I'm human, after all, and the smooth lines of his bare back and the way his pants ride indecently low on his hips are very eye-catching.

But that's more of an observation and most of my brain is occupied by a very novel, very strange, very uncomfortable tenderness.

Shit.

I walk home. In the dark. All alone. Couldn't get out of Blake's apartment fast enough. I close my door behind me and lean against it. My fingertips are as cold as my insides as I move through my home.

Everything is quiet. So, so quiet. The only sound is my breathing.

I stop, and the silence gets louder and louder.

And with silence comes loneliness.

It hits me viciously, like I've driven into a concrete wall.

I'm alone.

It's fine.

Everybody's lonely sometimes, Jude.

It'll pass.

I do run away from my thoughts this time. I shuck my clothes, climb into bed, pull the covers over my head, and will myself to sleep so I can get away from here.

ELEVEN

It's been a very long day, but it's not physical exhaustion that makes me feel like my bones are made of concrete.

Every time I go see Dad, my emotions run the gamut from guilt to anger to happiness, and everything else in between, and it drains every bit of energy out of me. I'm like a zombie walking the streets. Just a tired body with feet moving out of reflex and habit. Empty of everything. I've been feeling too much the whole day, so I've got nothing left to give.

The whole week's been a bit of a shitshow. Being in my apartment annoys me. Being alone annoys me. Being annoyed about those things annoys me. Which means I dug my heels in and ignored every single person I know to prove to myself I could get over this crap and get back to normal, but all I managed to achieve was to somehow make the fact that I was alone even more pronounced.

By now, I'm resigned to being disgusted with myself for being a supremely annoying person.

You know it's bad when you don't like to be around yourself anymore.

And I'm just tired enough to ignore the fact that my feet

have carried me to Blake's building. Nice going, feet. Back to the scene of the crime, clearly. Because Blake's apartment is the last place I felt good before I turned into this annoying, mopey mess.

I'm keeping my fingers crossed he's not home when I press my thumb on the buzzer. I give myself five seconds and if he doesn't answer, I'll get out of here.

"Hello?" he says when seventeen seconds have passed.

"Hey," I say. Nothing else comes to mind. No *wanna hang out?* No *let's go grab a bite to eat.* Nothing. Just sullen silence.

Even so, the door still clicks open.

Blake is leaning his shoulder against the doorframe and watches me trudge up the stairs.

"You're just letting anybody in without even asking their name?" I ask when I stop in front of him.

"I recognized your voice," he says, frowning with confusion like my question was weird.

"I only said one word."

"So?" he asks, still with the confused look.

Instead of waiting for my reply, he motions me inside with his head.

"Come on. Dinner's going to burn." He walks ahead of me, and I follow. In a few seconds, I'm sitting at the table with a glass of water in front of me while Blake moves around in his kitchen, bare feet softly slapping on the hardwood. He's wearing shorts and a worn T-shirt, his hair slightly messy. There's a faint blue line behind his ear that looks like it's been accidentally drawn with a pen.

"You look tired," he says.

I rub my palm over my face. "Long day. What are you making?"

"Stir-fry. It'll be done in five. You can make yourself useful and set the table."

While I work, he tells me about his day. A steady flow of

words that doesn't require any contribution from me. Like he's so in tune with me that he understands I just want to be quiet, but have somebody fill the silence.

Everything he says should sound mundane. It should be boring. It isn't. It's the exact opposite because I want to know.

Another first.

And the huge, lonely void that's opened up inside me and expanded over the past week starts to rapidly close up.

Blake puts a plate piled high with steaming vegetables and strips of chicken smothered in sauce in front of me. After a day of gas station beef jerky and soda, it smells like heaven and tastes even better.

"I could eat this every day for the rest of my life," I say through a mouthful of broccoli.

"I'm gonna venture a guess and say you were super hungry."

"From now on, I'll eat here. When do you serve breakfast?"

He looks down at his plate, a tiny smile tilting the corners of his lips upward. "I'll keep that in mind when I go grocery shopping."

"Seriously." I spear a strip of carrot on my fork. "This is really good."

"Thank you."

When we're done eating, I do the dishes, and he packs away the leftovers, all the while keeping up a constant stream of chatter about everything. His high school history classes. A magazine article he read about robots. His deep hatred for raisins.

Once the kitchen is clean, he throws me the remote.

"I have to send a quick email, and then I'm done. Find us something to watch?"

"What are you in the mood for?"

"I don't care. Anything."

I aimlessly click through Netflix for a few minutes before I toss the remote aside. I spend a little time staring at the ceiling before I give up on that, too. My mind won't shut up, so I do my best to distract it. There are a few sheets of blank paper on the coffee table, so I take one and start to fold.

In half diagonally. Triangle in half again. Open one of the flaps. I haven't done it in a while, but it's coming back to me as I go. The end result isn't half bad, if I do say so myself.

"Hey, that's cool," Blake says.

He takes the paper dragon and studies it from all sides. He holds it gently like he's afraid he's somehow going to break it.

"How did you learn to do that?"

"It's not that impressive."

"Let's agree to disagree."

"I learned it from YouTube. The source of all great human knowledge."

He grins. "Is it?"

"You can learn anything on there. It's like college but free."

"And what have you learned so far?"

"All things useless."

"Like?"

"I mean, take your pick. How to tie a tie. Fillet a fish. Repair a leaking faucet. Pick a lock. Make banana bread. Do those." I nod toward the dragon.

He looks down at the dragon he's still holding between his fingertips.

"It doesn't sound very useless."

"I also know how to juggle, roll a coin on my fingers, and make a cool blanket fort. How about that for useless?"

Blake tilts his head to the side. "I've never made a blanket fort."

I frown at him. "Never?"

He shakes his head.

"How? It's like, a childhood staple."

"I'm a foster kid, so I skipped a few of those staples."

I take one of the cookies and chew slowly while I process that piece of information. Blake shakes his head.

"Don't make that face."

"What face am I making?"

"The one that has pity written all over it. It's in the past."

"I don't know what that look is you're talking about, but it's definitely not pity."

"Well, good. It's unnecessary."

I take another cookie, toss it in my mouth, and get up. "Grab one of those bar stools." I point toward his kitchen counter as I stuff one more cookie in my mouth.

"For what?"

"It's high time you cross 'building a blanket fort' off the list of things you've never done."

"That is a hell of a blanket fort," Blake says about thirty minutes later when we're standing in front of the finished structure. He's grinning widely when he looks at me, and for good reason. This is a fucking awesome blanket fort. Good size and with lots of blankets and pillows. Blake even dug out some Christmas lights from somewhere to really get the full experience. Every couch cushion, pillow, blanket, and cover he owns is currently in the living room. I wasn't even sure he owned enough to pull it off, but it all worked out in the end.

"What now?" Blake asks.

"Now we get inside. Aren't you supposed to be the smart one out of the two of us? Because I thought it was obvious."

Blake perks up even more, and it's really fucking cute by now. When he goes down on his knees and starts crawling inside, giving me the perfect view of his very nice ass, it quickly goes from cute to hot.

I shake my head to get rid of all my perverted thoughts. I'm moderately successful. It'll have to do. I take the plate of cookies, turn off the lights, and follow him into the fort. The string of lights on the ceiling glows softly. It's quiet. Like we're cut off from the rest of the world and in hiding in our own secret spot. Nothing bad ever happens in a blanket fort.

You'd think it'd be weird to hang out in a blanket fort when you're technically a grown-up, but it's kind of the opposite.

I glance at Blake. He's staring at the ceiling, his body melting into the pillows, like he's found his spot and refuses to ever move. He turns his head toward me, his cheek pressing into the couch cushion, and meets my gaze.

"You know, this might be the single sweetest thing anyone's ever done for me."

"Yeah?" I ask.

He nods. Our eyes are locked. It's too intimate. Absolutely awful. Somebody needs to put an end to this. The sooner the better.

"Want to watch a movie?" I ask. "That's also a blanket fort staple."

"Bring it on. Give me the full experience."

He crawls out, then back in with a laptop stuffed underneath his arm. He hands it to me.

"*Armageddon*?" Blake asks after I've picked the movie.

"Have you seen it?"

"If I have, I don't remember anything. What's it about?"

"If you don't immediately know, you haven't seen it. This one leaves a mark, and it's amazing. Perfect for a beginner. They send oil drillers into space to destroy an asteroid that's heading toward Earth. Absolutely nothing in this movie makes sense. It's glorious."

"What's your deal with bad sci-fi?" He positions the laptop between us.

I want to shrug and leave it be. I don't. "My dad likes it. We used to have movie nights. And whenever any of the truly terrible ones made it to the theater, we were there on opening night. The ones where aliens land on Earth are great. The ones where people go to space are even better."

"What's your dad like?" Blake asks.

My eyes stay glued to the screen, even though I'm not registering anything about what's going on in the movie.

Just shut up and pretend you're watching the movie. He'll let it go. You've got the perfect excuse to ignore this shit. Just watch a shitty movie and then get out of his apartment, and you're done with this.

"On the outside? The embodiment of cool, calm, and collected."

Okay. You got it out of your system. Now shut. The. Fuck. Up.

"He has this really dry, dark sense of humor, but he's never cruel to people, even though hardly anyone ever gets that he's joking. Most people need some sort of indication you're pulling their leg. You can't just deadpan things with the straightest face imaginable."

Sharing is infinitely more disgusting than people make it out to be, and so far, I gotta say, I'm not a fan.

"And on the inside?" Blake prompts when I've been quiet for too long.

"On the inside... Kind. Through and through. He puts everybody else first. It's like he runs on love."

"He sounds like a great dad," Blake says.

It's been a while since I've talked about my dad to anybody, and suddenly, I can't seem to stop. Longing for the past pushes caution out of the way.

"He is. This one time, we were living in Colorado, and there was a snowstorm. We'd just moved there, so I didn't have any friends. Dad went door to door and asked people over and they stayed up the whole night and turned our backyard into a luge track. It snaked around the corner of the house, and you could go insanely fast. Next morning all the kids in the whole neighborhood were outside our house."

I'm sure the way the back of his hand brushes against mine is an accident, but he doesn't move it away. Not sure how I feel about that, so I just ignore the contact point and the strange lurch it causes in my stomach.

I don't move my hand either.

Somebody makes a rousing speech on the screen, but I hardly register it, lost in memories I've been trying my hardest to keep at bay for years, that are now making a coordinated mass escape.

A lot of the memories have been buried under a thick layer of bitterness for so long. They come out in random order, not much rhyme or reason to them, but I can't seem to stop remembering, and while I do, my mouth just moves.

"We used to go stargazing. The three of us. We'd drive out of the city, find a field, lay down blankets, and then just watch. Mom would pretend to know stars, even though she really didn't, but they'd both make up stories about constellations, and then we all tried to find new shapes in the sky.

"Sometimes they'd arrange a skip day. They'd pick me up from school and say I had to go to the dentist or something. Then we'd just drive around aimlessly, looking for new interesting spots.

"My mom... She loved butterflies, so Dad would draw them everywhere for her. Sometimes they'd sit outside on the porch at night, and she'd draw butterflies on Dad's skin. She said they were her good luck charms."

It goes on and on, one memory after another, until I finally run out of words.

The movie's over, and the laptop screen has gone dark.

"What happened to your mom?" Blake asks.

I really shouldn't answer that. I don't want to. I'm all talked out, and I've said too much.

"Cerebral hemorrhage." I take a slow, deep breath through my teeth. "I... I hadn't talked to either of them in—" I stop and shake my head. "A while. And then she was just gone." I aim my gaze at the ceiling, straight into one of the tiny LED lights until my eyes start to hurt from the brightness. "I always assumed... You never really think about it, do you? That you never get to say goodbye to most people. They're there, and then they're gone, and nobody cares that you're left behind with all those words you never got to say that are now trapped inside you for good."

"You miss her," Blake says softly.

"I miss my family." It sounds like the same thing, but isn't. I miss that life. I miss the person I was back then.

"This probably isn't what you signed up for," I say jokingly, but not really joking.

He shakes his head. "You're..." He frowns as if trying to come up with the right words. "You're a bit complicated."

"Am I?"

"A lot complicated."

"Aren't all people?"

"Depends."

"On?" I ask.

"Whether or not you care about their specific brand of complicated, I suppose."

"And do you?"

"About yours?"

I nod.

"You're pulling me in like quicksand."

His eyes turn me transparent like glass. Fragile like it, too.

"What are you doing?" I ask, because none of my friends have said things like that to me before. Or looked at me like I'm something new. Undiscovered. A treasure chest that hasn't been opened yet.

"I have no fucking clue," Blake says. His eyes move over the inside of our fort, and he smiles. "This really is great. I could stay here forever."

"Well, it *is* your apartment, so you have the option."

"Good point," he says, eyes shining like the brightest of lights.

"Too bad you missed the movie." I look away. "It was one of the good ones."

Blake shrugs and wiggles a bit, making himself comfortable. "There's a replay button."

I restart the movie, and this time we do watch.

About halfway through the movie, I glance at Blake.

He's asleep.

Fingers splayed on his chest, mouth slightly open, eyelids fluttering, breathing softly. His cheek is pressed into the pillow, and he looks so comfortable and peaceful that even though everything tells me to leave, I can't. Because I want a piece of that peace for myself. I want to absorb it through my skin or through the air or through osmosis. Something.

Just for a moment, I tell myself.

Move lower and closer.

Close my eyes.

I wake up to the smell of cinnamon. It takes me a moment to place myself and figure out why I'm inside a tent, but eventually last night comes back to me, and I crawl out of the blanket fort.

Blake's sitting at the kitchen counter, scrolling through his phone, but he looks up when he hears me.

"Morning," he says with an unsuitably wide grin for this time of the day.

"Okay, I have to ask. Are you ever"—I wave my hand toward him—"not happy?"

"When I have a reason not to be," he says.

"You sure about that? 'Cause I've yet to see proof."

"Stick around," he says before he gets up and pulls a pan of cinnamon rolls out of the oven.

Instead of getting out of his hair, I stay put for a little longer. We eat. He takes his laptop into the blanket fort and works, and I read one of his paperbacks.

"What do you have planned for today?" Blake asks once we've dragged ourselves out of the fort around noon.

"I've got work in an hour."

"Which one?" he asks.

"The sandwich place."

"Cool. I assume that means lunch is on you?"

I roll my eyes, but no matter how hard I try, I can't stop my smile. "Sure. Lunch is on me."

As promised, Blake stops by, and I make him lunch. He takes his laptop out and settles in one of the window seats, wolfing down two sandwiches while he does... whatever it is he does.

It's fun watching him. I've never seen anybody concentrate like him before. His eyes are on the screen, and he's completely oblivious to what's happening in the real world. There could be an explosion right outside the window, and I'm not sure he'd even notice.

"You're staring," Mina murmurs as she walks past me.

"Don't you have vegetables to cut?" I ask.

She settles in next to me at the counter and adjusts her apron. "I don't blame you. He's hot. Boyfriend?"

"Friend."

"So he's available?" She fluffs her blond hair, eyes trained on Blake, who's completely oblivious to our staring.

"No," I say. "He's seeing somebody. It's a very committed relationship. They're talking about marriage."

"Damn. All the good-looking ones are always taken." Mina walks away.

Once we close up shop a little after six, Blake stuffs all his things into his backpack and looks at me expectantly.

"Dinner? I'd kill for a taco."

"I hear you can get them for money these days, so you don't have to resort to crime."

"Smartass," he says and walks out the door, clearly assuming dinner is a done deal.

I suppose it is since I follow him.

We grab tacos from a food truck and eat them while we walk toward Blake's apartment.

"Are you coming upstairs?" he asks once we're at his front door. "I'm planning to be lazy for the rest of the evening, and I could use the help."

"I'm booked for a waitering gig in an hour." And then I do something that I haven't done in forever. I put myself out there. "Tomorrow?" I ask. "We should do something. If you want."

"Sure," he says. He drops his gaze to his feet for a moment before he meets my eyes again. "While we're making plans. I have a thing this weekend. A friend from high school... She's an artist. A few of her paintings are on display in a gallery. It's this 'thirty new artists under thirty' exhibit. Something like that.

Anyway, she's in town, and I sort of promised I'd be there. Want to come with me?"

"I don't know anything about art."

"Neither do I, but I'm pretty sure they don't have a test at the door to determine who's worthy of entrance."

"You better hope not because if there is, I'm copying your answers."

He smiles and toys with the strap of his backpack. "So you're in?"

"Sure. But if I say something dumb, you need to cover for me."

"I've yet to hear you say something dumb, so I'm not too worried."

"That's your first mistake. I say dumb shit all the time. Plus, I only know the most famous paintings, so unless they have the *Mona Lisa* on display, I won't have anything smart to say. And even if the *Mona Lisa* is there, my contribution will still be something like, 'Oh, look. It's that famous painting with that woman.'"

"I'm not sure what kind of impression I've made, but I'm not some kind of art expert either."

I snort. "You're a Stanford grad. I have a GED. One of those things is not like the other."

"I have a degree in computer science, so I spent zero hours exploring art galleries."

"Okay, good. Then we're equally ignorant. I can deal with that."

He shoves his hands into his pockets and rocks on the balls of his feet. "I'll meet you at your place at eight?"

I nod. He nods.

Neither of us moves yet. Blake looks down again, then up, one side of his lips quirking into a smile. My heart gives three quick thumps in a row before it settles into its old rhythm.

"I'll see you then." He turns around and runs up the five steps that lead to his front door.

He glances over his shoulder and sends me one more smile before he disappears inside, leaving me staring at his front door with the kind of stupid smile that has no business being on my face.

But I leave it be.

TWELVE

I SPEND way too long debating what to wear. My wardrobe consists entirely of casual clothes of the most casual variety. A few pairs of jeans. T-shirts for every occasion. Shorts. Plus, the dress pants and shirt from Blair and Nora's wedding. That's it. And when I Google 'what to wear to an art gallery,' to my great disappointment, none of the results say sweats are the way to go.

So I do something I haven't in a while and go clothes shopping. With Nora. She drags me straight to SoHo, where I slowly lose the will to live as she maneuvers me from one store to the next and disagrees with everything I like. In the end, I give up and just buy what she picks out for me.

Then I buy her lunch as a thanks for the privilege of having heard her complain about my taste in clothes for the past two hours. Money well spent.

But when I get dressed Saturday evening, I have to hand it to Nora. I look way more presentable than I usually do. Even if I don't know anything about art, at least I won't stick out like a sore thumb in my dark gray slacks, black button-down, and a forest-green blazer.

At eight on the dot, I go outside, and since Blake isn't here yet, I lean back against the wall and settle in. I scroll through my phone while I wait, but since I have no social media and the news is generally just depressing, I put it away pretty quickly.

I've just finished tucking the phone into my pocket when I look up and see Blake. He's a few feet away from me, standing completely still, looking at me, lips slightly parted, eyes moving rapidly up and down.

I straighten myself and spread my arms.

"This okay?" I ask, gesturing up and down my body. "I wasn't sure about the dress code."

The tip of is tongue peeks out, and he licks over his lips.

"You'll do." His voice sounds strange, but then he clears his throat and comes closer. "You look good."

"You too," I say, which is the biggest understatement anyone has ever made, but lately I haven't really been in the mood to objectify him. Obviously something's broken inside me.

"Anything I should know before we get going?" I ask, fiddling with the collar of my shirt. He steps closer, pats my hands away, and fixes it.

"There's an open bar, so if all the paintings suck, I bet we can drink them better."

I nod. "Say no more. Lead the way."

The gallery is in the Upper West Side, because of course it is. The moment we're inside a waiter shoves a tray of champagne in front of me. The maniacal smile makes me think he's poisoned something, but I take a glass anyway.

"Left or right?" Blake asks, looking in both directions. I follow his lead and check out both sides before I shrug. "No clue."

"Rock, paper, scissors. Loser decides?" Blake says.

"You're so classy. I'm so glad I dressed up for you," I say. "Let's do this."

He counts us down and promptly loses.

"Left it is," Blake says, so we head that way.

I can't claim to know anything about art, but it doesn't end up mattering much. Blake is more interesting to look at than the art anyway. By the time we've cleared the first wall, I have very little recollection of what was on it because I keep sneaking looks at Blake instead. It takes a lot of work not to be obvious about it. It takes a lot of work to get words out of my mouth when Blake says something. And I'm not interested in *just* saying words.

Lately, I have this new problem where I want to be interesting to Blake. I want to say intelligent things and make observations that will make him give me one of his wide, brilliant smiles. I want him to *want* to stick around and... Do what exactly? I don't know. Or maybe I do know and am just too much of a coward to admit it. Even to myself.

I've built a wall around me. Sturdy layers of bricks, one after another, year after year. It's safe here, hiding from the world and the people in it. Nobody can hurt you if you won't let them close enough.

But you're also never fully alive behind the wall. You exist, safe in your own bubble, and you think it's enough.

But what if it isn't?

"Jude?"

The voice sounds like it reaches me from a long distance away. I turn my head toward Blake and blink.

"Yeah?"

"You zoned out on me," Blake says.

"Oh. Sorry," I say.

He nods at the painting in front of me. "Is it because you like this one, or because you're bored?"

Neither.

I'm saved from answering by a loud and dramatic, "Blake? Blake McAdams?"

Blake's eyes don't move away from me for a few more seconds, but eventually, he turns his gaze away from me. There's a very tall, very blonde woman approaching us. Or, not us, she sweeps right past me without sparing me a glance and stops right in front of Blake. "My God, it's been ages," she says. "Is that really you?"

"Annika," Blake says politely. "What a surprise. I didn't know you were in town."

"A good surprise, I hope?" She sounds vaguely British, but not quite. Like somebody who's acquired their accent by watching BBC a lot.

"It's always a pleasure to see you," Blake says. It's the most formal I've ever heard him sound.

He kisses her on each cheek and moves past her toward me, so she's forced to turn around.

"This is Jude," Blake says. "Jude, Annika."

He doesn't explain who she is or how they know each other, so I'm going to assume she's the friend? Although, if they *are* friends, they must be the kind who don't really like each other.

"Nice to meet you," Annika says off-handedly before she turns her attention back to Blake. I might as well be a houseplant. "Mother and Father are around here somewhere. Did you see them already?"

Blake tenses. It's almost imperceptible, but it's there. Annika doesn't seem to notice.

"Not yet."

"What are you waiting for, then? Let's go say hi."

"I was looking at the paintings," Blake says.

Annika throws a bored look toward the wall.

"Yes. Wait until you see Sage's corner. It's certainly... interesting."

She says the word interesting the same way people would say a peanut butter and onion sandwich is... interesting.

"Come on, then," she says and hooks her arm through Blake's before she starts dragging him away. "To tell you the truth, I don't know why she insists on doing this. The world hardly needs any more artists. Painting is a nice hobby, but it doesn't really make a difference, does it?" She seems to consider what she's just said. "I sound like a bitch."

No argument from me, lady.

"I suppose I'm having a hard time switching back to this life. I've been completely wrapped up in the story I'm doing about the situation in Myanmar, so it's difficult to care about trivial things like this." She throws an eyeroll toward one of the paintings and shakes her head.

I'm not sure if I should go after them or not, but Blake says my name, and I just follow.

In no time at all, we're standing in front of a couple somewhere in their fifties. They're both whip-thin, tall, and painfully put together, with a badly disguised I'm-better-than-you air about them. Next to them is a young woman who looks like she's been forced at gun point to hang out with them, another couple who've perfected the snobbish look, and a few more people hovering on the fringes, not quite in the group, but not quite out of it either.

"Dominic. Daphne," Blake says. A round of handshakes and more air kisses follow before Blake turns toward the young woman. Finally there's a genuine smile on his face. "Sage," he says. She grins and practically jumps into Blake's arms.

"You made it!"

They hug, and she whispers something in Blake's ear that makes him shake his head lightly and whisper something back before he pulls away.

"Sage, a little decorum, maybe," Dominic says. "Blake. It's been a while." The words are polite. The look that accompanies them is not.

Blake nods. There doesn't seem to be any love lost there.

"How have you been?" Daphne asks, mildly less icy than her husband, which isn't to say the thermometer isn't still in the negative digits.

"Good," Blake says shortly.

"Still employed?" Dominic asks. I gape at him. And then at other members of the circle, who don't seem to think this question is nastily impolite and completely out of line.

"Yes," Blake says.

"I haven't gotten any calls from Sage saying she's in jail, so I'm assuming no more legal trouble lately?"

"No."

"Imagine that."

"Dad," Sage snaps.

"One has to wander, Sage," Dominic says. "Considering the history."

Sage mutters something under her breath before she aims a wide smile my way. "Hi. You're here with Blake?"

All eyes turn to me. This is nice and awkward.

"Uh... yes. Jude. Nice to meet you all."

"Blake is a homosexual," Dominic says loudly. I'm not sure if it's the homosexuality or the wildly inappropriate remark that's making people stare. I'd go with the latter, but you never know.

"Yes, here on a recruiting trip," Blake adds. "If anybody's interested."

"Blake!" Daphne gasps, because clearly it's Blake who's in the wrong here and not her sour-faced husband.

"Mother," Sage snaps. "We're going to mingle."

She sails past her parents, and I'm happy to follow her. We stop only once we're on the other side of the gallery, as far away from Dominic and Daphne as humanly possible.

"I'm so sorry," Sage says. "I swear, I didn't know they'd be here, or I wouldn't have asked you. They just showed up twenty minutes ago, completely out of the blue."

"To support you? That's nice. I take it they've finally come to terms with the fact you're not going to become a doctor or a lawyer or some other *useful* member of the society?"

"They have Annika for that. I'm still the disappointment of the family, but I'm a smidge more tolerable now that I've been featured in the *New York Times* as a young artist to watch." She rolls her eyes.

"Fancy," Blake says. "Can you sign something for me I can sell on eBay?"

"Shut up," Sage mutters before she turns her attention to me. "Sorry about that. My parents are terrible people." The statement is delivered matter-of-factly.

"Sorry?" I offer.

She waves me off. "I'm used to it. And they have their moments, as far and few between as they come. I got knocked up in high school, and they're kind of decent as grandparents. It helps that they live all the way across the country."

"Uh, so how exactly do you two know each other?" I ask.

"You haven't told your boyfriend all about me? I'm crushed. Crushed, I tell you!" Sage grins. "He was the broody bad boy, and I was the repressed rich girl. It was written in the stars. We were like Romeo and Juliet. My parents despised him, and I was in seventh heaven. It was teenage rebellion in its most beautiful form. Until I realized Blake, here, wasn't really into me. More like, he was trying to look out for me."

"An impossible task. She was a real pain in the ass," Blake says. There's clear fondness in his tone.

I see neither of us are going to address the boyfriend comment.

"A very traditional pain in the ass," Sage says. "I ticked all the boxes. Alcohol, weed, sex with the wrong guys. Really wrong ones. Daisy's father skipped town as soon as those two blue lines appeared on the pregnancy test. Still, all things considered, I'm a traditional gal and took the traditional routes of rebellion." She motions toward Blake. "This one hacked into places and had a penchant for stealing cars."

I whip my head toward Blake.

"One car," he says quickly. "It was one car, and I didn't actually steal it."

"Because you got caught," Sage remarks. "Not that I'm complaining. We would've never met if you hadn't had itchy fingers."

Blake looks at me almost pleadingly. "We already covered that I was exceptionally dumb when I was younger."

"You're a weird nerd," I say.

Sage bobs her head up and down, eyes sparkling. "Right?"

"Can you maybe try and not destroy the somewhat decent impression I've made so far?" Blake asks.

She waves him off. "It all worked out in the end. And besides, if you hadn't tried to steal that car, you'd have never met—"

"How's life in Vermont treating you?" Blake asks way too loudly.

Sage seems to find it just as weird as I do, but she shrugs it off after a bit. "Delightfully insane. We bought a cow."

"You're taking this whole farmer's wife thing extremely seriously," Blake says.

"Yeah, but the cow was super cute, so I figured, eh, a lawn mower. Daisy named her Bluebell. They're already best friends. You'll see once you *finally* come and visit."

Blake snorts and shakes his head. "Out of all the people I've ever known, you are the last person I would've pictured living in an orchard."

"It's very peaceful. Helps me with my art," Sage says. "Speaking of which. Did you see my masterpiece yet?"

"No. Annika steered us away before we got to yours."

"Figures." She starts to walk, and Blake and I follow her to the next room on our left. She leads us to a huge canvas and waves her hands dramatically in the air. "Ta-da!"

All black with slashes of red on it, almost as if somebody's torn holes in the canvas with a knife from the other side. Like bleeding wounds. Like somebody's been trapped underneath all this darkness and has finally had enough and has made their escape. Tried to make their escape? I suppose it's up for interpretation.

I take a step closer.

Fascinated.

Enchanted.

I've felt this way. The same helpless rage and anger that had no place to go and that grew and grew until it didn't fit inside me and filled... everything.

I jump at the hand on my shoulder.

"Sorry," Blake says. "Sorry. I didn't mean to startle you."

"It's fine." I turn away from Sage's painting and find them both looking at me. I point my thumb at the painting behind me. "Great stuff, that one."

I sound like an idiot, and I don't even care. I just want to get away from this place, and I'm not sure how to do it politely.

Sage tilts her head to the side, eyeing me with barely disguised curiosity. "There's a bar across the street. We should go there."

"I..." I hesitate.

"I'll tell you more stories about Blake's wild youth," she says.

Blake groans next to me.

I nod. I wouldn't pass that opportunity up for all the money in the world, but I need a quick second to get my head back straight. "Yeah, okay. I'll just stop by the bathroom before we go."

"Meet you at the exit?" Blake asks.

I spend a couple of minutes doing Blair's deep breathing exercises before I head toward the exit. Blake and Sage don't seem to be anywhere. I wait for a minute, but then when I glance out the window, I notice them outside. The two of them seem to be in the middle of a heated conversation. Sage's arms are crossed over her chest, and Blake's whole body radiates tension. He's scowling at her and says something, and she raises both her hands in the air like she's frustrated before she starts gesturing wildly with her hands as she replies.

I hesitate, not sure what to do. Go out there or wait until they're done? In the end, the decision is made for me when I see Sage's parents round the corner. I doubt they'll want to make small talk, but I'm not taking any chances, so I head outside.

"—the idiotic things you've ever done, this takes the cake," Sage is saying. "What the hell were you thinking?"

Neither of them has noticed me yet, and once again, I'm not sure what to do. Cough loudly? Pretend like somebody's calling me and take that imaginary call?

"Don't you think I know that?" Blake snaps "I know it's stupid. Believe me. I tell it to myself every fucking day. Look, I didn't plan on it, but he's..." He stops talking and drags his hand through his hair.

"He's what?" Sage demands impatiently.

"He's... he's different, okay?" he grits out. "I've never met anybody like him before. I can't just—"

I don't get to find out what Blake can't, because that's when Sage notices me and calls out a loud, "Hey, you! There you are!"

Blake whirls around and stares at me for a moment before he rubs the back of his neck and very clearly makes himself smile at me.

"Hey. I didn't even hear you," he says.

"I stepped out a second ago," I say. *No eavesdropping here. No, sir.* "Uh... everything okay?"

I don't think I can pretend I didn't notice they were arguing.

"Yeah," Blake says. "We were just..."

He seems to be lost for words and eventually he just clamps his mouth shut and leaves the sentence hanging in the air.

Sage sends him a quick scowl before she turns toward me. "Blake's ex is in town, so I was just trying to remind him why it's a bad idea to go there. He can be a real dumbass when it comes to this guy." She sends him a look laden with unspoken words. "A real fucking idiot."

"Oh," I say.

Somehow, it never even crossed my mind that Blake's reluctance to sleep with me might come down to something as simple as him being hung up on somebody else.

I mean, it explains a lot.

And I'm not...

It doesn't bother me. At all. So, Blake's still hung up on his ex. Big deal. I don't care. It's fine. We're friends. I don't do boyfriends, and he's not the dating type. Cool. I guess that works out perfectly.

"Shall we?" Sage asks. "I think I saw my mom peering out the window. We better skedaddle before she sees I'm escaping."

―――

By the time we stumble into my apartment, I'm pleasantly buzzed from all the champagne I've drunk this evening. Blake isn't any better. He trips on his own shoes right after he's taken them off and lands on his ass in the middle of my hallway.

"Oops," he says.

I snicker at the befuddled look on his face.

"Ah, shit. I was supposed to go home," he says, which makes me laugh even harder.

"You can stay here. I doubt you'd even find your apartment right now."

"As long as the Lyft driver finds it, I'm okay."

"Nope. I like you, so for once in my life, I'm going to be responsible. You're staying."

I reach my arm out and pull him to his feet. He sways a bit.

"Jesus. What was in that champagne?"

"Bubbles. Bubbles get you drunk fast."

He frowns. "Really?"

"Carbonation moves the alcohol into your bloodstream faster. The hangover will be shittier, too. Come on. Let's get you to bed."

He's still frowning when I push him toward the bedroom. Once there, I grab a clean T-shirt and hold it out for him.

"I don't think we should do this," he mutters, staring at the shirt with a frown.

"Sleep?" I ask.

"In one bed," he says. "I'm not going to sleep with you."

Well, sure you aren't. Not when you're still hung up on that ex of yours.

I pull the shirt back and clutch it in my fist while I cross my arms over my chest. "Believe me, by now, I've taken the hint. You take the bed, and I'll camp out on the couch."

He starts shaking his head even before I've finished talking. "It's not that I don't..." He still has that deer-caught-in-headlights look about him, but he also seems reluctant to leave. Eventually, he steps forward and takes the shirt off my hands before he retreats to the bathroom.

I don't get him. Not even a little bit. And right now, I'm too tired to try.

In the living room, I throw myself onto the couch. I close my eyes and will myself to stop thinking and go to sleep. The sounds somebody else makes while they're moving around in my apartment should feel weird. I've been alone for years now. I'm used to the quiet and being the only person around. Instead, Blake's presence is like a warm blanket after stumbling around in a snowstorm.

The bathroom door closes with a quiet click. Footsteps pad over the parquet floor. Then silence.

Eventually, I get up and pull off my T-shirt. I'm halfway done with taking off my pants when a sound from the doorway stops me.

"Uh..."

I look up and find Blake looking at me. I can't really see his eyes in the darkness of the room, so it's hard to say what he's thinking. It's hard to figure out why he's standing there, clutching the doorframe like he's trying to keep himself from moving.

"You need something?" I ask.

"No," he says slowly. "Everything's fine. Look, I'm an idiot. You can't sleep on that dinky couch. Let's just go to bed."

"I can handle my own fucking couch. Go get some sleep," I say.

"I'm not stealing your bed. You take the bed. I'll take the couch."

"You're a guest. And I'm already settled in."

"You're standing up," he points out.

Our eyes lock. A wordless challenge is thrown down. We both lunge toward the couch at the same time and land on it in a heap of bodies and limbs.

"I win," we say at the same time.

"I'm below you, ergo, I got here first," he says smugly.

"Easy fix," I say before I roll myself between him and the backrest and start pushing him down. He scrambles to hold on and hooks his leg over my hip. I struggle to get him down. He struggles to stay on the couch. After a little bit of panting and huffing and no clear winner, I give up and flop back, half on top of him, half squeezed between him and the couch.

"Truce?" he pants.

"Truce," I say.

A few minutes and a bathroom visit later, I'm lying next to Blake in my dark bedroom, wide awake. Blake and I are both lying very properly on our own sides of the bed, hands on top of the blanket like a virgin married couple on their wedding night.

Blake's voice breaks the silence.

"I've only ever slept with you."

I whip my head toward him so suddenly my neck cracks.

"I'm sorry, what?" I splutter. "When?"

"What?" he asks and turns to his side, frowning at me with confusion rivaling my own, before realization dawns on his face, and he starts to laugh. "No. I mean, literally sleeping in the same bed with another person. Or in the same blanket fort, as is our case."

"Oh," I say dumbly. I'm a bit slow on the uptake, but I do my best to process that new piece of information, even though, combined with what I overheard earlier from his conversation with Sage, none of it makes fucking any sense at all.

"I should warn you I have this thing where I have no idea what to say to people when they divulge deeply personal information, so I'll make a joke or say something stupid," I say.

"I'm aware."

"Not even a sleepover as a kid? Or sharing a tent on a hike?" I ask.

"Not even that."

"Seems I got to be your first, then. I hope I was gentle. Ah, see? Stupid joke. Right on schedule."

He smiles sleepily in the darkness. "I like your stupid jokes."

"So it's true. You really can't account for taste."

"Idiot," he says, full of affection and warmth. Oh, this thing is going so badly, because I shouldn't like it, and yet somehow, I still do. How's that for complicated?

"It's the second first you've given me, you know? The blanket fort and this," he says in a sleepy voice that manages to hit the hot-intimate-cute trifecta straight in the bullseye.

"Go me." I turn my head. He's right there. Only a few inches between our faces. He smells like champagne and peppermint toothpaste, looks like temptation, and feels like a bad decision. Even more so when his eyes find my lips and get stuck on them.

It gets worse because his own lips part and a soft exhale escapes and whispers over my skin. And he's still staring at my mouth as if hypnotized.

Morbid curiosity overrides common sense. I lick over my lips. Just to see what happens.

His eyes widen, and he zeroes in on my tongue like he's expecting there'll be an exam about its precise movements later.

My skin prickles and blood rushes through my veins.

What the fuck is happening?

And then he whips his head away from me, determinedly staring at the ceiling.

"This is cozy," he says, way too loudly. "I never feel like I'm warm enough, but this is downright toasty. Even my toes are warm."

I do my best to ignore the way my stomach jolts with disappointment—nobody needs that shit here—and clear my throat. "The apartment's in the middle of the building, so it's always warm. Even in the middle of the winter."

"That's good. If you have a smart heating system, it can save you a lot of money."

We're honest-to-God talking about utilities now. Riveting.

"I forgot to tell Sage I enjoyed her paintings," I say after a little bit.

"Next time," Blake says.

More silence.

"You two have known each other for a while," I say.

Blake nods, eyes locked on the darkened ceiling.

"Same high school. It was this super rich, preppy place, and I didn't really fit in, but Sage and I hit it off."

"And you're still friends."

He hums in response.

"How does a foster kid end up in a super preppy high school?" I ask.

"Scholarship. Most of those places have a few pity spots to show they're generous and inclusive. In return for the free tuition, they'll never stop rubbing it in. They even pointed it out during graduation. *And here's our scholarship student, Blake McAdams*. I can't complain, though. For all its faults, the education I got there was top tier."

I hesitate because I don't know if I should ask, but in the end, curiosity gets the better of me.

"What happened to your parents?"

He's silent for so long I'm beginning to regret I even asked.

"I don't know," he eventually says. "I was left in the mall. Food court. I don't really remember the details. Somebody found me when they were closing up and called the police. The cameras showed a grainy image of a young woman. Suppose that was my mother."

He's silent again. My hand moves. The back of it meets his. My pinky finger wraps around his pinky finger.

He clears his throat.

"There was a huge search, but they never found out who left me there. Splashed my photos all over newspapers to find relatives. Somebody to step forward and recognize me, at least.

Nobody ever did. So they put me in the system. Some of the families were nice. Others not so much. Not exactly horror story level terrible, but not great. Not enough food in some places. Or you can only shower once a week to keep the water bill low. Or just, like, months of junk food and nothing else. If I never see frozen TV dinners again, it'll be too soon. And there are those little things that all add up. You grow out of your shoes and nobody cares enough to get you a new pair. There's nobody ever there for science fairs or school plays. Sometimes little things like that leave big dents."

I don't say anything, because what's there to say? I just let him wrap his finger even more tightly around mine and listen to his breathing.

My mouth opens. I'll tell him about me. It only seems fair. Maybe not even just fair. I kind of want to tell him, which is a novel moment. I've never told anybody. Never discussed the whole ordeal with anybody either. Not even with Blair or Steph. They were there, so they know what happened, but I'd firmly put a stop to talking about it.

A soft exhale stops me.

"Blake?" I whisper softly.

Nothing.

THIRTEEN

IT FEELS like I've only been asleep a second when something wakes me. A thump, I think? Whatever it is, it's a foreign sound. One that shouldn't be there, especially in my otherwise quiet apartment.

I'd blame Blake, but he's still dead to the world, arm thrown over my chest, face nestled in the crook of my neck, thigh over mine like he's trying to trap me in place. And I don't mind.

Better not open that can of worms.

There's a clatter like somebody dropped something. It's followed by a muffled curse. A very familiar muffled curse. I carefully extract myself from Blake and make my way to the living room.

It's chaos. There's a backpack on the floor, most of its contents spilled out all over the place. Clothes, toiletries, books, a pair of sunglasses, coins scattered around an open wallet.

And in front of my couch...

"Nice ass," I say.

Steph snaps his head up and somehow hits it against the corner of the coffee table, even though it's a whole two feet away from him.

"Fucking ow!" he complains and rubs at the hurt spot.

I lean my shoulder against the doorjamb and study the chaos. "Whatcha doing?"

"Dropped my fucking earbud, didn't I?" he grumbles. "And now it's somewhere under the couch."

"Dumbass," I say, and I mean it with all the affection possible.

"You say the sweetest things. Make yourself useful, babe, and lift the couch," Stephen says.

"Babe? I'm not one of your one-night stands," I say as I go to the end of the couch.

"Time's a-wastin', love bug. Get on with it."

I obediently lift the couch, and he fishes his earbud out before he gets up and drops it on the coffee table.

"Thanks, sugarplum."

"You're welcome, boo boo bear."

We both grin at each other for a second before he tackles me and wraps me in a bone crushing bear hug.

"What the hell are you doing here?" I ask with a laugh. "Aren't you supposed to be in LA?"

"I absolutely should be," he agrees.

"So why aren't you?"

"I missed your face," he says, which is blatantly avoiding my question, but I'll let it go for now. He puts his palm on my ass and squeezes. "But most of all, I missed this ass."

I roll my eyes just as somebody clears their throat in the doorway. I turn around. Blake's... Yeah, he's all adorably sleepy and just damn fucking hot as he stands there and squints at me and Stephen.

"Sorry," I say. "Did we wake you?"

"No," Blake says. I've never heard him sound quite so curt. Then again, it's the middle of the night, and we just woke him up, so I guess that's to be expected.

Steph clears his throat before he takes a step back. "Oops. Next time warn a guy you've already got company. Guess it's a good thing I was all loud and woke you up. My plan was to sneak into the bed." He smiles widely and thrusts out his hand to Blake. "Sorry, man. Didn't mean to interrupt your evening. I'm Stephen, but don't mind me. You two can absolutely go back to whatever it is you were doing. I promise, I'm so beat, I won't even eavesdrop. I swear, I just took the world's longest flight from LA. A layover in fucking Anchorage. Kind of fucked up and missed my first flight. And to top it off, I've been up the whole time."

He's still holding his hand out. Blake's still staring. Which is about what you'd expect. Stephen's a lot to take the first time you meet him. I suppose the experience is even stranger when it's the middle of the night and you're teetering on the edge of asleep and hungover.

"This is Blake," I tell Stephen.

"Sweet. Good to meet you and all the other niceties," Steph says, upbeat as ever, before he gestures between himself and me. "No hard feelings, man. I swear, this thing between me and J is strictly platonic. We only sleep together if it's been a long dry spell, and neither of us has anyone better to do."

Blake blinks for the longest time.

"I don't think that's what platonic means," he finally says.

Stephen shrugs, completely unconcerned and at ease. "There's zero feelings, is what I'm saying. Just some regular old fucking. No intimate, kinky shit, I swear. It's like a friend helping a friend out. A helping hand. Or a helping mouth. Whichever does the trick."

"TMI, man. Nobody asked for details," I say with a sigh.

"Too much?" Stephen asks and winces. He sends Blake an apologetic look. "Sorry, sorry. I haven't slept in two days. The brain to mouth connection is tenuous. I almost propositioned a cop at the airport. Took a lot of talking to get him to believe I wasn't selling sex and just wanted directions."

"The brain to mouth connection is *always* tenuous, so you can't exactly put that down to sleep deprivation," I say dryly.

"J, please. I'm trying to impress your man-friend here. Be cool, okay?"

I snort. "Man-friend?"

"One-nighter?" He narrows his eyes at Blake and speaks out of the corner of his mouth. "Seems a bit rude to just outright say it."

"He's a friend," I say. "*Just* a friend. And definitely not a one-nighter."

Steph whips his head toward me. "You have friends?"

"It's insulting how surprised you sound." I shake my head and try to catch Blake's eye to subtly let him know Steph is not actually a crazy person, but it turns out to be mission impossible. Blake avoids looking at me like he's suddenly afraid my eyeballs have turned into plague rays.

Meanwhile, Steph looks from me to Blake. "Seriously, did I interrupt something? 'Cause I can get out of here for a few hours if you want some alone time to finish whatever you were doing. I could go for a burger right now. Is that weird food-poison shack on the corner still open? You know what? I'm gonna risk it, so you go ahead and do your thing."

"We were sleeping," I say.

"Shame." Steph grins and waggles his brows.

I decide not to address that. "I'll set up the couch for you."

"Couch? But it's uncomfortable!"

"Tough."

"Where's the love?" he asks nobody in particular.

"You can always go to Blair's and enjoy her guest room and all the love that comes with it."

"That guest room comes with a side of lecture. At least the couch keeps its opinions to itself."

"Well, then enjoy my non-judgmental couch without complaining."

"Damn. You've gotten all bossy in the last six months. I approve, by the way. Tell me to go to bed in a stern voice. Give me something for the spank bank while I'm out here all alone."

"Well, if that's all, we should get back to bed," Blake says loudly. "I'll get you a blanket."

In a remarkably efficient rush, he gets Steph a blanket, a sheet, and a pillow, throws them all on the couch, and marches me back into the bedroom where he pushes me onto the bed. He's just shy of tucking me in.

He climbs in himself and turns off the light.

"Night," he says in a tone rife with finality.

"Uh... night?" I offer.

What the hell just happened here?

FOURTEEN

It's the *but* kind of morning. You know the one. I slept for eight hours, *but* it feels like two. I ran for a mile, *but* it feels like ten. The man is forty, *but* he acts like he's twelve.

When I wake up, Blake is wrapped around me again, *but*... I still don't hate it.

The *but* kind of morning.

Blake's still dead to the world when I carefully untangle myself from him.

I drag my ass into the kitchen nook where Steph is burning pancakes. Him cooking is usually a clear sign something's up. I take one of the less burned pancakes. The thing's hard as a rock. I could beat a burglar unconscious with it.

Steph pushes a glass of orange juice my way. I eye it skeptically for a moment.

"It's from a bottle."

Which translates into edible. It might be the only thing on this table that is.

"Cheers." I lift the glass in his direction.

He throws another pancake on the plate. This one somehow manages to be both burned and raw.

"Your friend still asleep?"

I nod.

Steph frowns at the spatula he's holding. "I don't think he likes me very much."

"I don't think you can make that assessment based on one late-night encounter."

"Maybe," Steph says thoughtfully. "He looked pretty pissed, though. Give a guy one ass-squeeze and suddenly you're persona non grata."

"He doesn't care about that."

Steph lets out a snort. "Right."

I lean my tired head on my hands and close my eyes. "I spent weeks propositioning him, and I wasn't subtle about it. He's not interested. *And* he's made it abundantly clear."

I think. After the last few days, I'm not a hundred percent sure anymore.

"Why's he sleeping in your bed, then?" he asks and shovels one of the inedible pancakes in his mouth.

"Cause the couch is shit?" I shrug. "I don't know. You and I have slept in the same bed plenty of times. How's that any different?"

"You and I have had sex in the same bed plenty of times, too," he points out.

"Yeah, well, Blake and I just sleep."

Steph chews thoughtfully. "Fucking weird," he concludes.

"Why? Why is that weird? We're friends."

"I know. That's the fucking weird part."

"Because?" I ask.

"Well, first the obvious: you're voluntarily keeping somebody around for longer than it takes to get in their pants. *You.*"

"I'm no—"

"Unless you're playing the long game, which would also be a first."

"We're—"

"And if you *are* playing the long game, what's the point? I mean, you want him. He clearly wants you. What's the holdup?" He takes a sip of my orange juice and repeats, "Fucking weird."

I rub the heels of my palms over my eyes and chew on my words for a few seconds.

"I like him," I eventually mutter.

"What?" Steph asks and leans forward like he's hard of hearing.

"I. Like. Him," I say slowly. I make sure to keep my voice down. It feels like I'm trying to wrench the words out with pliers.

He stares at me like I'm speaking a foreign language. "Like, you want to hold his hand and boop his nose and sniff him? That kind of shit?"

"What? Why would I want to boop his nose?"

"Dude, I don't know what you people do when you're into that whole intimacy thing."

"Jesus Christ," I mutter. "I mean, I like him. I... want to spend time with him," I say in a whisper that quite efficiently conveys my panic at that development. "All the time."

"Oh, that's bad," Steph breathes with fascinated horror.

"Thank you!" I say. Finally, an appropriate reaction. "Now how do I... How..." I glance toward the bedroom door to make sure it's still closed. "How do I get rid of it?"

Steph takes another pancake. The guy clearly has no taste buds.

"Fuck him out of your system?" he suggests. I should've figured it'd be his first solution.

"I can't fuck him if he doesn't want to be fucked."

"Use somebody else to fuck him out of your system. I've got no plans."

I look away.

Steph starts to laugh. "Oh, this is good. Dude, you're already fucked!"

"Shut up," I say in disgust.

He raises both hands just as the bedroom door opens.

"Aww. Let Steph take care of this for you, baby boy," Steph says and winks.

"Yuck. About fifty percent of those words should never be uttered again. And don't even think about doing anything," I whisper frantically. I have no idea what he's planning, but it's Steph, so it's going to end up being a disaster no matter what.

"You're too uptight. Have some pancakes," Steph says a second before Blake walks into the kitchen.

"Hey, you!" Steph says brightly, making Blake wince.

"Yeah," he mutters before he slumps into one of the chairs.

"I made breakfast," Steph says and pushes the pancakes toward Blake.

"Nope," I say and push the plate back.

"Come on. They're not that bad," he protests.

"Not that bad would be an improvement. They're fucking awful."

"Are they supposed to be black?" Blake squints at the plate.

"Charcoal is good for teeth," Steph says.

"Sure it is." I get up. "I'm gonna go take a long shower, and then I'm gonna go to work. When I come back these abominations better be gone. And open the window. It smells like a coal mine in here."

Steph shrugs and stuffs another pancake in his mouth. "Your loss."

I start to leave when his pancake-muffled voice stops me. "We're going out tonight, by the way."

I turn around. "Are we?"

"Yup. I need a distraction, and you need to get laid."

My eyes involuntarily move to Blake. He's staring straight ahead. Honestly, I'm not even sure he's fully conscious. Either way, he doesn't react at all.

"Sure. Whatever," I say.

"I better get going," Blake says, abruptly getting up, too. "Long day ahead."

"You're welcome to join us," Steph calls after him.

He doesn't reply, just walks around picking up his things and stuffing them in the pockets of his borrowed sweats. It takes him less than a minute to get out the door.

I throw Steph a look, but he's too busy staring after Blake to explain himself, so after a few seconds, I give up and go to the bathroom.

FIFTEEN

Going out means we end up in somebody's house somewhere where Steph knows somebody. It's a lot of ambiguity, as is usually the case with Steph's acquaintances. He has a lot of them. Everywhere. And there's no point asking how he knows them. He just does.

Steph is one of those people that stands out from the crowd. He can be exceptionally charming if he wants to. A dazzling smile on his face. Impeccable memory, so he'll remember to ask about your grandmother's health, even though it's been seven months since you last saw him. He knows your dog's name and remembers where you were born. Knows your drink order and your birthday.

His phone is filled with invites to parties, so it's just a matter of choosing where we want to go.

"How do you know this guy?" Blake asks as we walk through some swanky area in Tribeca.

"Had a few threesomes with him and his girlfriend way back when," Steph says off-handedly. "He's a cool dude. Trust fund brat. Does PR for the Giants."

"A threesome *is* the perfect foundation for a friendship," I say.

"It was great. None of that getting-serious crap. Just good sex." Steph stops in front of an apartment building, doorman and all, and in a minute, we're heading upstairs. Private elevator. Penthouse. Why not?

The party's already in full swing by the time we get there. People are dancing, and loud music blares from invisible speakers. It's intense and disorienting. For me. Steph takes it in stride, and Blake... It's hard to say what Blake feels. He's been uncommonly serious and quiet ever since he showed up to my place earlier. I didn't think he would, but then he was there, dressed in a pair of jeans and a black Henley, a sort of determined air following in his wake.

"Let's dance," Steph says, and before I know it, he's dragging me into the throng of people, and when I look back, I don't see Blake anywhere.

"Wait," I shout over the music. "We lost Blake."

"He'll be fine," Steph says. He grabs my hips and starts to dance. Well, I say dance, but it's more like dry humping on Steph's side.

"Really?" I shout into his ear while he grabs my ass.

"Really," he replies with a wide grin. "Relax. And put some swing into your hips. We're being watched."

"I don't care who's watching. If you want to seduce somebody, you're on your own. I'm not doing the threesome thing with you today," I say.

"I know." He grins. "I have a feeling we won't even be doing the twosome thing anymore, so you owe me a little bit of fun. Now dance with me. Because we're being watched. And believe me, you want those eyes on you."

I roll *my* eyes, but I start to move.

I finally manage to pass Steph off to some guys and escape from the dance floor, sweaty and half-deaf from the loud music. I go through all the rooms, but I can't find Blake anywhere, and he doesn't pick up his phone when I call him, so I figure he's gone home. Maybe this isn't his scene. Maybe it isn't mine either, because once again, I find myself sneaking outside. There's a rooftop terrace, and it's empty because sometime in the last hour it's started to rain.

I hide under a narrow awning, sit down cross legged, and remain mostly dry. The glass wall I'm leaning against vibrates from the music, but the curtains are drawn inside, so I don't think anybody sees me.

I think I'm getting old.

An hour at a party, and I'm done.

At twenty-freaking-five. Nice going, loser.

The door slides open, and for a moment, the music gets louder before it closes again.

"Should've figured I'd find you here."

I turn my head to the side and look at Blake.

"I thought you'd already left," I say when he comes and sits down next to me.

"Nope."

The rain splatters all around us, hitting the wooden deck and the roof in steady, rhythmic rat-a-tat.

"Do you do yoga?" Blake asks, seemingly out of the blue.

I frown. "Not really?"

"How the hell can you sit folded up like that?" His eyes are on my lap where I've tucked my feet.

"Can't bend your limbs properly anymore, old man?"

Blake laughs and looks up at the sky. My gaze gets stuck on him. His damp hair and the birthmark right below his earlobe.

His wide shoulders and the defined curve of his biceps. The soft, blond hairs on his forearms.

I look away and reach my hand out, letting the cool raindrops fall on my skin, willing the sensation to remind me that playing with fire is how you get burned. Willing my brain to shut up. To not notice the way Blake keeps watching me when he thinks I'm not looking. The sharp awareness that I've done the exact same thing time and time again and have probably gotten caught the same number of times.

And now he's thrown all subtlety to the wind and is looking at me with a barely concealed, sharp *something* that makes my insides tighten and my skin sing.

"What's your deal with Steph?" he asks.

I lean my head back against the wall and close my eyes. "Why do you ask?"

"Call it curiosity."

"He's a friend."

"But you—" Blake pauses and frowns, choosing his words and finally landing on, "Fuck?"

There's a simple answer there, and I don't owe it to anybody. What I do and who I do is my own business, so why would I answer him? Why would he even ask? It's got nothing to do with him.

"On occasion," I say.

He chews over that for a while. Don't know why. It's not like it's exactly new information for him.

"Are you sleeping with him now?"

I take an exaggerated look to my left and right, then down at my lap. "I don't think so. Unless you see something I don't?"

His nostrils flare, and his fingers rap against the wooden decking boards.

"You know what I'm asking, so just fucking answer the question," he says.

I can't say I exactly appreciate the annoyed tone.

"I like you, Blake, but why the hell you think I owe you an explanation about who I'm fucking is beyond me." I start to get up, but he grabs my arm. I look down at where his fingers are clamped around my wrist and raise my brows at him.

He lets go, and I get up. Rain's coming down even harder now, so I have to raise my voice to be audible over the noise.

"What's your deal anyway? *You* said you didn't want me. So what? You don't want to play, but nobody else gets to either? This is some kindergarten-level pettiness. Give me a fucking break."

I've never been stuck on somebody like this, and it's pissing me the fuck off. There are so many other people I could have. People who want me back and come with no added complications. People who aren't so fucking confusing. There are plenty of people inside, so why am I even here?

I take a step back. Freezing rain pelts down my back. My T-shirt is soaking wet in a second as I stomp toward the door.

His voice stops me. "I never said I didn't want you."

I turn around slowly.

"I said I couldn't sleep with you," he says.

"Semantics," I snap.

"An important distinction."

I roll my eyes. "Sure. Thanks for the English lesson."

I turn around. Then turn back.

"What about your ex?" I ask.

He frowns and looks a hundred percent confused. "My what?"

"The dude Sage was talking about the other day."

He closes his eyes for a moment and his head drops forward. "There is no—" He sighs and clutches the back of his neck.

Christ, he's a fucking mess of mixed signals and confusion.

Everything I deeply dislike. I hover between staying and leaving.

Again.

His voice stops me.

Again.

"Have you ever wanted something?" He pauses. "Somebody," he corrects, eyes moving up and down my body with such intensity it makes my skin tingle. "So badly that you can't fucking think when they're around?" His voice hitches. Like he's suddenly very aware there are stakes. High stakes. But he goes on. "And even if you shouldn't, you can't stop it? Have you ever wanted somebody so much that your fucking body goes hot all over when you're around that person? Can't think clearly. Lie in your bed at night, jerking it until you're fucking raw? Ever felt like this?"

The blunt honesty of those words makes everything very sharp very suddenly. Sounds, sights—senses are overloaded.

"Have you?" he repeats in a voice so wrecked it's more shards than a voice. His voice is a rasp of desire that makes all the hairs on my body stand up. I can barely breathe through the haze of lust that fills my bloodstream and my lungs.

Instead of answering, I walk back to him. Uncertainty shines back from his usually laughing eyes.

If he wasn't talking about me, this is going to be awkward.

I push my hand into the hair at the back of his neck. His breath halts, eyes searching mine. The tip of his tongue peeks out, moving over his lips.

I press a quick kiss to his lips and pull back an inch. His eyes are wide on mine. It's his turn to lean forward and return the favor. His kiss is just as quick. It's testing the waters. His tongue flicks over my lips before he pulls back.

We're both breathing harshly, eyes locked, caution warring with need.

In the end, desire wins.

It always does.

We lunge toward each other at the same time. Blake's palm covers my cheek and my arm moves behind him, slamming our bodies together, head to toe, not an inch between us.

His breath tastes like whiskey and something sweet. The smell of his cologne fills my nostrils.

He lets out a guttural groan, and the bolt of lust that goes through me is flat-out painful. Blake's tongue flicks over my lips, and I open for him, overwhelmed with need, all common sense flying into the night.

If somebody parts the curtains and glances outside through that glass wall, they're going to get an eyeful.

Blake's muscles are rock hard beneath my palms, his body vibrating with tension that's looking for an outlet.

I'm the outlet.

And I can't fucking wait for him to use me.

My fingertips slide over his soaking wet skin, rivulets of rainwater running down my face and back. It's stupid and insane and amazing. Pleasure and desperation. Too much and not enough, all at once.

His grip on my hair tightens, twisting, pulling. It stings. I want more.

He pulls my head away from him by my hair. My scalp prickles. He closes his eyes and takes a step back.

We stare at each other through the haze of the rain.

"We're leaving," he says.

I have no argument with that.

SIXTEEN

The cab ride to Blake's place is quiet. Ominously so. It's the calm before the storm. A tornado in a box, and the lock is about to break.

We walk up the stairs, sopping wet, still silent. The sound of the key in the lock is deafening. He pulls the door open, and I go inside. Turn around in the narrow hallway. Blake's leaning against the door, eyes burning with intensity, chest rising and falling with each deep breath he takes.

"You're wet," he says.

"I am." I tilt my head to the side and grab the hem of my shirt. "Guess I better strip."

His inhale is knife sharp, but otherwise he's still as a statue, eyes fixed on me like he's afraid he'll miss something if he blinks.

That stillness won't last. Not if I have anything to say about it.

He breaks far quicker than I would've anticipated. I only manage to take my shirt off. The moment my fingers go to the button of my jeans, he's on me.

My back slams against the wall and his mouth is on mine, tongue diving into my mouth like he's planning to merge us into one. The jump from wet and freezing to hot and needy is so intense I feel lightheaded for a second.

The desperation is different and foreign to me, and I'm more turned on than I ever remember being. Is it normal to ache for somebody?

My fingers dig into his hips, and I pull him closer until his shaft grinds into mine. He arches against me. Thrusts. Rubs. Burns. Turns me mindless and thoughtless.

I wrestle his shirt off. He kicks off his shoes. Mine follow. Pants are next to go. He's gloriously naked and hard and hot against me.

Our mouths stay fused together when we stumble through the apartment toward the bed. Pants and groans echo from the walls, creating a deliciously dirty soundtrack.

"This is a terrible idea," Blake says, lips moving against mine. "Tell me to stop."

I let out a harsh laugh. "Fuck that. Finish what you've started."

It's like jumping out of an airplane without a parachute. I'm fucked once I get down, but until then, I might as well enjoy the ride.

In response, he digs his nails into the back of my neck and pulls my mouth to his again. We're sharing kisses and air, tongues brushing, teeth clashing, rushing forward. Each kiss gets more and more demanding. Blake takes. There's no hesitation and no doubt about how much he wants me.

For the first time in years, I let go. I trust him to figure out what I want and give it to me. For the first time, I don't feel like I have to be in charge. For the first time, I don't *want* to be in charge. The only thing I want is to stop thinking, and I'm doing an excellent job so far.

We land on the bed in a tangle of bodies, coiled together,

hot skin against hot skin, hips grinding. I seek relief. My dick is like a steel rod, my balls tight. I need to come.

Blake's hips punch into mine, our cocks rubbing together between us. My heartbeat pounds in my ears, and the sound gets even louder when Blake straightens his back, straddling me. My fingers are splayed on his thighs, moving through the soft hairs, digging into his golden skin. My eyes take in the smooth plane of his stomach, the ridges of his hips, the trail of golden hair that runs down from just below his belly button to his cock. Like an arrow pointing your eyes in the right direction. Not that I need a compass, but I appreciate the gesture.

He gives himself a few lazy strokes, eyes moving up and down my body.

"You got hands, right?" I can't believe that needy voice belongs to me.

"Two," he says.

"Then use them."

He laughs, some of the desperation from a few minutes ago replaced with his usual humor.

"Bossy," he says.

My chest tightens in anticipation when he leans forward. His left hand lands next to my head, supporting his weight. My bare cock brushes against his, and my back arches involuntarily. There's just one instinct, and it's to get closer.

Blake's smile turns wicked. He spits into his palm and takes my cock into his slick hand. He slides his palm up and down a few times. I scramble to push myself up on my elbows. No way in hell am I missing even a single second of this show.

Pleasure builds, starting from my spine, spreading, taking over my mind. The head of my dick moves in and out of his hand over and over again. He lets go, and I make a gurgling sound of protest. Coherency is a long-forgotten art by now. He spits into his palm again, lines up our lower bodies, and then both cocks are in his hand, sensitive skin against sensitive skin. He continues his strokes, and my head falls back from the mind-numbing pleasure.

"Fuck you and your long fingers," I groan, forcing my eyes back to where the show is happening.

"Like them?" Blake asks in a strained voice.

"What do you think?"

He falls forward and flicks his tongue over my lower lip before he pulls away and gets back to stroking our cocks. I approve. I fucking approve. I approve so much that all the compliments I plan to give him on his skills come out as moans.

The friction is just enough to bring me to the edge, but not quite enough to get me over to the other side. Blake leans forward again and starts kissing my neck, nipping the skin with his teeth.

"I have lube somewhere," he rasps in between kisses. "But it's so very far away, and I don't want to stop what I'm doing, so here's how it's gonna go. You'll hold off until I get myself off on you, and then I'll jerk you with my cum. How does that sound?"

I try to make words, but nothing comes out. In the end, I only manage a nod.

"Good boy," he murmurs into my ear before he bites the lobe.

All the air seems to be sucked out of the room. My body arches off the bed, and I come in a burning flash of pleasure that sears through my whole body. I shoot in Blake's hand, dick pulsing, cum covering his hand, his cock, my abdomen.

I flop back down with a deep inhale.

"Oh, fuck." The words are more of a garbled groan, but I'm firmly in that sweet spot of bliss after a fantastic orgasm where I don't care about anything.

Blake quirks his brow before he lets me go. He scoops up some of my release and then his hand goes into action, moving up and down his straining erection until his abdominal muscles tighten, and he comes all over my stomach.

For long moments, he just sits on top of me, chest rising and falling with each rapid breath he takes.

"You ruined my plan," he says once his breathing has calmed down a bit.

"My bad."

He flops down on top of me, lips against the side of my neck.

"You owe me."

"Put it on the list."

He laughs and snuggles closer.

And I let him.

SEVENTEEN

I haven't taken a sick day in years. I've worked through hangovers, head colds, and on one memorable occasion, a bout of flu, but today I'm tempted. Tempted to hide. Or better yet, take off altogether. Leave New York in my rearview mirror and go somewhere new.

I was an idiot last night. Messing around with Blake will not go down as one of my brighter moments, and I'm pretty sure I'm going to have to face him today, because unlike other people in my life, Blake knows my schedule, so he knows where to find me.

It'd be nice if he'd take me sneaking out this morning as a hint and wouldn't, but I'm not banking on it.

And it's a good thing I'm not. I'd be disappointed.

I'm in the back, drowning my thoughts in mundane prep work after lunch rush—cutting vegetables, filling the plastic containers with slices of ham and cheese and turkey—when Mina sticks her head in the kitchen.

"Somebody's looking for you."

I snap my head up from the tomato I'm slicing. I've got a bad feeling about this.

"Who?"

Please be Steph. Please be Steph.

"The hottie from the other day," she says.

I slowly put the knife down and peek through the illuminator window in the door.

Crap.

I lean back against the wall and drag my hands through my hair while I figure out how to deal with this shit.

I could… Yeah, I've got nothing. There's a glaring gap in my education. I skipped the lesson that teaches you what to do when your friend-slash-one-night-stand tracks you down the next day.

Mina comes and stands next to me and takes a look through the window, too.

"He doesn't look that happy, does he?" she remarks, craning her neck to get a better view. "What'd you do?"

"I fucked up," I say.

She turns away from the door and considers me for a second. "You can always say you're sorry," she suggests with the starry-eyed naivete of a twenty-one-year-old.

"Unless that sorry comes with a time machine that'll help me undo the last fifteen hours or so, it'll be useless."

"I don't think he's going to leave, so you better go see what he wants. I'll finish up here," Mina offers.

With a sigh, I straighten up and push the door open. Time to face the music.

Blake is standing in front of the counter, looking at me steadily.

And fuck me, of course he looks downright edible in his very proper khakis and blue dress shirt with rolled-up sleeves. There's a hickey below his collarbone. Not visible right now, but I know it's there, and it makes shivers of want run up my spine.

I stop in front of him. He doesn't say anything. Just keeps looking at me until I'm scowling.

"What?" I finally ask.

"I learned something about myself today," he says with a deceptively casual air to his words. "Turns out I don't like to wake up alone."

"I hear some people buy body pillows," I say. "Might be worth looking into."

Now he looks like he's not sure whether he wants to kiss me or wring my neck.

"Why'd you run off this morning?" he asks. Straight to the point.

I avoid his gaze and wave my hand around. "Some of us have jobs they can't do from their living room."

"At five a.m.?"

"It's a busy day. I'm a responsible employee and wanted to get a head start."

"You open at eleven."

"I'm slow. A better man wouldn't rub it in like that."

Why the fuck did I sleep with him? This is a new low in my hook-up career, and my track record wasn't anything to write home about to begin with.

"You want a sandwich or something?" I ask. "Because if not, I've got shit to do, and you're holding up the line."

He looks behind himself at the total emptiness before he sends me a withering look.

"Yeah, it's a real rush hour," he says before he stuffs his hand into the side pocket of his laptop bag. He comes out with something silvery between his fingers and places it on the counter in front of me.

I eye the key. By the way my stomach hollows out, it might as well be a wedding ring.

"What's that?"

"It's a key to my place. You're going to use it to let yourself in after you're done with work."

"Fuck no," I say empathically. "Look, we fucked. And now it's done. Curiosity satisfied. Let's move the fuck on."

Instead of getting out or being offended or any other normal reaction, Blake just laughs.

"No," he says like any of this is up for debate.

I cross my arms over my chest and scowl at him. "Were you lying, and you actually were a virgin? Because, newsflash, you don't have to get obsessed with the first dick you hold in your hand. There are plenty to choose from out there."

Blake's still smiling when he casually strolls around to my side of the counter. There's something determined in his grin, though. Something wild and feral that tells me I'm not going to come out on top.

"Employees only." I try to keep my voice even. Not sure if I succeed seeing that everything inside me is drawn to Blake, and he's so fucking close. I guess personal space isn't a thing we do anymore.

Instead of honoring the holy rules of the sandwich shop, he steps even closer, grabs the key from where I left it on the counter and then his hand slides into the front pocket of my jeans, where he turns the simple act of putting the key in my pocket into something downright indecent. There's grazing. And cupping. And chest pressed against chest. And my dick is pretty much convinced this might as well be a handjob, judging by how it salutes all Blake's ministrations.

"In case you change your mind," Blake murmurs. Still too close. Close enough for me to feel the outline of his cock through his pants.

I swallow and force the mix of irritation and lust down. "I won't."

He shrugs, pulls his hand away, and retreats to the other

side of the counter again, completely unapologetic and showing no remorse for the fact that I'm fucking aching.

"I have a meeting with a new client I need to get to," he says. "But I should be home by six. In my bed. Naked. With my dick in my hand. Feel free to use the key."

The bastard's lips quirk into a satisfied smirk when I suck in a loud breath.

"I'll see you," he says, hikes his laptop bag higher on his shoulder, and strolls out the door.

I glare down at the bulge in my pants.

"We're not going to do this," I grit out. "We have pride."

It's pretty much the only thing I have left.

EIGHTEEN

I UNLOCK the door and push it open. The apartment is quiet, but the lights are on. Maybe he's home. Maybe he left the lights on for my benefit? Do people do that? Nice people with fully developed empathy-bones might, but I wouldn't know anything about that. I drag my fingers through my hair and take a moment to really appreciate this situation. I'm exactly one step away from my next act of idiocy. A smart man would reassess and reconsider. Get the hell out of here. Stick his dick in an ice bucket and put his brain back in charge.

Not me, though.

I listen for a moment, my whole body tense with anticipation and apprehension. There's no sound of movement.

If he's not home yet, I'm leaving.

Under no circumstances will I wait for him.

My ears are starting to hurt from how hard I'm trying to see if there's any sound of movement.

I close my eyes and curse silently.

What is this shit? I don't get attached to people. I especially don't get attached to one-night stands.

Even if the one-night stand isn't exactly a one-night stand. Because Blake isn't, is he?

Then what? A fuck buddy? A friend with benefits? Just sex? Only he isn't. He feels like more, but what that means, I have no clue. It's not that I'm in love with him—thank fuck for small mercies because at least that's something I'm certain of—but I can't deny that I'm drawn to him. Like moth to a fucking flame.

He's an uncomfortable obsession I don't want to have, and I clearly have very little willpower, since I'm at his apartment and not at home where I should be.

I hesitate for another second before I give up. No point in postponing the inevitable.

Blake's in bed, like he promised. Very much dressed, not like he promised. Instead, he's reading a book. His long legs are crossed, encased in a comfy-looking pair of sweats and an equally comfy-looking T-shirt. And he's wearing those stupidly hot, nerdy glasses he only puts on when his eyes are tired after staring at a screen for too long.

Why the fuck do I know that? I don't *want* to know that. I want to have suitable distance between us where we wouldn't know personal details like that about each other.

I lean my shoulder against the partition wall and lift my chin toward him. "What's with the clothes? I was promised nakedness." Annoyance rings loud and clear in my voice. Good.

"I was, but you were late, so I already jerked off." He smiles smugly when I suck in a breath and puts the book down. "Was beginning to think you wouldn't come."

"The only reason I'm here is because I plan to come. Will you get undressed now?"

He gets up and puts the book away, but instead of taking his clothes off, he walks past me.

"Where are you going?" I ask his back.

"Dinner. I'm starving," he throws over his shoulder. "How does pasta sound?"

"I'm not here to eat!" I call after him.

"Tough shit," he replies.

He's laying out ingredients when I stomp into the kitchen. And like the willpowerless moron I am, I plop down at the counter and settle in. Because I'm here already, so I might as well wait him out and get some sex out of this ordeal. I send a glare at Blake's unfairly nice ass. He catches me. I glare some more.

I spent hours earlier trying to convince myself I had self-control and common sense and wasn't going to show up here. Clearly, I lack both. And I'm thinking with my dick. It made some pretty persuasive arguments earlier, so it won the debate in the end.

"What are you making?" I ask. A limp white flag after twenty-four hours of straight-up dick behavior. Aren't I nice?

"Steak pasta." He opens one of the cabinets and takes out a pack of pasta. "Store-bought, though."

"The horror. What kind of establishment are you running here?"

He grins and puts a wooden spoon in front of my mouth. I roll my eyes and taste.

"It's good," I say, doing my best to ignore the warmth that takes over my insides when he smiles. I watch him pour his store-bought pasta into boiling water. "People make pasta from scratch? In real life? While they're not auditioning for *MasterChef*?"

"It tastes better, but it takes time. Play your cards right, and I'll make it one of these days."

We're making plans now for date nights. Isn't that juuuuust awesome?

"Dating freaks you out," Blake remarks, cutting into my

thoughts. "Is it dating in general or dating me?"

"We're not dating," I say. "Besides, you're not the dating type, remember?"

He pops a slice of cucumber in his mouth. Doesn't argue but doesn't agree either. Just chews thoughtfully.

"Want one?" he holds a slice out toward me.

I don't know what possesses me to do it, but I lean forward and eat it out of his hand, lips grazing the tips of his fingers. His gaze is on me, smoldering hot.

"Thanks."

He pushes the cutting board and the cucumber toward me. I take the knife and cut a few more slices and eat those, too. I suddenly realize I'm starving. I haven't eaten anything today. Too busy sneaking out of apartments and freaking out about life.

"Where'd you learn to cook?" I ask.

"Well," he says slowly. "I told you about the hacking thing. I did a year in juvie, and then they put me back into the system. Only, I wasn't very interested in going back, so I figured I'd run away. You know, make my own luck." He grins, but there's not much humor in it. "Can't get very far without wheels, though," he adds.

"Is this the car theft story?"

He nods and grimaces. "As established, not one of my brightest moments. I got caught trying to steal this couple's SUV."

"When you say steal, do you mean full-on 'I tried to hotwire a car' kind of thing?"

"Oh, that would've been cool," he says, and for a moment I get a peek at that reckless fifteen-year-old he must've been once upon a time. Then he shakes his head and hides that part away again. "You can't really hotwire newer cars, so it was more of a 'somebody forgot their keys in the ignition' type of thing."

"I came, I saw, I conquered," I say.

"It went more like I went, I saw, I got caught."

"Then what happened?" I ask.

"The husband found me trying to drive his wife's car out of their driveway, so I figured I was on an express ride back to juvie." His eyes have a distant look in them, like he's transported back in time.

"But that didn't happen?"

He shakes his head and looks straight at me, more serious than I've ever seen him. "They gave me a chance. They had all sorts of connections, so they found me a spot at a group home for homeless teenagers." He shrugs. "It was different. You had to pull your own weight if you wanted to keep your room. You had to go to school. You had to learn all those basic life skills. Cooking." He nods toward the pot of pasta. "Cleaning. Bills. Budgeting. It felt like for the first time, I was responsible for my own life. It rammed home that I had to get my shit together if I wanted to make something of myself. I got lucky."

"Sounds more like you did a lot of work to get where you are," I say.

"Sure," he says, sliding a plate in front of me, "I put in the effort, but I still got lucky that I chose that particular car. And that they didn't call the cops on me. And that they decided to take a chance on me. I'll forever be grateful for that. Otherwise, who knows where I'd have ended up. Certainly not here." He sits down opposite me. His gaze catches mine and locks me in place. "I'd hate not to be here," he says.

Does he have to sound so sincere and vulnerable when he says things like that? It could just be a line, but the delivery gut-punches me and makes my heart do stupid things in my chest that I can't, for the life of me, stop.

This is one of those moments when you accidentally drop a match, and you think you have time to get something to put the flame out. No big deal.

You're back five seconds later.

The whole house is on fire.

It's too late to sound the alarm.

He cooked, so I clean. I take my time, trying to talk myself into leaving.

But when I put the last plate away and turn around, he gets up, grabs the hem of his shirt, and pulls it over his head. The shirt falls to the floor, his fingers move to the waistband of his sweats, and I lean my ass against the counter.

His gaze holds mine as he slowly pushes the sweats down.

Then he's naked. Every perfect, sexy, magnificent inch of him.

"Finally making good on your promise?" My voice doesn't sound like my own. Too hoarse. Too needy.

My insides are burning with want, and my hands are itching to touch. It's only made worse by that sexy confidence of his. Not sure why it turns me on so much, but the way he balances said confidence without ever being cocky gets me very hot and very bothered very fast.

He arches a brow, and I go to him. I stop when my toes touch his, reach out, and slide my fingertips over his thigh. The muscle clenches and vibrates underneath my touch. When I graze his balls, his breathing becomes uneven and his eyes widen. His lips part and a shaky exhale whispers over my cheek.

The tip of his cock brushes against my T-shirt-clad stomach, and he closes his eyes and curses softly.

I lean closer and press my mouth to his for a moment before I pull away and look down. I wrap my hand around his cock, drawing out more curses.

"You're too hot for your own good," I say.

He lets out a breathy laugh at that and quirks his brow. "What are you gonna do about it?"

"Blow you. Thoughts?"

His tongue peeks out and licks over his lips. "In favor. Go for it," he says in a rush.

I drop to my knees and wrap my hand around the base of his dick, ready for a taste, when Blake wraps his fingers in my hair and pulls me back.

"What? Did you change your mind?"

"Hell no. Bedroom," he says. "Please."

"Okay...?" Not sure what's wrong with here and now, but if a bed is what he wants, I guess a bed is what he's going to get.

I get up and head toward the bed.

"And get undressed," Blake calls after me.

I turn around. "Aren't you coming?"

"Give me a sec."

"You're being weird."

"Just get undressed," he orders.

"Yes, sir." I turn around, grab the back of my shirt, and pull it off. Blake's loud inhale sucks all the air out of the room. I smile and walk away.

There's a thump from the hallway and then another one, and a few seconds after that, he rushes into the bedroom. He stops by the partition wall and swallows hard. I quirk an eyebrow at him and give myself a slow stroke. He's on me in a flash, kneeling above me, mouth hovering over mine.

"What were you doing?" I ask. "Rearranging the furniture for better sex feng shui?"

"I hid your shoes," he says and starts to kiss me, but I rear back.

"What the fuck?"

"I hid your shoes," he repeats patiently and tries to kiss me again.

"Why?"

"If you don't have your shoes, you can't run out on me in the middle of the night," he says.

I should be pissed off, but he looks so damn proud of himself that I just don't have it in me. Especially when he catches me off guard and kisses me while he grinds his cock into mine.

I grab his hips though, and flip us so I'm on top. And in charge. I lift both his hands above his head and pin them there with one of mine. The other one is free to roam over Blake's side.

I bend down and flick his nipple with my tongue. His hips punch up and he lets out a breathless chuckle.

"What are you gonna do to me?" he asks.

"Whatever I want. You're mine."

"Yes. I'm yours," he breathes out. I shouldn't like it this much.

"And you'll pay for that little stunt with my shoes," I continue.

"Do what you want," he says, but he doesn't really sound that sorry. There's anticipation in his eyes. Anticipation and desire.

I flick my tongue over the shell of his ear and bite the lobe before I lean my forehead against his.

"I think I'm going to use you."

He nods eagerly. "That sounds like an excellent plan."

"I'm going to make myself come as many times as I want."

The nodding grows more intense, his eyes traveling up and down my body. "I'm on board with that."

"But you don't get to come."

His gaze snaps to mine. "At all?"

"Not until I'm finished with you. And I'm going to take my time."

He closes his eyes, and his cock jumps against his belly.

"You like that," I say.

He nods again, almost as if he's unable to form words anymore.

Seems like as good a starting point as any. I kiss my way down his body, and he pushes himself up on his elbows as I go. Once at my destination, I drag my tongue from the base of his cock to the very tip. I look up then, and the pure, uninhibited need on Blake's face is like a kick in the throat. It's hard to breathe for a moment.

Attraction is a scary thing. It can so easily grow out of control. You can so easily find that you've gone too far and there's no way back. That you're in too deep, and there's no way out.

I have a feeling this ride is already flying off the tracks, and there's not much I can do about it other than hope the landing will be soft. But as long as we're still midair, I won't worry about what's to come too much. Instead, I dig my fingertips into his hips and swallow him down.

"Holy shit." Blake's hips jerk up, forcing his cock deeper into my mouth. "You're really good at this," he rushes out in one single breath.

I better be. I've had enough practice to get the technical side sorted out, but it's also that I just fucking enjoy this. I like using my mouth and tongue on him. Love that he turns from coherent and put together into a moaning, panting mess. Love the silky feel of his cock sliding between my lips. Love going down on him and tasting the salt of him on my tongue.

I smooth my hands up his thighs, tongue flicking over the tip of his cock again and again until his arms give out underneath him, and he falls to his back on the bed, his chest heaving like he's at the finish line after a race.

He spreads his legs wider, every muscle under my palm taut and vibrating with tension. I roll his balls between my fingers and his breathing gets louder. I lap, suck, and lick. I'm going to make a mess of him. That's my one motivation right now.

"I'm gonna..." he gasps.

I pull off and admire my handywork. He's spit slick and rock hard. Perfect.

"What the fuck?" he groans and lifts his head.

"Can't come yet. Remember?"

His head falls back to the bed again. "Are you fucking kidding me?"

I smirk. "Frustrated?"

He takes a slow, measured breath. "You know you're going to pay for this, right?"

"I'm counting on it," I say right before I swallow him down again, hard and sloppy, head bobbing up and down. Blake's palms slam on the bed, fists twisting the covers. My own cock rubs against the sheets, taking the edge off but not much more. His low moans urge me on, and once his body grows taut again, I pull off to the sound of sweet, sweet cursing.

I go down on him again. He wraps his thigh around my back, keeping me locked in place. Fucking hot. The hands in my hair tighten, and he pushes into my mouth. I let him use me. Want him to use me. He's the most beautiful man I've ever seen. Especially now, all sweat-slick and desperate.

"Fuck, please," he says, urgent and frantic. For me. This is all for me. I did this.

Shivers run over my back. His dick slips from my mouth. I lean my forehead on his abdomen and take my cock in my hand. It only takes a tug, and I come all over the sheet between his legs, cock pulsing, fingers slick with my own release before I flop down on Blake.

He sucks in a breath and rocks against me, his cock rubbing against my chest. I push him down and keep him as still as possible.

"You fucker," he pants, his whole body tense as a strung wire, and I laugh, body buzzing, spine tingling from the rush of orgasm.

"Warned you," I say.

"Don't you dare fall asleep right now," he grouses.

I hum and leisurely make my way up his body, licking and kissing his chest, every perfect inch of him. Once we're face to face, he brings his hands to the back of my neck and pulls my head down. He distracts me with a kiss that bleeds into another one. And another. His tongue goes into my mouth, licking and teasing, plunging in and out. His hips grind against mine. We're making out like two teenagers.

He distracts me just enough to roll us over again so I'm lying underneath him. He's straddling me, dick jutting up toward his navel.

I put my hands behind my head and study him. "What are you gonna do with me now?" I ask.

"Torture. Turn over."

I'm too satisfied to argue. And I want to see where this goes. So I roll over onto my stomach.

"Get on your knees," he says. "Head down."

I see where this is going. A shiver of anticipation moves over my skin, leaving goosebumps behind. Blake's palm slides up my back, pushing my upper body closer to the mattress, manhandling me into exactly the position he wants.

"You have a magnificent ass," he says, massaging one of the cheeks. I glance over my shoulder. He lowers his head and presses a kiss to the base of my spine. Kisses up, and then down again.

I grunt, anticipation stealing my words. My cock stiffens, and I spread my legs even farther.

I know where this is going.

I *know*.

But when he lowers his head and flicks his tongue over my rim, my whole body still jerks.

It's been a long, long time since anybody did that. This is fucking intimate. Maybe the most intimate thing of all, so I've only ever allowed it a handful of times, and even then with a lot of reservation. All of that's gone now. Only need remains.

"Fuck," I breathe out.

Blake licks me again. His hands spread my cheeks wider, and I sink into the mattress. The pleasure is a slow burn. Starts with a flicker and grows into a flame. My hips won't stay still anymore, pushing back, fucking his tongue as he slowly works it inside my hole. His fingers grip my ass cheeks as he works me open until I'm a shivering, quivering mess beneath his touch.

His panting breaths are just as loud as mine, his tongue pushing in and out quicker and quicker. His forehead lands on my lower back.

"Can I?" he asks. "Do you... Can I?"

"Yeah," I say. "Do it."

Yes, yes, yes. Do whatever you want with me. Anything. I'll take it.

Wet with spit, needy, and desperate like I've never been before.

He scrambles to the nightstand. Lube and condoms land next to my head. The lube disappears for a second before it's tossed back and slick fingers replace his tongue.

One.

Then two.

Stretching. Scissoring. Stroking.

Until I'm twisting the sheets between my fingers, spread open, ready for more.

By now, my cock is hard again.

"Look at you," Blake breathes out. "Waiting for me with my fingers in your ass."

He strokes over my prostate, and my ass clenches around his fingers.

He groans. "Shit. I'm gonna lose it the moment I get inside you."

"Aww. Short fuse?" I ask, throwing him a look over my shoulder. It's a miracle I can keep it together myself at the smoldering look he sends me. He laughs, and his fingers vibrate inside me. Fucking hell.

"It's all because of you."

"I'll take that as a compliment."

His palm slides over my back and his dick presses against my hole. "I've wanted to do this since the first time I saw you."

If the goal is emotional distance... well, safe to say this is not the way to do it.

"What took you so long?"

This is also not a conversation to have with somebody's cock pressed against your ass, but that doesn't seem to stop me.

Blake doesn't reply. His hips move, and he starts pushing inside me. Thank fuck. This part I know. This part I'm good at.

I widen my legs. Push back. He lets out a guttural groan. Sinks inside me, slow inch by slow inch. He takes his time. Careful. Until he's all the way inside me. I close my eyes. Get used to the fullness.

Thoughts scatter and disappear. Only Blake remains.

He's still for so long I have to push back to urge him to move. Steely fingers dig into my hips.

He gives a slow, almost lazy thrust. Every nerve ending is immediately at attention. He does it again. And again. Faster. More forceful.

Wildfire burns in my veins, turning something that's supposed to be quick and easy into something violent and unmanageable. Creating a hunger inside me I've never felt before. Overwhelming in its intensity. Uncontrollable.

I turn my head back, and he leans forward. Kisses me. Thrusts. Somehow hits the exact right spot.

I'm a goner. My elbows give out, refusing to support my weight anymore, and I drop down, shivering with aftershocks and the ecstatic rush that sweeps through my whole body.

Blake follows me with a few hard, erratic thrusts, his dick jerking inside me. He collapses on top of me, sweaty and sated, his heart pounding against my back.

As far as decisions go, this was still a terrible one to make, but it's hard to care when you've just had every thought fucked out of you.

Blake's lips press against the nape of my neck.

"Wanna do it again?" he mutters against my neck.

I snort. "You're either really optimistic or overly confident in your ability to get it up."

"I can absolutely get it up for you."

I reach my hand back and squeeze his ass. "You keep telling yourself that, buddy."

He smiles into my shoulder and keeps his mouth pressed against it.

"Stay?" he whispers into my skin.

"You stole my shoes. I kind of have to stay, don't I?" I glance at him, gaze catching his.

"Stay because you want to," he says softly.

In the end, the decision isn't that difficult.

"I'll stay."

This time, when I leave, I let him know. He makes me breakfast even though it's so early, being up should be considered blasphemy.

He kisses me as he passes me on his way to the fridge, while

I stare straight ahead and try to will my brain to wake up. Kisses me between cracking eggs in the bowl and kisses me while he waits for them to cook. Kisses me in the shower and kisses me while I get dressed.

He retrieves my shoes from the hallway closet and watches me put them on.

Kisses me again before I head out.

The subway is almost empty.

My couch is empty when I get back home, but I find Steph hogging all the blankets and pillows in my bed. He gives me a bleary look when I accidentally drop my phone.

"Hey," he says hoarsely, taking in my most definitely disheveled appearance. "Fun night?" he asks with a grin.

For the first time, I don't want to have our usual interaction. The one we have whenever we happen to cross paths after a one-nighter. Whatever Blake and I have... I don't think I can say it's temporary. Not anymore. I don't think I can keep away. I don't have enough self-control. And I don't want to joke about my night. Don't want to discuss Blake with Steph. Instead, I want to keep Blake to myself. Protect whatever it is that's brewing between us from everybody else's eyes. So, no. I don't want to talk about him. Not before I figure out what's happening and how to deal with it.

Steph pushes himself up on his elbow and regards me with a seriousness he hardly ever displays.

"It was good," I finally say.

"Just good?" he asks and quirks a brow.

I look away from him. "I stayed the night."

Covers rustle as Steph gets out of bed. He comes and leans against the wall next to me. Nudges me with his shoulder.

"That's a good thing. Isn't it?"

I lean my head back and stare at the ceiling.

"Fuck if I know."

NINETEEN

I'm determined to be careful. Like walking on barely frozen ice. One step at a time, always ready to run at the slightest hint of cracks.

But days pass. And the surface stays intact.

No cracks.

No suspicious sounds.

So I get bolder.

I venture further away from safety. Deeper into whatever it is Blake is offering.

The wall starts to come down. Layer by layer. Brick by brick.

Steph moves his crap into my room. Why wouldn't he? It's not like I'm ever really there anymore.

Instead, every night, I somehow end up at Blake's apartment. I say somehow, but it's more a result of deliberate action. It's difficult to stay in my own place when the moment I step in the door at Blake's place, he's all over me. By the time we're done with each other I have zero motivation to drag myself out of his warm bed and away from the strong arms he wraps around me every night.

I try to keep things casual. Try to keep at least some distance and set at least some boundaries. I really do try. But every night, Blake and I inevitably end up in bed together and spend hours getting each other off, talking, watching TV, reading, eating, laughing.

It's not a hookup. It's not casual. Even if I'm not ready to admit that to myself. Not yet anyway.

It's lucky I don't have time to ponder it too much, because Blake walks into the bedroom, and he hasn't bothered to tie a towel around his waist. Instead, he uses one to dry himself while he walks, which I thoroughly appreciate. I roll onto my stomach and prop my chin on my arms.

"You have the prettiest cock."

Blake stops rubbing the towel over his hair and raises his brows at me. "I'm not sure that's the term I prefer."

I shrug. "It's just an observation."

He drops the towel and comes to me, gloriously naked. We spent the day in bed. Fucking. Talking. Napping. And—it bears repeating—fucking.

It's not the first day like this. Ever since I gave myself permission to start this... situation, things have quickly gotten out of hand. I'm in way over my head, but every time I manage to gather a smidgeon of willpower to consider putting some distance between us, that resolve is quickly overpowered by a single hot look over the dinner table or a quick kiss in the middle of the street.

He climbs onto the bed and lies down on top of me. Kisses the shell of my ear. Moves down to my neck and ends with pressing his lips to my shoulder.

"Want me to put my pretty cock inside you? I could be persuaded."

I smile into my hands as shivers of pleasure move over my back. "Yeah, I'm sure it'd be a tough negotiation."

"It would. I'm not easy, you know. You'd have to seduce me. And just rubbing your ass against my cock won't do the trick. You'd have to really put some effort in. 'Cause I have standards."

"Those are important," I agree.

He hums against the back of my neck.

I groan and push my forehead into the mattress. "I have to get to work."

I'm at the Barclays Center tonight, setting up for the Nets. I'd much rather stay here.

Blake nuzzles my neck.

"Hmm? What was that? You have to get naked? I can help you with that." He slides his hand into my boxer briefs and squeezes my ass while he keeps kissing my neck. I roll myself over, and he falls onto the bed next to me with a huff. I press one more quick kiss to his lips before I roll off the bed. He pushes himself up on his elbows.

"Okay, new offer," he says. "Cancel whatever you have lined up, and I'll hire you myself for the night."

I snort. "To do what?"

"Fuck," he says.

"This offer comes with extra strong sex worker vibes, and that's not really my area of expertise."

"I strongly disagree. You're excellent at sex, so you'd make for an excellent sex worker. Don't sell yourself short."

I make a thoughtful face. "You know, it's not the worst idea. Instead of being paid peanuts for grunt work, I should totally become one of those high-end escorts. Because I *am* good at sex. I also look good in a suit. And I wouldn't mind a lavish life of leisure."

"I assume since I gave you the idea, I'll get dibs when you start looking for clients? I'll take all the available time slots."

I pull on a pair of jeans and button them. "Aww, babe, you can't afford me."

"Well, that backfired," he says. "Actually, I should probably tell you... You're not that great in bed."

I send him an amused look. "That's an abrupt one-eighty."

"Didn't want to hurt your feelings before. But yeah, you're terrible. Your skills could really use *a lot* of work. I'm talking months and months of rigorous daily practice. But I'm a benevolent guy, so I'll volunteer to help you out with that."

"You're a real do-gooder."

"Enough with the compliments. Time's a-wastin', so get undressed, and let's get cracking."

I go to the bed, put my knee on the mattress, and bend down, mouth hovering above his.

"It's a tempting offer," I say. "Very generous of you to sacrifice your time like that."

"I know. I'm great. I bet we can find a way for you to show your appreciation."

I catch his lower lip between mine and suck gently. His breathing picks up. I slide my hand down his chest. Down, down, down until I wrap my fingers around his cock. I give a slow stroke, and he bites back a groan.

"Seems even my subpar skills are doing it for you," I murmur against his lips.

"Think what you could accomplish with a little practice," he replies breathlessly while he tilts his head farther back and searches out my lips again.

"Spontaneous combustion?" I grin and pull back. "Guess we'll find out. Later."

He falls back with a dramatic sigh. "Tease."

I straighten myself and start gathering my stuff. My stuff, which is everywhere. For years, all the apartments I've lived in have looked like glorified hotel rooms. I don't leave my things lying around. Or rather, I didn't used to leave my things lying around. Blake's home seems to invite clutter, and lately I've started producing my own.

Blake gets up and pulls on a pair of sweats. He follows me to the front door, where he leans his shoulder against the wall and watches me while I put on my sneakers, dig out my backpack, and stuff my things into it.

He takes the keys from the hook by the door and throws them to me. I roll my eyes and slip them into my pocket. I've been trying to forget the keys every now and then in the hopes it'll discipline me a bit and make me go home.

It's not really working, but a false sense of security is still a sense of security, I guess.

"Wake me up when you get back," he says.

"With my substandard bedroom prowess?"

"The first step is admitting the problem. And we already agreed I'm willing to help hone your skills. I'll pencil you into my calendar for the foreseeable future. But also, I need to talk to you about something. Tell you something."

I raise my brows. "Sounds ominous."

"It's not..." It seems like he's finding it somewhat difficult to explain what it's not, and after a few seconds he just shakes his head. The smile he aims my way is a touch tense. "Not ominous. Just... I'll explain later."

"Okay," I say slowly.

I'm still not fully convinced it's not something bad, but then he steps closer and says, "I already miss you," and I forget everything else.

I have to get going, so I kiss him again because lately, I can't seem to keep my mouth away from him.

"I'll be late."

"Don't care. Wake me."

With a final kiss and a nod, I jog down the stairs and into the night, a smile on my face, and a skip in my step.

I actually quite enjoy my gig at the Barclays. I'm the lowest guy on the totem pole, so it's mostly heavy lifting, but it's a good workout, and everybody is determined to get the job done quickly and efficiently, so time usually flies when I'm here. The money isn't terrible either. All in all, it's one of the better jobs I have.

There was a concert here earlier tonight, so first all the chairs need to be removed from the floor before press sections and TV screens will go up.

It's choreographed chaos, with trucks and forklifts bringing everything in and people moving around, assembling the court, and putting up the nets on the hoops. It's tough, physical work, and there's limited time to do it, so there's hardly a moment to breathe, but that's what I like about it the most. Leaves me less time to think.

We're laying down the last of the court panels when my phone rings. Who the hell is calling me at five thirty in the morning? I get an uncomfortable feeling in the pit of my stomach. When, in the history of the world, has a call in the middle of the night meant something good has happened?

The hollow, uncomfortable anxiety gets worse when I see Nora's name on the screen. I take a few steps away from the half-finished court and lift the phone to my ear.

"Yeah?"

"Don't freak out," Nora says.

"Perfect way to get me to do just that." I do my best not to freak out, but it's not going too well.

"Okay, my bad. Look, Blair's in the hospital," she says. *"She went into labor."*

I freeze. I can't say I'm an expert at making babies, but even I know they're supposed to cook for nine months. There was something Blair said about weeks a while back, but I honestly can't remember right now.

"But... that's too early. Right?" I wouldn't say I'm completely freaking out, but I'm not exactly chill either.

"She's thirty-four weeks along, so kind of but it's not too bad. Blair and the baby are doing great. Not even in the NICU, so she's a trooper." She lets out a loud breath and rambles on in a very un-Nora-like way. *"It was kind of crazy how fast it all happened. We were asleep and then suddenly Blair's all, the baby is coming, and there was an ambulance, and now I have all this leftover adrenaline, and I don't know how to handle it. And she's so tiny. I've never seen such a tiny baby, Jude."*

That's a lot of information to get in such a short time.

"Did you say 'she?'" I ask.

She laughs for a second. *"Yeah. She tricked us all. Surprise. It's a girl."*

Relief rushes through me, and I laugh out loud, drawing some looks, but I don't even care.

"Dude, you're gonna have to come up with a whole new batch of stripper names now."

"Oh, for sure. A whole new world has opened up for us."

"Candy Rose," I suggest.

"Or Trixie Crystal."

"Or go with a classic like Bambi."

She's quiet for a moment before she lets out another breath. *"We'll be in the hospital for a week, at least, but Blair really wants you to come and see the baby, so can you?"*

"Do you even have to ask? Text me the visiting hours, and I'll be there."

"This is one beautiful baby," I say softly, looking down at the bundle of sunshine-yellow blankets in my lap. Nora left to get some things from their apartment and pick up Steph—who's somehow managed to get himself stranded somewhere in the Hamptons—as soon as I arrived, so it's just me and Blair and the baby in her hospital room. It's still early. I came straight from work, so I had to flirt my way inside at the nurse's station since it's not visiting hours yet.

Blair slides her fingertips over the tiny white beanie on her daughter's head, looking at her with a very soft, un-Blair-like smile. "I know. Other babies are screwed, because I just gave birth to the ultimate baby."

"From now on whenever parents see her, they'll look at their own kid and be all, 'Why can't you be more like Blair's baby?'"

"Poor little losers. But what can you do?"

I chuckle and adjust my arm. The baby's eyelids flutter softly.

"What are you gonna name her?"

"Hazel." She looks up and smiles.

I gaze at the sleeping baby. It fits. "She looks like a Hazel."

"I mean, hazelnuts are superior nuts, so it's a suitable name for a superior baby."

I laugh, and the baby stirs, so I clamp my mouth shut and sway her gently. When I lift my gaze, I find Blair eyeing me with a funny look on her face.

"What?" I ask. "Am I doing it wrong? Do I have to hold her differently?"

"Jeez, no. You're doing it perfectly." She looks down at Hazel and slides her fingertip over her head again like she can't stop touching her. "I just... I just want you to know that even though Hazel is with us now, Nora and I aren't going to turn into those people who'll be all about the baby and forget the rest of the world even exists. We still love you and Steph both so, so much, and Hazel will never change that. I guess what I want to say is that you and Steph are both a part of our family, and..." She frowns and opens and closes her mouth for a little while. "We love you all equally, no matter what, and it's a different kind of love, but it's all equal in size. And there's not, like, a finite amount of love. I mean... It grows. And expands."

I raise my brows at her. "What are you... Are you giving me the older sibling speech?"

"The what?"

"You know. The one parents give to the older kid when the new baby is born?"

She glances at me quickly and then away. "I might've gotten some inspiration from Google," she mutters. "Don't laugh, you ass. You know I don't do emotions well. I Googled how to say I love you before I said it to Nora. In the end I wrote her one of those stupid poems where the first letters of each line make up the phrase 'I love you.'" Something about that makes her perk up. "Should I do one for you? Nora seemed to like hers, so I can basically just insert your name in there and presto, a love declaration."

"Idiot," I say with all the affection in the world. "I'm an adult. I get that Hazel comes first. She's your fuc—freaking child. She's supposed to get all your attention and love. And don't even tell me you love us all equally. It's not possible, and that's okay. I mean, if the three of us are in that only-one-door-that-holds-two-people-in-a-shipwreck situation, I fully expect you to yeet me into the sea and save Hazel. That's how it's supposed to be."

Blair sniffs and dashes the back of her hand across her eyes. Then again. And again.

"You okay there, B?" I ask after she keeps sniffing and dashing.

"Great," she says in a clipped tone. "Happiest day of my

life," she adds before she swallows hard, and then it's seemingly out-of-the-blue waterworks, and she digs her fingers into my arm. "You're going to dump us," she wails so suddenly I jump. Hazel stirs again but remains asleep. Blair tries to smother her crying in her hands, which creates a weird, hollow, snotty sound, what with all the sniffing and tears.

I am so confused.

"I'm going to dump you?" I ask slowly.

"Yes! You do that. You push people away, and so far I haven't let you, but now with Hazel, what if I won't have the time to force you to be in my life? Babies take a lot of time. What if now it's my time to become one of the casualties? You're like my brother, and I love you, but you can be such a callous asshole when you cut people out of your life, so what if you start to distance yourself from us, and I don't notice until it's too late?"

I blink and try to process... all of that.

Introspection usually doesn't give me great results, so I rarely venture to those grounds.

This time's no different.

A hot flash of shame goes through me like a lightning bolt. What kind of a fucking person am I? Apparently the kind whose best friend seems to think I can just drop her without a second thought and go on my merry way. Guilt digs its claws even deeper when I'm forced to admit to myself that I can't exactly be indignant about Blair feeling this way. She's witnessed all my lowest moments. With my parents. My biological mother. Friends. Potential friends.

Maybe I haven't pushed Blair out of my life, but I haven't exactly made it abundantly clear she's a part of it either.

I take her friendship—take it for granted, no less—and I don't give anything back. I mean, sure, if she needs help or a favor, I'm there, but I don't ask for her help. Ever. Which kind of sucks, doesn't it? Because people in your life also want to feel that they're needed, and I never let myself need anybody, because what if one day they're not there anymore?

"Blair," I say helplessly and maneuver Hazel so that my left hand is free. I take Blair's hand in mine and squeeze until she looks at me. "I promise you, you'll never get rid of me. Unless you get sick and tired of me yourself and ask me to leave you the fuc—the fudge alone. Man, I swear way too much. Are you sure you want to keep me around? Because there's a chance I'll make sure Hazel's first word is something wildly inappropriate."

She sniffs and sends me a long, watery look as if she's assessing whether I'm telling the truth before she swallows hard and sends me a tremulous smile. "Are you kidding me? Have you seen those videos of toddlers saying fuck? Those things are hilarious."

"Language," I hiss while I try to cover Hazel's ears.

Blair rolls her eyes. "She's a few hours old and asleep. I don't think I'll scar her for life."

"Class-A parenting right there. You know what? Even if I did want to dump you, I clearly can't anymore. Somebody has to make sure Hazel has a good role model."

She very ungratefully snorts. "Who? *You?*"

"Yes, me."

She's still laughing. "Yeah, okay. Sure."

I look down at Hazel. "Don't listen to your mommy. I'm awesome. You'll see. And I promise, I'll look after you until the day I die."

And Blair is crying again, but then she leans her head on my shoulder, and I lean my cheek on the top of her head, and... it feels pretty damn nice.

TWENTY

When I get back from the hospital, I find Blake behind his screens. He's wearing his nerdy glasses again, so lost in his work he doesn't even seem to notice I'm there. It's cute.

I take advantage of the moment and just watch for a little while. Time for some harsh truths. I don't think I've ever liked somebody quite as much as I like him. And instead of arguing with myself or trying to play it down, I let myself enjoy the way my heart jumps in my chest and the feverish rush of blood inside my veins.

My socked feet barely make a sound on the floor. I slide my palms over his shoulders and wrap my arms around his neck from behind.

"Good morning."

He turns his head and smiles. "Is it?"

I kiss the side of his neck in reply. He tilts his head and sighs happily. I move my lips over the sensitive skin, up and down, until his breathing starts to pick up, and he maneuvers his office chair around until he's facing me. He catches my mouth with his and kisses me. His tongue swipes over my bottom lip before it slides into my mouth. His fingers grip the hair at the back of my head, pulling me closer.

He pulls until I climb into his lap with my knees on either side of his thighs, straddling him. His eyes are hooded as he slides his hands under my T-shirt, his thumbs moving over my abdominal muscles, leaving small shivers of pleasure in their wake.

"Long night?" he asks.

I nod.

"How are Blair and the baby doing?"

I smile. I love that he asks. I love that he cares. "They're perfect."

His eyes get a soft look in them, and he squeezes my hip for a moment.

"Tired?" he asks.

"I'm past that point."

He nips at my lower lip and hums. "Even so, you should probably sleep. Take it from the expert in terrible sleep habits."

"Shh," I say in between kisses. "I'm a bit busy for sensible life advice right now."

"With?" He sounds amused.

"If you can't tell, I'm doing it wrong."

I nip at his neck, and he groans. "Definitely not doing it wrong."

And then he locks his hands around my thighs and stands up so abruptly I barely have time to grab onto his shoulders.

I laugh when he takes a few quick steps across the floor and drops me on the bed.

"That was fucking sexy," I say breathlessly.

He climbs on the bed, kneels over me, and starts to undress me, and I try to return the favor. Arms and legs tangle with clothes, and we laugh and struggle and laugh some more and then he's above me.

His eyes roam over me like I'm a feast, and he can't seem to decide where to start. Honestly, I'll be fine with anywhere as long as he samples everything that I'm offering.

I wrap my legs around him and drive my heels into his lower back, and he follows the wordless order and kisses me. A very good place to start. But instead of ravenous and wild, his mouth is slow and gentle, lazily exploring, and for some reason it makes me oddly apprehensive because of how terrifyingly vulnerable I feel. Like a layer of skin has been scraped off, and everyone who looks can see everything.

This feels very intimate all of a sudden, and I'm not sure I'm equipped to handle it. At the same time, I don't have the will to pull away, so we just kiss for a long, long time, and somewhere in the midst of the kissing, the doubts and dread dwindle and ebb until they're not there anymore. Instead, it's just Blake and his body above mine. His lips against my lips and his ragged breaths in my ears.

He kisses his way down my body until his hot mouth is on my dick, sucking like his life depends on it, cheeks hollowed, eyes on mine. It's a filthy sight, and I'm not willing to miss a second. Pleasure swirls through my body as he pulls me deeper into his mouth. He licks and sucks. His tongue swirls around the tip of my cock before he pulls off and pops his finger into his mouth. I watch him take my cock back into his mouth and feel the tip of his finger dragging down my balls to the crease of my ass.

His finger probes, there's more spit, and then he's inside, and I'm writhing under his touch, hips jerking upward when he swipes over my prostate. He moves back up, and then it's his tongue in my mouth, and two lubed fingers in my ass, and it's fucking incredible, and my body tingles and melts into his touch until I'm only capable of moans and other incoherent noises and shoving my hips up so he'll finally take the hint. Which he doesn't. I think he just likes to torture me. Not that I mind. Not too much, at least.

"Blake?" I gasp as the pads of his fingers hit the jackpot inside me once again. I'm starting to feel like I might lose it if he doesn't do something about it soon.

"Yeah?" he whispers against my lips.

"You think you could fuck me now?"

His eyes glint in the sunlight.

"You think I should?" he asks almost conversationally.

"Either fuck me or add more fingers to the mix and get me off that way."

He laughs. "See, I told you I liked your straightforwardness."

"Less talk, more dick," I say, true to form.

He pushes himself up on one arm, still laughing, and rummages around in the drawer of his bedside table. Then he's back. No longer laughing. Instead, his eyes are clouded over with desire as he kneels between my thighs and watches.

I drop my head back and groan. "I swear to God, if you don't get moving, I'm..."

"You're what?" He quirks a brow.

"I..." But it's hard to make any threats when he presses the tip of his cock against my hole and starts rubbing it up and down.

"I..." I repeat, determined to concentrate. He pushes all the way inside me, so I give up. I recognize a lost cause when I see one. His palm lands on the bed, next to my head. His breath hitches, and his eyes get that unfocused, pleasure-filled look in them. I squeeze my muscles around him, and he lets out a string of curses. He pulls almost all the way out and squeezes the base of his dick for a second before pushing back inside.

"Fuck," I groan in a dazed voice once he bottoms out.

When I look up, there's so much naked emotion on his face

that for a moment it's hard to breathe. My chest tightens and my heart hammers, and it's scary as fuck but...

It's worth the risk.

If it means I get to keep Blake, it's worth the risk.

"Kiss me." My voice is a rasp. Blake's mouth comes down on mine, wild and demanding, and he starts to move his hips. Long, torturously slow thrusts that turn the pleasure swirling inside me into an inferno that I can't control anymore.

He buries his head against the side of my neck. He's everywhere. All around me, inside me. Just him and me. I've never felt this way before, because I've never done this with anybody who mattered.

And Blake matters.

More than anybody else.

I can't believe I'm putting myself in this position. Voluntarily. But here we are.

So I wrap myself around him in return. Cling to him as the pleasure builds. Forget myself in the moment.

He lifts himself up on his elbows, and I wrap my leg around him. His slow thrusts turn erratic. Faster. Harder. Until we're a mess of sweaty, shaking limbs and bodies, kissing sloppily, cursing loudly, mindless from the rush of release once it crashes over us. It steals thoughts and words and breaths. Leaves me gasping for air, cock pulsing, back arching before I fall back on the bed. A boneless, breathless mess, Blake collapses on top of me, and I wrap my arms around him.

We're quiet for the longest time before I break the silence.

"Blake?" I murmur softly.

"Hmm?" he mumbles against my neck.

"Remember how you said you weren't really the dating type?"

He lifts his head and studies me curiously before he nods.

"Well, I was wondering," I say. "If, maybe… you'd make an exception for me?"

I sound uncertain and kind of pathetic, and I'm sure that could've been said in a better way. A more memorable way. A more heartfelt way. Or at least in a hotter way. In a way that'd indicate I'm worth taking a chance on.

Sure, Blake seems willing, has for a while, but it wouldn't hurt to do some extra advertising.

Too bad I've got nothing more eloquent to add.

Even so, Blake's eyes are glimmering in the late morning sunlight, and his smile is equally brilliant as he nods again, thumbs still moving over my skin. "Okay."

"Yeah?" I ask.

His smile grows even wider. "Yeah." He looks down at where his thumbs are playing on my skin and then up again. Serious now.

"You already are my every exception."

TWENTY-ONE

"But if I gave you a name, you could potentially dig up all sorts of dirt about them, right?" Blair tilts her travel mug and drinks the last of her coffee before she looks at Blake expectantly.

"Technically," Blake says, smiling at Blair.

"Real dirt? Not just an Instagram photo they forgot to add a filter to?"

"Depends what you consider real dirt," Blake says. To his credit, after a twenty-minute interrogation about hacking, he's still answering all Blair's questions with a smile and the patience of a saint. Even if most of those questions seem to revolve around elaborate plans to screw over anybody who's ever wronged Blair. Sorry, Troy Can't-remember-your-last-name. Serves you right for breaking Blair's Barbie dream car in kindergarten. Honestly, the only reason I'm not worried about Blair's avid interest in Blake's skills is that I think Nora will put a stop to her plans before they get truly illegal.

"Anything incriminating. Or scandalous. Or embarrassing. Or illegal. Anything goes." She looks way too invested in the answer.

"If information is stored online, it can be found," Blake says. "Your data from dating sites, porn sites, potentially embarrassing things you've bought—it's all there. I mean, people have hacked into webcams and taken incriminating photos. But the truth is you don't even need a hacker for a lot of that. Most of the information is already out there, being freely shared by people themselves and obtainable through perfectly legal means. You can buy data for very little money. The fact is, you're tracked everywhere you go and if you're doing"—he waves toward Blair—"scandalous, embarrassing, incriminating things online, that data is available."

"Really?" Blair says, even more intrigued now. "And how would one approach buying that data? Hypothetically speaking, of course."

I scrunch my hot dog wrapper into a ball and throw it in the trash can while Blake launches into a rant about online privacy and all the ways it's lacking. I've been on the receiving end of a fair few of those lectures by now. I've also started a fair few of those lectures. Because it turns me the fuck on when he gets going. Sometimes I mention downloading one of the apps that are known to leak your data like a broken faucet just to watch his head nearly explode. It always ends up in the most awesome sex once I've generously let him convince me to abandon that plan.

"You realize there's a very real possibility Blair's going to end up in jail because of your boyfriend." Nora and I are walking a few steps behind Blair and Blake, half-listening to the conversation, and in my case, mostly just admiring Blake's ass.

I take a sip of my coffee and tear my eyes away from Blake for a second. "You're the one who wanted to meet him, so now enjoy meeting him without complaining. Besides, if the worst happens, you're a lawyer."

She adjusts the baby wrap where Hazel is sleeping on her chest. "I deal with art, not criminals."

"Well, sucks for you." I shrug.

She rolls her eyes, lips twitching. We walk in silence for a little while, and Nora keeps throwing me looks when she thinks I'm not watching. While smiling. Like I'm some adorable puppy frolicking around in the grass.

"I like him," she says after a few more minutes of silent looks.

There's the asshole part of me that wants to scoff and claim I don't care. That it doesn't matter what she thinks. That despite what John Donne says, I *am* an island.

But I'm determined to be a better version of myself.

"He's pretty great," I say, eyes locked on Blake's back and the wild hand gestures he's executing in the middle of Central Park. The words are surprisingly easy to say. They're even easier to mean.

I'm starting to suspect I could watch him forever and not get bored, and isn't that a terrifying development?

"And I like him with you," Nora continues.

"What does that mean?"

She shrugs. "I've known you for four years, and I've never seen you actually, truly happy. Not until now."

I can't even argue with that because, well, I *am* happy. Actually, truly fucking happy. I didn't even know it was possible to feel this way. That another person could so seamlessly fit into my life. That I could like somebody this much.

Like him in a way that's new and scary and exhilarating all at once.

Like him in a thoroughly inconvenient way that makes me want to do anything for him just to see him smile.

Like him in a way that, even through all the uncertainty and fear, makes me look at him calmly and feel *everything*.

You're finally here! I've been waiting for you. Just you. Nobody else fits, but you do.

There's a chance I should tell all of this to Blake, but I stay stubbornly silent. About the way I'm *aware* of him. About the way my heart speeds up whenever he walks into the room, even if I'm not looking, because somehow I just know he's there. About all the things I know about him. About how I collect every scrap of information he gives me because I want to know everything. About how much I like the way he says "hi" to me in his gravelly morning voice when he opens his eyes and how I live for the sleepy smile that always goes with that greeting. How cute it is when he sometimes laughs at his own jokes. How my favorite time of the day is the night now, because that's when he's pressed against me, head to toe, seeking me out like he can't get close enough.

How every time he wraps himself around me, it feels like home.

"Earth to Jude!" I snap my head up at Blair's voice and blink. She quirks her brows at me for a second, but then she's all business.

"What was that one dude's name we all hate? The one who played soccer at Portland High," Blair prompts. "The pretty boy."

"Ca—" I stop as my brain catches up and I narrow my eyes at her. "Why?"

"No reason," she says innocently. Too innocently. "Just reminiscing."

"Sure," I say slowly. "You *are* the sentimental type."

"Uh-huh," Nora says at the same time, with equal helping of sarcasm. "You're not going to screw up some poor man's life just because in high school he told you ballet was dumb or stole your spot in the cafeteria or whatever other stupid grudge you're holding."

Blair's innocent smiles morph into a scowl. "But Jude's boyfriend's a hacker! What, we're just going to let all this revenge potential go to waste?"

"Yes," Nora says, "because we're adults, and I'd like to think you're going to be a good role model for our daughter."

Blair glowers at her, but then she blows out a breath. "Yeah, okay."

Nora looks surprised for a second before she perks up. "Wait. That actually worked?"

"Yes. But you're only allowed to use it twice a year."

"Deal," Nora says quickly like she's afraid Blair might change her mind. Hazel hiccups and lets out a small whimper. Nora gently kisses the top of her head and looks at Blair. "We should probably get going. She'll wake up soon and will want to eat."

"Are we still on for dinner on Tuesday?" I ask Blair because the new, better version of me is making an effort to actively be a part of people's lives. At least the few I actually, truly care about.

"Absolutely. Oh, before I forget, Mom and Dad are coming to see Hazel on Sunday. You two should come, too. They'd love to see you." She throws me an expectant look.

"Can't. Out of town on Sunday. But tell your parents hi for me?"

"Consider it done," Blair says.

They wave at us and get going, and we head in the opposite direction toward the subway. It really is a beautiful day. Not too cold, not too warm. Fall is in full swing, and the park has wrapped itself in a golden late-November hue. Before you know it, it's bare branches, cold days, and even colder nights, which has its own kind of beauty.

I glance at Blake just as he looks at me.

"I need to talk to you about some—" he says just as I say, "Can I ask you some—?"

We both grin.

"Great minds," I say.

"Clearly." He gestures toward me. "You first."

I'd insist he goes first, but if I do that there's a high chance I'll chicken out.

"Okay. Well," I say, "I was thinking maybe you'd want to come out of town with me on Sunday."

"Sure," he says with an easy shrug. Just like that.

My shoulders relax a bit. I don't know why, but somehow I expected this to be more dramatic. I'm glad it's not, but I've turned it into this pivotal moment in my head over the course of the last week while I was trying to decide whether asking him was a good idea or not, and it's a bit disorienting that it plays out so calmly.

"Are you going to tell me where we're going?" Blake asks.

In my haste to get this thing over with, I've clearly forgotten to add some key details. Scratch the dramatic part. We can still get there, it seems.

I throw him a look. "You just agreed to come with me, even though you don't even know what this is about?"

"Yeah." He meets my gaze and sends me a small smile. "You'll be there."

"I'll also be there if it turns out I'm inviting you to a cannibal convention."

He stops and widens his eyes. "Hold the phone. You're telling me you got tickets to Peeps for Meats? Being in this relationship has finally paid off!"

"Is that a real thing? Because if it's not, it's disturbing how quickly you came up with that name."

He steps closer, still grinning. His hands go to my cheeks, and he tilts my head up a fraction before he plants a small kiss on my lips. He pulls away and starts walking again, and after a second, I take a few quick steps and catch up with him. My left hand, dangling uselessly by my side, sneaks toward him until the backs of our hands touch, then I slide my palm against his and link our fingers. He squeezes my hand, and my heart skips a few beats.

"So," he says after a little bit. "Sunday? What are we doing? Should I pack a knife and fork or not?"

"That'd be a no. Knives aren't allowed. I'm pretty sure forks aren't either." I hesitate before I take a big gulp of air. "You might want to change your mind and say no, but I'm gonna go see my dad, and I was wondering if you'd maybe, possibly, perhaps want to come with me and meet him?"

TWENTY-TWO

Prisons and airports have a lot in common. Fences. Barbed wire. Stern signs and cameras everywhere. Guards. You wait in line. You go through security, complete with metal detectors and x-ray scans.

I've heard strip searches are a thing in both, but so far, I've managed to avoid those. I should probably knock on wood.

But you suffer through all of it, and once you're done, you get your reward.

A trip to a foreign country.

Or a new adventure.

Or... you get to see someone you love.

Ever since I parked the car, Blake's been quiet.

I should've told him. Prepared him. Warned him.

Needless to say, I didn't.

I spent the last week worrying about how to ask him if he wanted to come with me—worrying about *if* I should ask him to come with me at all—and in doing so, I completely forgot to figure out how I'd handle the aftermath if he said yes.

Well, now I have my answer: not well.

But this is Blake, so he somehow takes it all in stride. Instead of running for the hills or asking me a thousand questions, he takes my hand in his over the center console of the car, links our fingers, and squeezes.

"Ready to go?" he asks like we're headed to a picnic in the park and not a goddamn prison.

"Aren't you going to ask me why we're here?" I keep my eyes fixed firmly on our entwined fingers.

"I can connect the dots," he says gently.

I look up. He doesn't look worried or judgmental or any of the things people should when their boyfriend brings them to meet his dad. In prison.

"Are you going to ask why he's in there?" I ask.

He studies me with the same gentleness that softened his words a moment ago.

"Do you want me to?"

I hesitate for a moment but nod. "I think you should."

He turns himself so he's facing me, thumb moving over mine in soft swipes. "Why's your dad in prison?"

I'm pretty sure other people aren't having this conversation with their boyfriends on a sunny Sunday, so if nothing else, at least we're original.

"Kidnapping," I say.

I can feel Blake's eyes on the side of my face. "Kidnapping who?"

I look up. Face him head on. He can probably guess the answer, but still.

"Me."

I've been coming here for so long that I'm at that point where I know most of the guards. Today it's Victor Curtis standing by the wall of the visiting area. I like him. He's one of the nicer ones.

We settle in at one of the round tables in the corner, and where Blake didn't look nervous before, he definitely does now. His fingers tap against the table, but the rest of his body is completely still, as if he's trying to act like statue to go unnoticed. Eventually, when his fingers start moving so quickly they're more like blurry lines and the rattle of his nails starts to turn heads, I cover his hand with mine.

"Are you okay?"

"Sorry," he says with a wince.

"It's fine. I was nervous when I visited the first time, too."

"I'm not nervous," he says quickly.

I look down at where his knee has started to bounce up and down. He stops and looks at me.

"Okay, I'm nervous."

"No shit. It's fine, believe me. It's prison. It's not exactly a good time for anybody. And if you'd rather not be here, I get it."

"Yeah, no," he says. "It's not that."

"Then what?"

He leans toward me and lowers his voice. "I'm meeting your dad."

"I know?" I say, unsure where he's going with this.

He starts tapping the fingers of his other hand against his thigh.

"What if he doesn't like me?"

I lean back and, unbelievably, a slow smile spreads on my face.

"Wait. You're nervous because you want to impress my dad?"

"I've never been introduced to anybody's parents before."

"Neither have I, but I hear people do it all the time, so it can't be that bad."

"Easy for you to say. I don't have any parents you can meet. Fuck, you're so lucky!"

"The fact that you're a foster kid was what tipped the scales." I brush my palm over his back. "He'll like you."

"Like me," he scoffs. "I don't want him to just like me. I want to impress him," he says. "And I'm going to warn you right now, I will do anything to make it happen. He doesn't like blond hair? I'm in the salon tomorrow morning. He needs something smuggled inside? I'm his man. If he asks me to tattoo a map on my back and get myself thrown in jail in order to break him out of here, I will do it. Also, if you happen to hear me lie to make myself look better, feel free to keep your mouth shut."

I laugh out loud. I've never laughed in this place.

"Good plan. What if he doesn't like suck-ups, though?"

He throws me an incredulous look. "That's ridiculous. What kind of person doesn't like to be admired and revered?"

I look down, shoulders still shaking with laughter. "You're kind of an idiot, you know that?"

He leans back and smiles. "Got you to laugh though, didn't I?"

My heart does that weird thing—skips a few beats and then starts beating insanely fast. It seems to be a symptom of some sort of Blake-related heart disease, because it only ever happens around him.

Ah, sweet self-delusion. My oldest and dearest friend.

I'm still laughing when Dad arrives, which makes him stop a few feet away from our table and stare at me for a moment with something I can only describe as astonishment on his face.

I get up and give him a quick hug. He squeezes me tightly for a moment before we have to let go. There are rules here. Hugs are supposed to be brief.

"Dad," I say.

"Son," he replies.

It took me a couple of years before I could hear the word without wincing. Most days I'm still not a hundred percent sure how I feel about it, even though we've talked and cleared the air, forgiven and forgotten. Today... I like it. Or maybe it's more that I'm finally allowing myself to like it. Lately I've been allowing myself to like a lot of things, so one more doesn't seem like that big of a deal.

Dad sends a curious look Blake's way and then looks back at me.

"I want you to meet somebody," I say, and my lips pull into another grin completely of their own accord when I look at my boyfriend. "This is Blake."

Dad stops, his eyes moving up and down Blake. His brows furrow into a frown like he's trying to catch up to what's happening before he drops down on one of the chairs, eyes still moving between me and Blake as we settle in opposite him.

"Well," he says slowly. His shoulders slump and he sags like somebody's just placed a huge burden on him. "Your mother always warned me this was a possibility." His eyes venture to Blake once again, and he shakes his head. "I just never thought you'd choose to tell me like this."

Blake's eyes widen as he glances my way.

"It's nice to meet you?" he says. He might've been joking about impressing my dad by any possible means, but now he looks like he's giving that strategy a second thought.

"You could've prepared me, at least." Dad's eyes move to Blake's chest and the midnight green and silver T-shirt he's wearing underneath his dark blue jacket, before he shakes his head again and lets out a heavy sigh. "An Eagles fan. It's like spitting in the face of my ancestors."

Blake blinks in surprise, and I take pity on him.

"Did you have your fun?" I arch my brow at Dad.

He grins. "It'll tide me over for a good while." He leans forward and reaches out his hand to Blake. "It's good to meet you, Blake."

Blake's smile is back, and it's so brilliant it's hard not to stare. "If it helps, the shirt's a hand-me-down. I just like the color."

"It doesn't hurt. How do you feel about the Giants?"

Blake throws a glance my way, and I give him a brief nod.

"Love them."

Dad laughs. "I choose to believe you." He looks at me and smiles, then. He always does that. Every time I'm here, he looks at me like it's the first and last time he'll ever see me. Like he needs to do all the looking he can in case I decide to walk out and never return.

"How are you, son?" he asks.

"Good." I nod. "Work's good. And..." I glance at Blake and shrug and smile, because that's what I do around Blake—I smile. "Life's good, too."

Dad closes his eyes for a second and hangs his head and when he looks up, his eyes are shining with unshed tears. "Good," he says roughly. Clears his throat. "Good. Tell me everything. How did you two meet?"

I can't seem to find my words, but Blake seamlessly takes over.

"On a rooftop," he says.

Dad smiles and nods. "Jude's always liked high places. When we were living in Wyoming, we had a huge maple tree in our front yard. This one gave me and Abby daily heart attacks with his climbing. Fifty feet up in the sky and he just kept going."

Blake glances my way, eyes shining brightly, before he leans forward on his elbows. "What was Jude like as a kid?"

Dad's eyes flick to me. Unbearably tender and filled with

infinite pride, but also tinged with sadness that'll probably never truly disappear from his gaze. He's lost too much to ever be the same man he used to be. But he keeps going. I know it's largely for my sake.

"Never in my life have I seen a more curious child. He was interested in everything. He was the kid who'd ask a question, and the moment you answered it, he'd have ten follow-up questions locked and loaded. Abby called them the 'but, Dad' questions." Dad's eyes get that faraway look in them that always appears when he thinks of Mom. "That's how all Jude's inquiries into the great mysteries of life started," he continues. "Half the time I didn't even have the answers when he really got going."

"But," I interrupt, and Dad's gaze flies to me in surprise. "Then you'd look them up with me. You never just said you didn't know. You said 'I don't know *but*,' and then we'd find the answer."

We don't do this. We don't talk about the past. Haven't for years. In the beginning, yes. We covered all the whys and hows that led to him ending up in this place, but all those happy memories of our life that made the three of us *us*? We avoid those.

But now Dad is nodding slowly and smiling before he concentrates back on Blake and launches into stories about my childhood. Mom. Our life.

He talks. And talks. And talks. And I realize I haven't heard him talk this much in years. That he hasn't looked so alive in years. That we haven't touched on anything personal for about the same amount of time, both too afraid it'll rattle the somewhat tenuous status quo where we sort of pretend we're still the same people we were seven years ago. But now I get a completely unfiltered look at myself through my dad's eyes.

I also realize Dad *wants* to talk about this. Wants to relive the happier times. Wants to get lost in the memories. Wants to remember Mom and our life like it used to be.

And I want to hear it too, but I've been too much of a coward to bring it up. I'm not even sure who I've been protecting. Me or him.

Blake doesn't have any of my reservations. Whatever he wants to know, he asks. He makes Dad laugh, and makes me laugh, and somehow turns this miserable, sterile room into something bright and warm for the time we're here. And he does it the same way he does everything else. With quiet, stubborn determination. The same as he's been using to turn my muted, invisible existence into a life actually worth living.

Our allotted two hours pass too quickly. I hug Dad and promise to be back in two weeks. Like I always do.

"Love you, kid," he says. Like he always does. Like he's done my whole life.

And I believe him. Always have.

Once outside, I lean against the car and close my eyes for a moment. Blake takes up position next to me and just lets me be while I sort through my emotions and slot each feeling into its designated compartment.

When I'm ready to face the world again, I open my eyes and glance toward him.

"Ready to go?"

He nods, looking contemplative.

"Can I drive?" he asks.

I fish the keys out of my pocket and throw them to him. "Knock yourself out."

"Do you have to go to work today?" he asks as we pull out of the parking lot.

I shake my head.

"Then how do you feel about a getaway?" he says.

"I do have to work tomorrow," I say.

"We'll make it a short one." He aims a grin my way. "Trust me?"

Isn't that a loaded question?

In the end, the answer is the easiest of all, though.

"Yes."

TWENTY-THREE

HE TAKES me to one of those luxury hotels in the Upper West Side where it's better not to think about how much spending the night in one of those rooms even costs.

I stand in the doorway, look around, and let out a low whistle. "Fancy."

"Of course it's fancy," Blake says. "We can't do a proper staycation in a roadside motel, can we now?"

I watch him walk to the bed and throw himself on it. He splays his arms and legs out like a starfish and sighs happily.

"This will do," he says. "This will do very well."

I watch him, spread out on the bed, his T-shirt riding up a bit, exposing a sliver of his abdomen. He's so beautiful in the low afternoon sunlight that it nearly takes my breath away.

"You're a bit of a hedonist, aren't you?" I ask.

He opens one eye and peers at me. "I've been known to enjoy the finer things in life on occasion." He stretches slowly and lets out a contented sigh before he pushes himself up on his elbows. "When I was growing up, I never had anything. Most days the necessities were covered. Food. Clothes. Roof over my head. Some days I wasn't so lucky. So now that I can afford it, I indulge when I feel like it."

I cock my head to the side. "Am I an indulgence?"

"An indulgence," he says. "And a necessity."

"And will you? Indulge."

Instead of answering, he gets up and stalks toward me. I love the way he moves. With graceful purposefulness. He barrels straight into me and backs me into a wall, mouths colliding, one hand gripping my hip, the fingers of his other hand digging into the back of my neck.

The need is urgent and fierce, and I throw myself into the kiss with equal wildness. I wrap my leg around his hip and pull him closer. I throw my head back and Blake's lips latch onto my neck, devouring me with open-mouthed kisses.

My mind goes blissfully empty, and I close my eyes, enjoying the sensations and the moment.

I shove my hand between our bodies and flick the button of Blake's jeans open. The sound of the zipper lowering makes shivers run over my back, anticipation boiling in my blood. I push my hand into his pants and find his stiff cock. My movements lack any kind of finesse—my grip rough, movements fast and harsh.

Blake's forehead lands on my shoulder for a second. His gasps move over my skin, his panting breaths muffled in that spot where my shoulder and neck meet.

He stiffens and slams his palm down on mine, forcing me to stop. Next thing I know, my hand is out of his pants, and Blake is on his knees in front of me. He fumbles with the button for a second but then my pants are around my ankles, and my cock is in his mouth.

"Jesus," I groan.

Blake looks up, the corners of his lips curling. He runs his palms up my thighs, grips my ass, and pulls me toward his mouth while sucking me deeper. My fingers grapple for something to hold on to. There's nothing but a smooth wall, so instead, I wrap my fingers in Blake's hair.

My brain becomes a wasteland in a second. The suction and the wet heat destroy the last connection between my brain cells. This is the best blowjob in the history of blowjobs. The tight ring of Blake's lips, the suction, the flicks of his tongue, my cock going so deep into his mouth he gags around it but keeps going. My heart beats so wildly I expect to see the outline of it through my skin when I look down.

This is how I'm going to die.

But what a fucking way to go.

I'm running out of breath, toes curling into the soft carpet underneath my feet, balls tightening painfully because I'm trying to hold myself back. At least for a second longer. I'll regret it if I don't.

Blake has no mercy, though. He keeps sucking me, head bobbing up and down, fingers digging into my ass.

He's not bringing me pleasure. He's forcing it upon me with single-minded focus.

I try to warn him. Pull his hair. Gasp an, "I'm—"

That's all I have in me.

He sucks me even deeper, and I can't...

My vision blurs, and the sound that comes out of my mouth is more a howl than anything else. I slam my head back, and it hits the wall with a loud thud, but I barely feel it under the mind-numbing rush of pleasure that sweeps through me like a tidal wave.

"Fuck," I say weakly once I manage to get my mouth to cooperate.

Blake's still kneeling in front of me. Lips swollen, cheeks flushed, skin coated with saliva, and a trickle of my cum on the corner of his mouth. He's never been more beautiful.

"Fuck," I repeat, voice still shaky. "Fuck. That was…" I have no words. I know they exist, but I don't have them.

I reach out, and he lets me pull him to his feet.

"Want to see if that bed is as soft as it looks?" he asks.

"Of course. Spoil me," I manage.

Later, when it's gotten dark outside, I'm lying on my stomach and Blake is lying half on top of me.

His fingertips flutter over my back, sliding up and down everywhere he can reach. I squirm whenever he hits a ticklish spot, and then he repeats the motion.

He fucked my brains out on the huge, luxurious bed. I don't have to think anymore because everything outside of this room feels far away and not really connected to me. Somewhere out there is that other Jude with his messy life and endless issues, and you know what? Good luck to the fucker. This Jude here is calm and content and happy.

"Tell me a story," Blake murmurs into my shoulder.

"What kind of story?"

"A story you want to tell me."

"I don't know any fairytales."

He presses a kiss on my shoulder blade. "Never liked those anyway."

I stare out the window into the night, chin propped on my forearms.

A non-fairytale.

I can do that.

TWENTY-FOUR

D<small>ECEMBER</small> 2001

Abigail Riley has always been a firm believer that the world, at its core, is a beautiful place.

That everything in life happens for a reason.

That what you give is what you get.

That good things happen to good people.

So excuse her if she's having a bit of a hard time adjusting to this new status quo. Excuse her if she can't seem to keep the faith right now. Excuse her if she can't really fight off the anger and the betrayal and the deep feeling of unfairness that's made a home inside her chest over the course of the past five months, festering and spreading like an infection that's slowly taken over her body, bit by bit and inch by inch.

The little boy on her couch stirs, lets out a tiny whimper, opens his eyes, and sends Abby a bleary look, but when she puts her hand against his cheek, he burrows closer, lets out a long sigh, and falls asleep again. Abby leaves her hand in place, trapped between the couch and the little boy. She'd keep it there forever if she could. If only, by some miracle, she'd be allowed to do that.

He's tiny. His hands are small. His toes are small. Even the dimples in his cheeks are small. He's perfect and Abby's heart aches when she looks at him.

How is it possible for anybody not to love him? If he was hers, she'd move heaven and earth to keep him safe. But that woman... That fucking woman.

Abby's fingers roll into a fist. They do that a lot lately. The crescent moon-shaped nail markings are tattooed in the soft part of her palm by now.

The front door opens, her head snaps up, and she lifts her index finger in front of her mouth as she looks up. Grant stops in the doorway of the minuscule studio apartment they're renting in Brooklyn. His eyes immediately move to the couch, and his shoulders slump. He quietly toes off his shoes and comes to Abby, his socked feet shuffling on the floorboards.

He sits down next to her, wraps his arm around her shoulders, and kisses her temple.

"Again?" he whispers.

Abby nods, eyes locked on the little boy.

"He was crying when I got home after my shift," she says. They share a wall. Abby and Grant on one side, Adam and... that woman on the other. A wall that might as well be a curtain since it hardly blocks any sounds. They've heard it all over the past few months they've lived in this apartment. Parties. Sex. Shouting. Crying. Screams. Drug-fueled babbling. Drunken fights.

"I went and knocked, and nobody answered. Must've pounded on that door for a good ten minutes, but nothing. So, I picked the lock."

Grant lets out a deep sigh and rubs his palms over his face. "Abs..." He's well aware of his wife's proclivity for creative solutions.

"What was I supposed to do?" Abby whispers. "I bet she's been gone all fucking day. Maybe last night, too. She still isn't back. You should've seen Adam. He was in his crib, couldn't get out. His diaper was overflowing, he was filthy, and hungry." Abby's voice breaks and she angrily scrubs at her eyes. "I made him a plate, and he inhaled it all. I would've given him more, but I was afraid he'd be sick. I..." She swallows. "I don't know when she last fed him."

"We have to call CPS again." Grant's head falls back, and he looks at the ceiling.

"Yeah. You do that. I'm sure this time they'll finally do something." Sarcasm is thick in her voice, and Grant doesn't deserve it, but she can't stop herself from lashing out. It's been months of helpless anger because nobody cares and nobody helps and there's nobody to turn to, and Abby doesn't know what to do anymore. How to help this little boy who's done nothing wrong. CPS keeps sending people over, but the mantra is always the same. Can't prove anything. No obvious signs of neglect. Separation is the last resort.

A part of her understands it. She wouldn't want to be in their shoes. Wouldn't want the responsibility on her shoulders. Logically, she knows they're doing their best. Emotionally, she doesn't think their best is nearly enough.

She's afraid of going to work because if she's at home she can at least listen on the other side of the wall and make sure everything's okay. Not to mention how little she's been to school lately. Her supervisor isn't exactly happy with her, but she can't just stand by and do nothing. If anything happens while she's gone... she'll never forgive herself.

The first time she saw the little boy was five months ago. A few days after they'd moved into their apartment. She'd been running late and had stormed into the hallway and nearly tripped over the child. A small boy in nothing but a diaper, *playing with a plastic fork and a cup on the cold stairs. The door left of her apartment had been open. The boy had looked at her with wide, serious eyes that somehow seemed too old for his face.*

"The kid's seen some things," Abby had thought jokingly.

She'd knocked on the door and a girl barely out of her teens appeared. She'd seemed impossibly young. Maybe eighteen at the most to Abby's twenty-nine. She'd seemed confused and not really all there, but when Abby had pointed at the kid, she seemed to snap out of it at least a little bit. She'd hugged the boy to her chest, the prongs of the plastic fork digging into her skin as the two of them stood there.

Sleep deprivation, Abby thought. Felt sorry for her. Waved her off and smiled supportively when she blabbered something about nodding off. And Abby had tried to be encouraging. No worries. Happens to everybody. Next time maybe make sure the door is locked.

Sarah and Adam. Adam and Sarah. A Mom and her son and not brother and sister like Abby had initially thought.

It wasn't the only thing she'd misjudged that day.

Because it wasn't sleep deprivation.

Abby would learn that soon enough. Would hear neighbors whispering and see them shaking their heads but never actually doing anything to help. Never stepping in. Never opening their doors when social worker after social worker walked through these halls after yet another useless call to the CPS.

"CPS has procedures and rules they have to follow," Grant repeats, even though he's starting to sound less and less convinced every time he's forced to say it. Abby loves him more than life, but there are some things she'll never fully understand about her husband. His unwavering belief in the system is one of those things. He's the best man Abby knows, but there are things he just refuses to see. The system only works if people in it honor *the rules that keep the system going. In Grant's world, people do. Abby knows better.*

"They won't do shit," she whispers, and now she's full-on crying, her shoulders shaking, her lips pressed together in a thin line because otherwise she'll sob out loud, and she can't wake Adam.

"I'll make the call," Grant says quietly and goes to get the phone.

Abby slides her palm over Adam's soft hair.
He's safe right now.
For tonight, that'll have to do.

The fact that the world isn't black and white proves to be the most difficult lesson to learn for Abby. That people don't slot into neat compartments of good and bad, virtuous and evil.

Because Sarah and Adam have their good days. Days when instead of shouting, there's laughter. When all Abby hears on the other side of the wall is Sarah singing a lullaby to Adam. Days when she sees them walking to the park and going to the playground. Days of bedtime stories and Sarah drawing Adam chalk pictures on the sidewalk in front of their building. Days when Sarah throws out all the bottles and wipes away the remnants of suspicious white powder, and cleans and vacuums and opens the curtains and windows so her apartment is sunny and bright.

Days when she promises she's done. This is it. She's going to get clean and get her life together. From now on she'll do better. Because she loves Adam. And Abby really believes she does. She sees it in Sarah's eyes when she looks at Adam. Hears it in her voice.

Those are the days when Abby hopes so hard it hurts. Hopes that this time the peace will stick. That this time Sarah keeps her word.

Abby and Grant try to help Sarah. They make sure their work and school schedules always have one of them at home. For Adam, but also for Sarah. They drag her to support groups and meetings. They scrape together enough money to pay for therapist appointments. It never sticks. She won't go. She doesn't have a problem. She's just young and they don't understand, and doesn't she deserve a night out every once in a while? Doesn't she deserve to relax and have fun every now and then?

And maybe she does. Maybe everybody does. But Sarah's fun is destructive. It's loud and it's scary even for Abby, let alone for Adam. And once Sarah gets going, she doesn't care about anything anymore. She doesn't care that Adam is scared of the people Sarah calls her friends. That he's terrified of that asshole Sarah calls her boyfriend. That Adam shouldn't see any of the things happening at her parties. That he's a curious little boy and could get his hands on any number of things lying around in that damn apartment. That a two-year-old can't just hang out by himself while Sarah goes to a club and forgets to come back for a day or two.

And those aren't isolated incidents. When Sarah gets going, it can take weeks for her to come down to earth again. It's not a one-party-and-done situation. It's a weeks-long bender that goes on and on and on, and Sarah doesn't seem to notice that Adam's practically living with Abby and Grant on those days.

She has no idea how much it hurts when she finally comes looking for Adam, sheepish and defiant at once. And then takes him away. How much it hurts to hope the playground visits and lullabies will replace ugly, drunken laughter and fear for good and at the same time knowing they never do.

Yes, there are good days. There are even great days. But at what point does the bad outweigh the good? At what point does love turn too ugly for it to be called love at all? Who gets to decide enough is enough?

It's the grotesque laughter that wakes Abby. For a moment she's disoriented, but then she's out of bed, not bothering with getting dressed. Her Garfield T-shirt and sleep pants with pictures of lasagna on them will have to do.

Grant's still at work, covering a shift at the bar, and she'll get an earful later for being impulsive and not thinking, but she can't stop herself. Something lands against the wall with a thud and a woman screeches. She tears out of the apartment. The hallway floor is ice cold under her bare feet, but she doesn't feel it.

She pulls the door open and lands in chaos. There's no music, but people are swaying in the middle of the floor in some strange uncoordinated, jerky dance while a slasher movie is playing on the TV. Every available surface seems to be covered in bottles and debris. She steps in something wet and slimy. She doesn't want to know what it is.

Her eyes sweep over the small apartment, searching frantically, until they land on Adam. Abby's already erratic heartbeat grows wilder, and she barely swallows down her terrified cry. She pushes forward to where that waste of space Sarah calls her boyfriend is holding Adam by his forearm on the windowsill, right next to a wide-open window.

"Never take my shit," he screams, spit flying everywhere. Adam jerks like a ragdoll in his hold while the guy shakes him, his eyes wide with terror, too afraid to make a sound.

Abby charges forward, pushes past people until she's right behind the guy. Oh God, she doesn't know what to do. Doesn't know how to stop the man and get Adam to her safely. Adam sees her and now he's crying. He reaches for her and while the man blearily looks around, Abby scoops Adam into her arms. Little, grimy fingers twist into her shirt. His pants are wet, and his little body is burning up.

"Yo, what the fuck?" the man shouts. He looms over Abby, and she's ready to take Adam and run, only then there's Sarah, and she wraps her hands around the guy's torso.

"Baby," she coos, not blackout drunk yet, but well on her way there. "Come and dance with me."

"Kid took my shit," the guy keeps repeating. "Needs a lesson."

His shit turns out to be a gun dangling limply between his fingers. Abby's hands start shaking so badly she's having a hard time holding Adam.

"He's fine. I'll make you a drink," Sarah says. "Let him play. He's having fun." Her eyes finally land on Abby. "It's not loaded." Sarah frowns. "We're not stupid." She takes a step forward and reaches out like she wants to take Adam, but the boyfriend grabs Sarah's ass, and she giggles, and Abby and Adam are forgotten.

Abby walks out of the apartment with Adam.

Nobody stops her.

Nobody cares.

Nobody even notices.

She's been desperately searching for help for months, but when Adam is wrapped in blankets, clean and dry and softly snoring in her and Grant's bed, she realizes something.

Help isn't coming.

Because she is the help.

Abby's grandmother used to say you could tell a lady is a lady by the state of her fingernails. Based on hers, Abby's no lady. Not that she ever was, but over the last few days, she's chewed off most of her nails.

They have a plan. A terrible, horrible plan. A plan concocted in the middle of the night with Abby wrapped tightly in Grant's arms, all cried out after the CPS lady came back from her inspection and told her there was no gun in that apartment and it's her word against Sarah's.

And now Sarah's angry and grumbling to Abby about people being too nosy and not minding their own business.

"*I wish we could just take him and go,*" *Abby whispers. Wishful thinking on her part. She's never broken any laws in her life. Not the serious, real ones, at least.*

Grant is silent for the longest time before he hugs her closer. "*Do you mean it?*" *He sounds so serious all of a sudden.* "*Really, seriously, truly mean it?*" *he asks.*

Abby thinks about it. Really, seriously, truly thinks about it.

And then she nods.

So now they have a plan.

For the first time, Abby's glad neither Grant nor she has any family. It makes disappearing so much easier. Because that's the plan. To disappear. To take Adam—no, to kidnap Adam—and go. It's better to call it what it is. They're going to kidnap a child.

Abby's grandmother would say it's a sin, and that they're going to burn in hell. But here's the thing: Abby doesn't care. She's aware there will be consequences for their actions. In the library, she looks up punishments for kidnapping. Makes sure she understands what she's in for. Even spares a thought for hell and the afterlife. Even though she doesn't really believe in that stuff, she wants to cover all her bases. To really, truly make it clear for herself that if they're going to go through with this, she accepts what's going to happen to her and Grant.

She still doesn't care. When the consequences of their actions catch up to them, they'll take their punishment. What matters now is they're going to save Adam. Take him and go far, far away and make sure he'll have a good life and never, ever have anybody wave a gun in his face ever again.

It's surprisingly easy, in the end.

They start telling their neighbors about their plans to move away from the city when they run into them while getting their mail. About a great job offer Abby's considering taking because it's too good to pass up. Just occasionally drop it in the conversation. Nothing too overt, just a remark here and there. Over the course of the following weeks, they both quietly drop out of school and quit their jobs. Sell everything they can to have as much cash in hand as possible.

When all the preparations have been made, it's really just a matter of waiting for the perfect moment. They say their goodbyes to Sarah and Adam and a few of their other neighbors, and they leave. A few days later, they drop tickets to a club opening in Sarah's mailbox. A part of Abby is hoping Sarah stays put. That this is the night that changes things for Sarah. That she finally sees the immeasurable treasure she has in Adam. That this time, she won't leave.

Mostly, though, she's not surprised at all to see her walk out the door that evening.

Abby sneaks inside late at night, hoping and praying she won't run into any neighbors. Grant's waiting in the car around the corner.

She picks the lock. Adam is asleep in his crib, but he opens his eyes when Abby softly touches his cheek. He sees Abby, and he smiles, and when Abby dresses him, he doesn't protest and listens to her with wide eyes as she whispers about going on an adventure. She doubts he understands her, but it doesn't matter anyway.

Once they're back in the hallway, they hear footsteps, and Abby's heart threatens to stop while they're hiding in a corner, but then a door opens and closes somewhere, and after a little while Abby sneaks outside without any problems.

She tries to look as natural as possible, walking through the dark streets with Adam in her arms. She has no idea if she's pulling it off, but she makes it to the car.

She puts Adam in the car seat and straps him in. Gives him a stuffed butterfly. She's always liked butterflies. She once read they symbolize change and transformation. Comfort. Hope. Positivity.

They need all of that, so the aquamarine butterfly seemed like a talisman when she picked it out in the store earlier on a whim.

Adam cuddles the butterfly to his chest, his eyelids already drooping.

Abby gets in the car, and they're off. She can't even really believe it all plays out so smoothly.

With every mile they drive, breathing gets easier, and once they leave New York in their rearview mirror, Abby hopes with everything she has inside her they'll never have to return.

For the next few weeks, they lie low and keep an eye on the news religiously.

It takes Sarah ten days to report Adam missing.

By that time there's no Adam anymore.

Just Abby, Grant, and Jude.

TWENTY-FIVE

BLAKE IS quiet for the longest time. He hasn't said a single word since I started talking, just kept on lying on top of me, blanketing me from the rest of the world with his body.

"So... Adam is...?" he eventually says.

"My real name."

"How'd she find you?" he asks. "Sarah," he adds as if it wasn't clear.

"I found her. Wrote her an email," I say with a grim smile. "Thought I was adopted. Took one of those at-home DNA tests, and lo and behold, found Sarah. There's a kind of poetic justice to it. The kidnappee rats out the kidnappers."

"You love them, though. So it couldn't have been great."

"No," I agree. "Then again, finding out your whole life is a lie is never a good time for anybody."

Blake's fingertips run up my spine and into my hair.

"Your parents were arrested," he surmises.

I nod. "Ten years in prison. It's been almost eight now."

I can feel him thinking. Can practically hear his thoughts moving around in his head as he tries to orient himself in the landscape of my life.

"Okay," he says slowly once he's decided he's placed himself on the correct latitude and longitude. "Then what happened?"

"I was shipped off to Seattle. It's where Sarah had ended up. She was living there with her husband, and I was underage and had nowhere to go, so what better place than the home of your biological mother, right?"

His fingers still for a moment where they've been combing through my hair at the back of my head.

"But it wasn't?" he asks.

I blow out a lengthy breath. "I guess I see where everybody was coming from with this. And I went willingly. I wanted to go. I didn't know what I was in for, but at the same time, I figured I owed it to Sarah—and myself—to at least try. And I wasn't eighteen yet, so I had to go somewhere. Mom was raised by her grandmother, and she'd died a long time ago. Dad's parents were dead. There were no aunts or uncles. I had nobody. It's just that..."

"She was a stranger," Blake guesses after a few beats of silence when I search for the right words to describe Sarah.

I nod slowly. "Not even just that. To me, she was a stranger. To her, I was her long-lost son, and she... she had this image in her head, I suppose. About what kind of person I'd grown up to be. What our relationship would be like now she'd found me. What kind of things I would like. It was this idolized version of her son, and nobody can ever live up to that image because real people come with flaws and messy emotions, and they'll want to make decisions you don't necessarily agree with.

"Whenever I deviated from that image of me she'd created in her head, she'd look completely lost. Like she didn't know what to do with me. Like I'd improvised instead of following the script and suddenly her lines didn't fit anymore. And then she'd try to paint over that image she had of me, but the lines of the last picture were showing through the new coat of paint, so the result was always a little bit disappointing for her. It's not like she outright said it, but you could feel the tension lingering in the air."

"It couldn't have been easy for you," Blake says. "To go from having a family to living with strangers."

"She kept calling me Adam," I say softly. "And I swear I tried, but every time she did it, my brain just short circuited for a moment. *Who the fuck is Adam?* Every damn time. I'd try to remember it was me, but I just..."

"You're not Adam," Blake says.

I close my eyes and shrug apologetically, even though it's not Blake who should be at the receiving end of that apology.

"No," I say. "It was like walking on eggshells. And I was just so tense and anxious all the time. So afraid of making the wrong move or saying the wrong thing. It's not like anything would've happened if I had, but she was this woman who'd had her kid taken from her, and I didn't want her to be disappointed in who she got back. Which is not really a viable way to live or build any kind of relationship. I suppose you can pretend to be somebody you're not. It's not an impossible task, but here's the catch. I didn't *know* who she wanted me to be, so I couldn't even pretend. I just knew I wasn't him."

He slides his palm over my back and leans his forehead against the nape of my neck.

"You're enough," he says very quietly. "Just you."

I didn't even know I needed to hear that so badly. Something seems to crack inside me. That last stubborn piece of resistance I've been holding on to. Poof. Disappears.

There's freedom in it when you're allowed to be a mess in front of somebody you trust and you know they won't think less of you because of it.

"I started to resent her," I say, handing over my ugly truths one after the other. "Every time I looked at her, I thought, 'If you'd been a decent mother to me while you had the chance, none of this would've happened.'"

He's quiet for a long time before he says, "Yeah, I can see how you'd feel that way."

"It's very confusing. Hating somebody you don't necessarily want to hate."

"I can see that, too."

"But even more than Sarah, I hated my mom and dad."

His fingers start moving again. "I'd say you had your reasons."

"But then I also missed them. More and more as days and weeks passed. Eventually, I sucked it up and wrote them both a letter. Just... vomited everything I was feeling out on the paper, stuffed them into envelopes and sent them. I figured it'd take some time for the letters to reach them, so I'd also have time to prepare myself for whatever they'd say. Seems stupid now, but it made sense back then..." My voice trails off. But then I shake my head and snap out of it. "The reply didn't come. Neither of them wrote back. So I figured the letters somehow went missing before they reached them. I wrote again. Nothing. I emailed. Nothing. It didn't make any sense. Yeah, I was pissed, but *they* didn't have any reason to just ignore me."

"No, it doesn't make any sense," he agrees.

"I went to Sarah. I asked her to help me, and she said she would. But then it took so much time, and she kept saying she was handling it, and I just had to be patient, but I started writing and calling everywhere I could think of anyway. I mean, I was seventeen. I had no idea who to call or how the system even works, so it was a lot of dead ends, but eventually I got my answer. Turns out there was a no-contact order in place, so they weren't allowed to write, call, or basically contact me in any way. *A criminal defendant is not to directly or indirectly contact or be within sight of the protected person and their residence.*"

"I'm guessing you weren't the one who asked for that," Blake says.

"No, I wasn't." I stare at the mattress with a deep frown. "I hate when people do that." Words burst out more vehemently than I was planning. "Lie," I add in a more measured tone. "It's the one thing I can't handle. Liars."

Blake's gone very still above me. I don't think he's even breathing for a moment. Can't really blame him—it's safe to say this is not what he signed up for—but then he nods, and I can feel his forehead move against the nape of my neck.

"Makes sense," he says, so softly I barely hear the words.

I clear my throat and swallow down the anger and hurt.

"Anyway," I say. "Turned out it *was* Sarah who requested the no-contact order. And then when I confronted her about it... Let's just say it didn't go well. She pretty much told me she thinks I have Stockholm syndrome, and I should keep my distance from my parents and give myself time to heal, and generally it'd just be better if we all close that chapter of our lives, leave the past in the past, and move on." I stretch out my fingers and glare at the carpet. "I didn't have fucking Stockholm syndrome. I was just..." I don't know how to describe what I was succinctly, but Blake comes to my rescue.

"Living with strangers, coping with major life changes and loss, and homesick?"

I rewind and play his words in my head again. It's a pretty good summary.

"That about covers it," I say before I sigh. "It'd be easier if there were actual villains in this story. Not just people who made terrible choices."

He nods again, and his hair tickles my skin. "What happened next?"

"I bailed," I say, point-blank. Look down at my fingers. "I do that. When going gets tough." I clear my throat. "I went back to

Maine. Camped out on Steph's couch. I dropped out of school and worked two jobs so I could hire a lawyer and get that fucking no-contact order lifted. Finally got that taken care of once I turned eighteen." I look down at my hands. "And then my mom... One moment I was seventeen, and we were having breakfast, ready to move to Michigan. The next, there were cops and jail cells and court dates and nothing was ever the same again. And then she died. And I never even got to talk to her again. Because of that fucking no-contact order."

Seems it's time to contemplate again, and this time Blake really takes his time.

"I'm sorry," he finally says, but where it'd sound like a pointless platitude from any other person, Blake sounds completely sincere.

"Yeah, well. It's not like I handled it well or anything." I pause. Stumble over my next ugly truth. "I haven't seen or talked to Sarah since."

"Do you want to?" There's no judgment in his voice. To Blake it's not about whether it's wrong or right that I've cut her out of my life. What matters to him is whether or not I want to do something about it.

So here's one more ugly truth for the road.

"No."

He doesn't say anything in response to that, but his fingers are back in my hair, and I close my eyes and just let myself sink into the sensations they create.

"I should be a better person, right?" I mutter. "I *should* want to be her son."

His fingers still for a moment before they start combing through my hair again.

"I don't think there's a wrong or right answer to that. Sometimes you just have to do what's best for you regardless of what other people think or want. It's not a crime to put yourself first."

I mull that over for a bit before I flop onto my back, turn my head, and look at him.

"If your biological mother found you, would you want to meet her?"

"I've thought about it," he says after a second.

"And?"

He blows out a big breath. "Some days I'm curious. I'd like to know why she did it. Most days I think not. Let sleeping dogs lie, and all that."

I nod, and a short laugh escapes. "We're quite a pair."

I don't know what response I expect to that, but it's not the wide smile that appears on his face. I also don't expect him to lean over and kiss me. I welcome it, but I don't expect it.

And I don't expect him to look at me and feel like my heart is going to burst out of my chest when he says, "I like us."

"Yeah," I say with a nod. "I like us, too."

TWENTY-SIX

Life has a funny way of throwing things at you. You go about your days, not bothering anybody. You try to avoid making waves or noise or anything. You just want to get by. Quietly mind your own business.

Maybe life's a bit muted, but you don't really see it because you don't *know*.

And then life throws you a curveball. On some random roof, at some random party.

Here's a person who just fits. He'll seamlessly slot into your life.

All his corners match yours.

You click.

It's easy. So, fucking easy.

It just makes sense.

And maybe it's stupid, but it feels inevitable. Of course you were supposed to meet him. How could you have not?

After all, he's yours.

Simple as that.

"Are you almost done?"

I press the phone between my shoulder and ear and nod.

"Are you nodding?" Blake asks with a laugh.

"I am. Because who needs words when you can read me like a book anyway?" I ask.

"Very economical. So are you? Done?"

I lock the door of the small office building where I've been temping as a cleaner for the last week.

"Closing up shop right now. Why?"

"I'll be there in five," he says, and hangs up.

I loiter on the sidewalk while I wait. It only takes him about two minutes to round the corner. He walks straight into me, not even slowing down, just colliding with me, toes against toes, chest against chest, lips against lips.

"Hi," he says once he pries himself away from me. He stays close, though. Close enough that I can see my reflection in his eyes.

He presses another kiss to my lips. Like he can't stay away. I'm addicted to being wanted like this.

"Come on." He grabs my hand and pulls me forward.

"Where are we going?" I ask as he drags me after him through the streets.

He throws me a glance over his shoulder. "I saw something just now, and it reminded me of you."

"Okay. I'm sufficiently intrigued," I say.

"It's a surprise," he adds.

"Yeah, I gathered from all the mysteriousness."

He laughs and marches on, dragging me along, and I follow through the night.

We end up in front of Grand Central Station.

I turn toward Blake with a frown. "Are we going somewhere? Not to be a party pooper, but it's almost one a.m. and I smell like artificial lemons and bleach."

"You'll see."

And then I'm being dragged again. He's practically vibrating with excitement, and I'm not sure why. He's never seemed like an especially avid train enthusiast, so I have no idea why he looks so pumped about being here.

I find out in a minute when we reach the main concourse and stop in front of a grand piano.

"What's this?"

He throws me a look, lips twitching.

"It's a piano," he says.

"I can see that. Why's it here?"

"They're having a piano concert here tomorrow. Students from Juilliard and Manhattan School of Music come in and play for the commuters in the morning."

"Okay," I say slowly. "And we're here in the middle of the night... because we want to nab really good spots?"

He smiles and nods toward the piano. "Play me something."

I take a step back. "What?"

"Play me something," he repeats.

I look around. There aren't many people around, and I don't see any security guards anywhere, but nevertheless, I am about a hundred and seventy percent certain this piano is not for playing. At least not by me. It's a Steinway, for crying out loud.

"Come on, Mr. I-can-play-the-piano," Blake says. "Time to put your money where your mouth is."

I take another glance around. "I don't think the piano's here for random passersby."

"It's not," he agrees.

"Then I don't think they'll be happy about me playing it."

Blake's smile is outright smug now. "But I thought you were... What did you say again? Refresh my memory a bit. Was it... extremely talented? Because I'm pretty sure those were the words you used."

I narrow my eyes at him. "You're enjoying this, aren't you?"

"So much. You have no idea. So? You told me you'd prove you can play if I produced a piano. Here it is. Your move."

"And when we're arrested, then what?"

"Then we can relive these beautiful moments in our jail cell."

"*Our* jail cell. You're mighty optimistic."

"Or romantic. We can be together in the holding cell before we're ruthlessly torn apart. It'll be tragic *and* romantic."

"Not sure how many people try to woo the other with the threat of getting arrested," I point out.

"It's a buyer's market, Jude. You need to stand out from the other losers."

"Is that how it works?"

"Clearly. I got you, didn't I?"

Can't really argue with solid facts like those, so instead, I glance at the piano. I'm already so tempted my fingers are itching. Playing piano was one of the casualties when my parents were arrested.

I used to be good. Piano lessons were the one constant, even with all our moving around. I never wanted to be a famous pianist or anything, I just liked to play. Liked the effect music had on people. Loved the power of communicating emotions and memories when words couldn't do them justice.

I'd had plans. But... being a music student doesn't really pay, and I needed the money, so that was the end of said plans.

"You know you want to." Blake cuts into my thoughts.

"Fuck you." It's more a term of endearment than anything else. "You'll bail me out?"

"Consider it one of my indulgences."

I take another glance around before I head toward the piano. I clear the rope that's been hoisted up around it and slide my fingertips over the keys without making a sound.

I take a seat on the bench. It's all so familiar. Blake sits down next to me and when I look at him, he waggles his brows.

I hesitate before I place my fingertips on the keys. Wrists raised slightly. Back straight. Elbows and shoulders relaxed.

It's like riding a bike.

I raise my brows at Blake. "Any requests?"

"You choose," he says.

So I do.

It's like a first date with your best friend you've had a crush on for ages. At first, you're nervous and your heart is beating uncomfortably hard, but then you take that first step, press that first key, and suddenly you're lost in the sound and the keys and time flies, and you have no clue where it went, and you don't understand why you were ever nervous about something that feels so natural. You stop thinking in English and instead think in music.

And you remember. You remember how much you fucking love the piano. Love the feel of the keys underneath your fingers. Love how versatile it is. The rhythm and the melody mixing together perfectly. And the sound of it... You fucking love the sound of a piano. The sweet, dark richness that moves through your whole body. The resonance. The beauty.

And once your fingers still, you only have one thought. Why the fuck did you ever stop? This was—

"Hey! What the hell are you doing?"

I snap my head up at the loud shout and my eyes land on an extremely pissed off security guard heading our way.

I whip my head toward Blake.

"Get the bail money ready," I say.

"Relax," he whispers. "I can fix this."

We both get up and back away from the piano.

"This piano is not for playing." The security guard's face has taken on a pretty unpleasant puce hue. "There are signs!"

"How exactly are you fixing it?" I murmur out of the corner of my mouth.

"Have a little trust," he says reassuringly. "I've got this."

"This is unacceptable," the security guard goes on. "I'll have you—"

That's when Blake grabs my hand and shouts, "Run!"

For a moment, I'm stumped, but then my feet are moving as we storm past the late-night travelers toward the exit, a chorus of angry shouts following us. I take a quick glance over my shoulder. We have a bit of a head start, but the security guard seems exceedingly motivated to catch us.

Then we're outside, running down the street. We round the corner, and we don't stop until we've put a few blocks between us and the station.

Blake puts his hands on his knees and leans forward, trying to catch his breath, and I slump against a wall, doing my best to get my breathing back under control.

"That was you fixing it?" I ask once I can speak again.

He waves his hand above his head and quirks his brow at me. "Were you arrested?"

"Not yet."

"You're welcome. I accept gratitude in the form of blowjobs."

"I bet they have cameras here, so keep it in your pants for now."

"You're such a fucking pessimist."

He straightens himself up and looks at me. My lips twitch. And then I'm laughing. Loud, noisy laughter that echoes off the walls of the surrounding buildings. Blake joins me. I laugh until my stomach muscles start to cramp and I run out of air. I laugh until it hurts to laugh.

Once I've calmed down, I lean against the wall next to Blake.

He turns his head toward me. "What was the song? The one you played."

"'Time.' Hans Zimmer."

"It was beautiful. And you were right. You *are* extremely talented."

My heart picks up speed at the praise, and it's good it's relatively dark out here because I'm pretty sure I'm blushing. "Always with the surprised tone."

"Well, yeah. Why are you making sandwiches and cleaning offices when you can play like that?"

"Maybe I like making sandwiches and cleaning offices?"

"Do you?" he challenges.

"I don't mind it," I say.

"But is it the end goal?"

I want to bristle in dignified contempt. What? I'm suddenly not good enough for him while I make sandwiches? Only, that's not how he means it, and I know it. I also know we're both aware making sandwiches isn't what I want to do with my life. Maybe if I had a love for food and a knack for inventing new, interesting recipes, but I just generally don't care about food. Unless somebody makes it for me, and I get to eat it. Same goes for everything else I occupy myself with. I'm adequate at all of it. Not great. Not terrible. I don't hate any of my jobs, but I also don't love them.

"I wanted to be a music therapist," I say.

"But not anymore?" Blake asks.

"I don't know what I want anymore."

"But you still like playing?" he asks.

"I think I wanted to forget just how much I like it." I clear my throat. "It doesn't matter. I haven't practiced regularly in a long-ass time, and it's... it's better like this. I don't have the time anyway. Maybe I'll pick it up as a hobby one of these days. We should get going."

He doesn't say anything to that, just sends me a calculating look. I want to know what he's thinking, but he doesn't seem keen to share, and I don't plan to pry.

Instead, I'm determined to enjoy the high of playing and the adrenaline rush of running. I roll myself off the wall and kiss him. Or more like maul him, because that's what you do when you want to really show your appreciation for somebody, and he clearly went to the same school of manners I did, because he welcomes my appreciation with gusto.

He hails a cab before things can get too indecent, and we manage to behave almost like civilized human beings on the drive to his apartment, but once the front door closes behind us, all bets are off.

He's on his knees in front of me, my pants end up somewhere around my ankles, and my hands are in his hair, clutching the strands as he swallows me down. It's a real sight—his head bobbing up and down, the tip of his nose tickling over my abdomen every now and then. His eyes have that hazy look of pleasure in them like *he's* the one getting head, not me.

Although... that can be arranged.

I pull at his hair until he looks up, and for a moment I lose my train of thought. It's a sinful sight—his lips stretched around my length, a needy look in his beautiful eyes.

"Bed," I rasp. "Want to taste you too, while you do that thing you just did with your tongue."

His eyes widen for a second and then he catches my drift and is up ridiculously fast. There might be flames under his heels as he books it to the bedroom, but I don't have time to check.

Then we're on the bed on our sides, and his fingers dig into my ass cheeks as he maneuvers me right where he wants me. He does it with such precision that by the time I'm where he wants me, I only need to open my mouth and his dick is right there, primed and ready to go.

Then it's just hands and mouths and mind-numbing pleasure so intense I wouldn't be surprised if it ended with my brain exploding. And when he noisily sucks two fingers into his mouth, maneuvers said fingers to my entrance, and sinks them into my ass, I'm mentally leaving all my worldly possessions to him. He deserves them. Not that being in possession of my crap is much of a prize, but it's the thought that counts. I'm pretty sure I babble something about it to him because he chuckles, and his mouth vibrates around me, and dear God, that should be illegal.

I groan, and I gasp, and I moan, and make all sorts of other noises while trying my best to make my sloppy blowjob at least a fraction as good for him.

He's determined to one-up me, clearly, because he pulls another skill out of his bag of tricks and swallows around me, and that's all she wrote.

I come with a round of expletives that'd make even the most experienced sailor blush, before I gather all my willpower and suck him back into my mouth. It's a good thing he's already on the edge, because he only needs to buck his hips a few times before he comes down my throat.

We both flop onto our backs.

"Fuck. Me," he says weakly.

"Not tonight, honey. I'm tired." My voice is more a slur than anything else.

He laughs, turns his head, and kisses my thigh, and I'm either extremely sensitive to thigh kisses or just crazy, because I'm having a very hard time swallowing down some very serious declarations. The kind I can't, in good conscience, make right after a blowjob.

So I keep them to myself for now, crawl on top of him, and let him kiss me to sleep.

TWENTY-SEVEN

Turns out my *I'm fine with my life the way it is* narrative has so many holes in it, it might as well be made out of swiss cheese. Ever since Blake took me to play the piano at the Grand Central Station, I've been restless. And to add insult to injury, more and more, I catch myself playing air piano on counters and tables, armrests and backrests. Blake's back and stomach and arms.

Why? Fuck if I know. It's like my fingers suddenly have a mind of their own, and they just keep doing their own thing, even if I disapprove so hard.

Eventually, pissed off to the max, I give in and rent one of those studio rooms with a piano in it for an hour. I just need to get it out of my system, and then I can go back to the way things were.

I go to the studio. I waste time and glare at the address on my phone.

Then I look up and glare at the building in front of me. Then at the address again. It goes on for a while. Let nobody say I'm not determined to be a stubborn asshole. No, sir. I want that shit engraved on my headstone.

I nearly jump out of my skin when my phone pings in my hand.

Blake: Just go inside. Stop being a stubborn asshole.

I glance around, but I don't see him anywhere. I frown at my phone.

Me: Where are you?

Blake: At home. Working.

Me: Then how do you know I'm being a stubborn asshole?

Blake: Lucky guess.

I send him a raised middle finger emoji. He sends back a kissy face. So I do the only mature thing I can think of. I stick my tongue out at the phone before I sigh and head inside the building.

When I played at the station it came easily, mainly because I'd played that particular piece so many times in the past it was apparently in muscle memory.

But then I'm sitting in front of a borrowed piano in a borrowed room, and I might as well have borrowed myself new fingers while I was at it because I keep fucking it up and making dumb-ass mistakes. Chopin is whirling in his grave.

So I go back the next day. Because I deserve a do-over.

I abandon the challenging classical pieces for now and go back to something more manageable. Études and minuets I remember from a long time ago. The Beatles. "Fur Elise" and "Moonlight Sonata."

Fuck up some more.

Go back.

Before I know it, I'm a regular. With a regular time slot. And the redhead at the front desk wants to know how my day is going. And other regulars smile at me.

They shouldn't. I'm not here to chat. I'm here to give a metaphorical middle finger to a bunch of dead composers by practicing the piano. My revenge skills could really use some work.

Anyway, people wouldn't be so unreasonably friendly, but I made the mistake of having Blake with me a few times, and that guy hasn't met a person he doesn't want to smile at and make small talk with.

Every time I go to the studio, I swear it's the last time. Then I end up going back.

It's like learning to walk again after an accident. Muscles I haven't used in a while have to remember movements that were once second nature. My brain has to restore some paths and lanes that haven't seen maintenance in years. Yes, muscle memory is a thing, but the finer points of technical skills have decayed over time, and I need to put in some serious effort to get them back.

I'm not exactly terrible, but I need to be better.

"Why?" Blake asks in an amused voice after I've settled in on his couch after yet another rant about my stupid fingers, and since I'm no one-trick pony and like to keep things interesting, I also had some choice words about people who don't understand you have to stand to the side to let people off the train before pushing in.

"Why do you need to be better?" Blake asks.

For a moment, I'm stumped.

"Because," I say with all the grace of a nine-year-old having a tantrum.

He quirks a brow.

"What's the point otherwise?" I ask.

He shrugs. "I don't know. To have fun?"

I scoff at the sheer stupidity of that statement. "Yeah, I'm sure that'll fly at the—"

I clamp my mouth shut. He sends me a knowing look before

he shakes his head and starts typing something. And then he's handing me the computer.

"Just fill in the fucking application form," he says with a sigh. "You're so unbelievably stubborn about the stupidest things. You know you want to, so just take the fucking laptop and fill in that fucking application form to Berklee you've been secretly reading and stop fucking pretending like you're not fucking interested."

I blink at all the fucks he just laid on me.

He doesn't even look apologetic. Just shrugs. "Tough love," he says. "Sometimes it's the only thing that works with you."

With how many fucks there were, you'd think this doesn't invite tenderness, but it does. It so does. I'm starting to think my love language does not come in the form of beautiful words and candlelit dinners but well-placed sarcastic remarks and exasperation. Blake has clearly mastered both.

I wordlessly take the laptop. Put it down on the table.

Blake quirks his brow and opens his mouth, but I don't let him speak. Instead, I kiss him. Thoroughly. It's the kind of kiss that merges into another kiss and makes your heart jump in your chest and your spine tingle.

"Thank you," I say.

"For?"

"For putting up with me."

He snorts. "It's not exactly a hardship."

"No?" I ask. "And here I was trying to think of a way to make it up to you." I slide my palm suggestively over the front of his sweats. "Then again, if you say it's okay..."

"It's been so hard," he says immediately. "So, so hard."

"I can feel that."

He laughs and kisses me again, and the words are right there, on the tip of my tongue.

I love you. I love you. I love you.

He drags me to the bedroom, and later, while I lie on top of him, his heartbeat steadily ticking against my ear, I let the feelings wash over me in a joyful rush.

I love you.
I love you.
I love you.

TWENTY-EIGHT

"Do you think a marriage proposal while you're preoccupied counts?"

My hand stops halfway to my mouth, and I stare at Steph, a slice of pizza dangling from my fingers.

"What?"

"I think I might've accidentally asked some dude to marry me last night."

I put the slice of pizza down. "How do you accidentally propose to somebody?"

"I don't know. I say things. You know I'm not good at multi-tasking."

"Okay. Walk me back a bit. What were you doing while you were proposing?"

He looks around the sunny pizza place with an assessing look before he curls the fingers of his left hand into a loose fist, opens his mouth, and starts moving his hand up and down, making it painfully obvious exactly what he was up to at the time the proposal took place.

I raise my brows at him. "And you still had time to propose

with your mouth full? I'd say you're doing well on the multi-tasking front."

"I was on the receiving end, so my mouth was free to say all kinds of things. Somewhere between 'deeper' and 'harder,' I also threw in a 'marry me.' I mean, I guess he got it right, so I wanted to show my appreciation?"

I'd be surprised, but this is Steph, so it absolutely sounds like something that'd happen to him.

I take a moment to consider his predicament.

"I don't think it counts," I say, and pick up my slice of pizza again. "I'm pretty sure you're not the first one to promise things when orgasms are involved."

Steph nods thoughtfully and picks up his phone. He slides his thumb over the screen and pushes it in front of me.

I look down with my innocent, unsuspecting gaze and nearly choke on the mouthful of pizza at the dick pic now in front of me. I cough and force down some water before I glare at him.

"Warn a guy next time, would you?" I take another drink. "Why are you showing me this?"

"I want your opinion. Duh."

The things I do for friends. I take a quick glance at the screen again before I slide it back to Steph.

"It's a nice dick. Not sure if it's worth a lifetime commitment, but to each their own. I'd also consider his personality before jumping into wedding vows, but that's just me."

He rolls his eyes. "He says he got us matching rings. I mean, it's a joke, right? He can't be serious with this shit."

I'm lost again.

"What?"

The phone is back, so I take another look. I've seen this stranger's junk way more times than I would like by now. But then I start to laugh.

"Okay. Matching cock rings. I get it now."

I go back to my pizza and Steph keeps looking at me while chewing on the inside of his cheek.

"So?" he finally blurts. "Serious or not?"

"I'm leaning toward not. I think he's flirting with you."

Steph looks almost ridiculously relieved at that as he nods. "Okay. Phew. Dodged a bullet, in that case. I should probably never see him or talk to him again, though. Just in case."

I snort and grab another slice of pizza. "Yeah, or you could be a decent person, and tell him you're not interested. Don't just ghost him."

"Since when are you pillar of morality?"

"I have hidden depths."

"I know you do. I'm just surprised you're exploring them."

I smile at him sweetly and raise my middle finger. "You should get a roll of duct tape for next time you sleep with somebody. Slap it on your mouth to keep all the love declarations at bay."

He grimaces at the prospect of future stumbles. "Ha. Funny. You know, this could happen to you too, so I wouldn't be so smug about it."

I shrug. "I only sleep with one person, and honestly, I don't think he'd mind the love declarations."

Steph's brows rise to his hairline.

"Would *you*?" he asks.

I grab a napkin from the holder and wipe my hands, crumple it into a ball, and drop it on the empty plate.

"It's not that I'd mind them. It's more that I don't need them."

Steph purses his lips and studies me like I'm a fascinating science experiment gone wrong.

"I don't need grand declarations and over-the-top romantic gestures," I say. "I'm pretty sure I'd just be really uncomfortable with those." It's difficult to put my feelings into words because I don't know if there are even words for what Blake means to me, and I'm not sure it's really something I want to explain to Steph. "The bottom line is I like being with him. I'm happier than I've ever been, and I know I make him happy, too. That's all I need."

Steph is quiet for the longest time before he says, "Well, damn. You're actually in love."

I shrug one shoulder. "Go figure."

"I'm happy for you two." Steph considers me. "You gonna tell him? *He* might want to hear it."

I nod thoughtfully. "Hey! Maybe I'll let him blow me and then propose?"

Steph throws a piece of pizza crust at me. I dodge to the side, and it hits the back of some old lady's head, so we spend the rest of our lunch apologizing to her, and luckily, the matter of my love life is forgotten.

But when I walk home, Steph's words linger. Sink their roots into my brain and anchor themselves in place.

He might want to hear it.

He probably does want to hear it. Deserves to hear it. Feelings might make *me* uncomfortable, but it'd make Blake happy to hear me say the words.

And I want to make him happy.

More than anything, I want to make Blake happy.

TWENTY-NINE

I WRESTLE the bags of groceries through the front door of Blake's building. The handle of one of the bags is on its last legs, so of course I end up crawling around the hallway, chasing onions.

I hardly pay attention to the mishap. My mind's too busy with plans and trying to figure out all the ways I can screw things up.

Romance isn't my forte. Neither is cooking, but I figure if we're already stepping out of the comfort zone, might as well go all in. So I'm going to build a blanket fort. And I'm going to cook Blake's favorite mushroom risotto. And I'm going to romance Blake so hard he'll be ruined for all other men for the rest of eternity.

He said he was going to be out all day, so I'm hoping that's the case and I have enough time to set everything up with extra time for ordering dinner in case my grand cooking plans don't work out the way I want them.

I start with the blanket fort, and once that's done, I head to the kitchen. I've just laid everything out when my phone starts to ring. I glance at it and frown at the unknown number before I pick it up.

"This is Jude," I say as I shimmy the phone between my shoulder and ear.

"Jude! Thank God somebody knows how to pick up their phone," a woman's voice rushes out on the other end.

She says that like I'm supposed to know who she is, and I can't exactly say I do. Luckily, she doesn't leave me guessing but barrels straight on.

"This is Trisha from Rossi Catering. You've worked with us in the past."

"Uh, yes?" I say. I know Rossi Catering. They were one of the first places that offered me a job when I moved to the city, and I worked for them on and off for a few months, but back then I'd always been in contact with the owner, Jack, and not a Trisha.

"Well, Jude, I'm sure glad I got a hold of you. See, I'm in a bit of a pickle here, and I was hoping you could help me out."

She sounds excessively perky.

"Sure?" I say carefully.

"You're a gem. You truly are. Dad always said you were one of his most dependable guys."

"Jack?" I confirm.

"That's Dad," she says. *"He had a stroke a few months back. He's on the mend, don't you worry, but he's now handed the reins over to me, and we're catering an event today, but three of my waiters just called in sick. It's the last time I hire roommates, I swear to God. Anyway, I'm going through Dad's list now trying to find replacements, and I know it's practically no notice at all, but is there any way you can come in today?"*

"Oh." I glance at the blanket fort and the food and then pull the phone away from my ear to look at the time. "I—"

"I'll pay you double," she says. "Dad truly always spoke so highly of you."

I'd be lying if I said the flattery doesn't work.

"What time?" I ask.

"Two. It's a family day at a retirement home. It's only two hours, so you'll be free at four."

I sigh and drag my hand through my hair. "Yeah, I'll be there."

"Thank you, thank you, thank you! You really are a lifesaver."

I get the details and hang up.

Well, new plan, I guess. I'll order dinner. It's better this way. I bet it'll be more romantic if I serve something edible anyway.

"Thank you, thank you, thank you," Trisha keeps repeating as she sends me on my way at four.

"It's fine. I was happy to help," I assure her over and over again before I get out of there.

Dusk is falling, the temperature is dropping, and when I walk, a snowflake falls on my nose. I look up, and I smile. There's something magical about the first snow. Especially in the city, where the pristine white blanket only lasts for a very short time.

I pull out my phone and text Blake to see if I still have time to get back home before him and surprise him.

Me: Are you home yet?

It takes him a bit to reply, but eventually he does.

Blake: I'll be there around six.

Another text follows shortly after.

Blake: I miss you.

I smile and pocket the phone. Plenty of time, then.

Okay. A new game plan. I'll head to Bianchi's and get dinner, and then I should get back home right before Blake. And I just earned enough cash to pay for said dinner. Honestly, this catering gig might've been divine intervention to prevent any cooking disasters. Probably wouldn't have been very romantic to burn Blake's apartment building down.

By the time I arrive at Bianchi's, the snow has gone from beautiful to problematic. Wide, wet flakes are mixed with little round pellets of ice. Pretty to look at, but not very pleasant to walk around in.

I step in the door and shake my head, spraying half-melted snow everywhere, and wipe my palm over my face.

One of the waitresses sends me a sympathetic look.

"Take a seat anywhere," she says. "I'll be right with you."

I open my mouth to explain I need the food to go when I spot a very familiar face. The smile on my face is a reflex by now. I see Blake. I'm happy. I smile. That simple.

He lifts his eyes as if sensing I'm there. Looks straight at me.

My smile widens, and I give a small wave.

He doesn't.

Instead, he's gone completely still, lips slightly parted, eyes wide. Guess he didn't expect to run into me.

I suppose my romantic dinner plans need a bit of an overhaul now. I don't think Blake will want a second dinner if he's already eaten.

The woman he's with waves her hand in front of Blake's face.

I'm a distraction, and he clearly doesn't need that. I should get out of here and leave him to his business.

I guess I could get the dessert for later. That sounds like a plan, too. Drop by the bakery and get the chocolate cake he likes.

Blake slowly gets up.

I shake my head and wave my thumb toward the door to tell him I'll be going and not to mess up his meeting for me.

I open my mouth.

Words are on the tip of my tongue.

I'll see you at home.

The woman sitting across from Blake turns her head and looks at me.

Time freezes.

I freeze.

My breath gets stuck somewhere in my throat.

I don't remember moving, but I must have because I'm outside, hurrying down the street.

Away.

Away.

Away.

"Jude!"

I stop, turn around slowly, and face Blake.

He stops ten feet away from me.

He knows, a little voice says in my head. He knows because if he didn't know, he'd be more surprised. He would look startled, instead of resigned.

The door of the restaurant opens again. I look up. At *her*. And away.

"You know who she is," I say, that hollow *knowing* creeping through me.

Blake's lips part, but no sound comes out.

"Jude," he says. Pleads.

"You know who she is." I repeat. It's not a question.

Blake closes his eyes for a second before he looks at me again.

"I know who she is," he says quietly.

It's like a punch in the lungs. All the air wooshes out of me. My legs feel like they're not mine. Like they're having a difficult time figuring out they should be holding me up.

I flick a glance at the door of the restaurant. At Sarah.

She hasn't changed much. The same dark hair. The same slim, almost fragile build. The same large blue eyes. The eyes I see every time I look in the mirror. Sarah's gaze moves between me and Blake, but otherwise she's completely still.

Blake pushes his wet hair out of his eyes. "Please, just let me—"

"Is she a client?" I interrupt.

Tell me she is. That you just met her. Fucking lie to me! I don't care. Just don't ruin us.

He shakes his head.

I double over for a moment before I drag both hands through my hair and pull as hard as I can before I straighten myself up. My scalp stings.

"How long?" I ask.

Blake opens and closes his mouth without a sound.

"How long have you known her?" I say through gritted teeth. My voice is strangled like somebody's cut off all my air.

"Ever since I tried to steal her car a decade ago," he says, so softly I barely hear him over the noise of the street and the roar of blood in my ears.

A laugh escapes. Harsh and bitter and ugly.

"Did you know who I was?" I choke out.

Please, fucking say no.

I'm hopelessly hoping, even though I already see the answer on his face.

"Yes," Blake says. "I knew who you were."

Each of these quiet confessions is another kick to the chest.

You fucking idiot. You trusted him. You knew better. You fucking idiot.

"Jude, please." Blake steps forward. Reaches out his hand. I back away so quickly I slam into a lamp post.

"Just let me explain," he says.

"Explain?" I shake my head. "Explain what? Is this some sort of sick game? What the fuck is this?"

"Please," Blake repeats. "She asked me to find you—"

"Oh? Oh! Was fucking me also part of the deal? Did she pay you to fuck me?"

He winces like I've thrown stones at him. I want it to hurt. I want to say every cruel thing I can think of and hurl it in his face.

Hurt him like he's hurting me.

Break him like he's breaking me.

"It's not like that," Blake says. "It's not like that at all. Just please, let me explain. I knew it was wrong, but I fell for—"

"Don't you fucking dare!" I snap so viciously he takes a step back. I try to gulp in air. Try to make myself breathe because I can't seem to get enough air. The best I can manage are shallow breaths that tease my lungs with the promise of relief but never fully deliver.

I should've known better.

I should've known that this is how it ends. This is how it always ends.

Once again, I'm in pieces. Scattered on the street, in the puddles of half-melted snow and dirt. Trampled under somebody else's whims, a pawn in someone else's game.

I'm so fucking stupid.

I clutch the back of my neck with icy cold fingers and stare at the sky for a moment. I have a horrible feeling I'm about to cry, and I can't. Not here. Not right now. Not in front of him. And her. I can't. I can't. I can't.

I take one more look at him.

He says my name wordlessly, lips moving, no sound coming out.

I turn around. My limbs feel like they weigh a thousand pounds, but I force myself to move.

"Jude!" he calls after me.

His hand grabs my arm, and I wrench myself free.

"Don't fucking follow me." I walk away without another look.

By the time I get home, my teeth are rattling from the cold, and I'm soaked to the bone.

The apartment is dark and empty. Steph's gone for the night.

My fingers refuse to cooperate when I try to peel my wet clothes off. I wrestle uselessly with the buttons of my shirt before I give up.

I sink down on the floor on my ass, back against the door, staring at nothing.

Everything is numb.

Cold and numb and empty.

THIRTY

THE NEXT MORNING, I wake up to a ray of sun on my face. For a few blissful moments I'm confused. I'm in my own bed. That hasn't happened in a while. Why am I—

Yesterday crashes down on me like a bucket of ice water.

Every single moment of pain and anger in glorious Technicolor. There's no filter that'd dull the sharp edges of every blade of truth that was rammed into my brain last night.

My eyes sting, and I squeeze them shut.

Deep breaths.

In through the nose.

Out through the mouth.

Until I can think again.

This is... this is better. Like this. Finding out now.

Because what's the alternative?

Discovering the truth months from now?

Or years down the line?

After I'd had weeks, months, years of Blake? Years of Blake laughing happily, holding me at night, watching shitty sci-fi movies with his head in my lap. Years of Blake and his nerdy glasses and greedy kisses and mischievous smiles. Years of shrewd comments and nights spent talking and kissing and fucking. Years of loving him and being loved in return.

Then coming home one day, way down the line, and finding out the second life you've built on the ashes of the first one also turns out to be a lie?

No.

This is better.

If I repeat it enough, I'll eventually believe it.

I stuff a pillow over my head and try to fall asleep again. My life's infinitely more manageable if I'm not actively present in it.

It doesn't work.

After I've spent twenty minutes staring blankly at the ceiling, I get up. I pull on a pair of sweats and a sweater I find on the floor—fucking Steph—and head to the bathroom where I hold my head under cold water for a bit to clear it. After that, I drag my ass into the living room.

And stop short.

Blake slowly gets up from where he's sitting at the kitchen table and gives a helpless shrug.

"Stephen let me in." He sounds rough. He looks rough. Still in last night's clothes. I wonder how long he's been here.

I stomp down the unwelcome urge to offer him tea. Or a hug. Something. Anything.

"What do you want?" I ask.

"To talk."

"Is it going to make anything better?"

He looks down. Taps the tip of his thumb against his fingertips before he looks up again. "Most likely worse."

That stumps me for a moment. I expected excuses and apologies, not honesty.

I go and flop down on the other side of the table and gesture toward him with my hand. "Go ahead, then. Surprise me."

He takes a seat and places his elbows on the table, leaning

forward a bit. Like he wants to get closer. I push my chair back a few inches. He stops, eyes me carefully, and straightens up.

"Did you know hackers help search for missing people?" he says.

I blink in complete confusion at the direction this conversation has taken. "Huh?"

"For fun. It's turned into sort of a game. You have a team and a—" He starts to lean forward again, that spark in his eyes that is always there when he talks about something that interests him, but then he catches himself and settles back down. "There are events. I've participated now and then. It's doubly beneficial. You help locate missing persons, but you also learn how to gather open-sourced intelligence."

"Good for you?" I say slowly. I'm not sure where this is headed.

"It's why Sarah turned to me. To find you. Because she knew I had the experience. And I couldn't say no. Not that I really planned to, but even if I'd wanted to… She once saved me, and…"

"And you're loyal," I say, remembering what he told me all those months ago on that rooftop. "That's your best quality and your worst quality."

He nods wordlessly.

I study him for a few seconds before I ask, "How did you find me?"

"You were in the background of one of the photos Blair posted on her studio Instagram page. It was easy after that."

I process that for a bit. Try to navigate this new landscape where I didn't meet a stranger on a rooftop, but somebody who already knew me.

"So when we met?" I ask, leaving the question hanging in the air.

He shakes his head. "Sort of an accident but not really. I

knew you'd be there that night. There was no friend asking for a favor. I was working there as a barback that night, true, but I applied for the gig because it was a private party, and I needed an in." He scrubs his palm over his face and lifts his tired gaze. "I just wanted to see you, I guess? Get a glimpse of you."

"Why? What was the point?"

"To see if you were okay." He looks down at his hands. "And I was curious. About you. About Sarah's son. I realize you two have a very complicated relationship, but for me she's... Sarah and David were a lifeline for me, so I suppose I wanted to see what was wrong with you that you didn't want them in your life. See if you were an asshole."

"A stupid fucking asshole," I say, and yes, I mean me. That assessment was spot-on. I *am* a stupid fucking asshole.

He almost smiles at that. "*That* was an accident. You were the fifth person I'd had to send away from that roof that evening. It gets old fast."

"So when you closed the door?" I ask.

"I knew we'd be locked out."

I drop my head back and let out a mirthless laugh before I look at him again and nod. "Well, aren't you clever," I say with as much sarcasm as is possible to insert in that short sentence. "Then what?"

He gives a helpless shrug. "You weren't what I expected." He hesitates for a second before he continues. "After we got back down? On the staircase, when I walked into you—"

"Ooh, ooh, ooh!" I say with an even bigger helping of sarcasm. I'm sensing a theme here. "Can I guess? It wasn't an accident?"

"It was to distract you so I could steal your watch," he says.

I stare at him.

"I'm sorry, what?"

"Your watch. You didn't lose it. I stole it. I wanted an excuse to see you again."

For long moments, I have no idea what to say.

"You were right. You made it worse. Congrats. I didn't think you could."

Another helpless shrug. "No more lies."

"That's a novel approach."

He winces. I don't feel bad.

I don't.

"That evening at the gallery," I say slowly. "The argument you were having outside with Sage... That was about me, wasn't it?"

"Yes," he says.

I don't even know what to think of that, so I leave it be.

We're both silent for a long time after that. Waiting. For what? I don't know anymore.

He breaks the silence first.

"I fell for you," he says quietly.

My heart gives a traitorous thump. I'd rip it out and throw it at him if I could.

"Fuck you," I reply softly. "Fuck. You." More forcefully.

He nods as if he expected that. "I tried not to."

"Yeah, okay," I snap. "That makes everything better. You're forgiven. Let's get married."

His shoulders slump, and he gives a resigned nod. I don't think he's stupid enough to actually think coming clean now, after getting caught, is going to make anything better, but maybe there was still hope, because there's always hope, isn't there?

"Were you ever going to tell me?" I ask. "If I hadn't seen you yesterday, would you have told me?"

"I tried," he says and looks down at where his fingers are linked, nails digging into the backs of his hands. "Every time I had a plan that I was going to tell you, every time I told you I needed to talk to you, something seemed to come up. It only got more difficult with each passing day. And I was a coward, and I didn't try too hard, obviously."

I remember all those times he *did* say those words. Told me that we needed to talk. That he needed to tell me something. But we never got to that. I don't know if it makes anything better.

"Was it all a lie?" I ask. "Everything you told me about yourself? Everything?" I don't know why I'm asking this. Don't know if I even want to hear the answer.

He's shaking his head well before I'm finished speaking.

"No. Christ, no! I swear, everything I told you about myself, it's all true. I never lied about any of that. And everything you told me about yourself? I didn't know that. I just knew Sarah had a son, and she didn't know where you were. That was it. The only things I lied about were Sarah and all the social engineering that was involved in meeting you."

"Social engineering," I say slowly. "What a nice way to put it."

"People hacking is a part of my job," he says quietly. "I trick and manipulate people into doing things they shouldn't to discover weaknesses in the system."

I nod. Fuck. And I thought I couldn't hurt any more. "And I'm a job."

He's in front of me then.

On his knees.

Fingers digging into my thighs.

It hurts.

I wish it'd hurt more. Enough to drown out the crushing feeling inside. Because that pain is infinitely worse.

"No. Please. It's not like that. It was never a job. I needed to repay some of my debt to Sarah for everything she's done for me, and this was my way to do that. I was never supposed to get to know you. I was never supposed to love you—"

"Get out," I grit out through my teeth.

"I love you," he repeats, and I push him.

Off me.

Away from me.

If I don't, I might break.

I might shatter.

"Get the fuck out!" My voice echoes off the walls.

He gets up. Painfully slowly. Looks at me. I refuse to look away.

I hate him.

I want him to see it.

I want him to know.

I hate him.

He swallows hard. There are tears in his eyes now, falling down. Maybe he'll cry me a river, and we'll both drown.

He walks out.

I hate him.

I hate him.

I hate him.

And look at that.

Now he's made me into a liar, too.

THIRTY-ONE

You'd prefer to be angry.

You want to be furious. You want to *want* to throw shit and punch stuff.

But you don't. Instead, you move through your days with some kind of newfound lethargy.

Completely lost.

What next?

What now?

All the plans you'd tentatively started to make, all the visions for your future, are suddenly null and void. You drafted a picture in your mind about what your life was going to be like, and it felt so real you could almost touch it before somebody else put a match to all your plans, and you were left to watch everything go up in flames.

So where does it leave you?

What do you do?

I spend my days on autopilot. Book as many temp jobs for myself as humanly possible so by the time I finally get into my bed late at night I won't have the energy to think anymore. Then I get back up a few hours later and do it all over again.

I tell myself I just have to get through *this* day, and then the next one will be better. A little more tolerable. A little more manageable. Because it has to be. *Please, somebody tell me it gets better.*

The not-thinking turns out to be the most difficult part, but at least once I'm dead tired I can separate the emotions from my thoughts.

So I spend my nights studying my bedroom ceiling and the debris of Blake and me with the detached air of a scientist taking in a failed experiment.

The subject seems to have fooled himself into believing there is a happy ending. In an interesting example of how fleeting the human memory is, the subject seemingly forgot all his hard-learned lessons and jumped headfirst into trusting another human being again. The subject is clearly dumb as a rock.

I start sleeping with the weather channel on because it drowns out my thoughts and is just boring enough to put me to sleep. And it has the added benefit that it drives Steph away from my bed because he's fed up with the noise and me walking around the apartment in the middle of the night, trying to distract myself from not sleeping. By the end of week one, I'm so sick of Steph eyeing me carefully while I roam around at night that I kick him out.

I should feel bad, but being alone is a relief. At least this way I'm not constantly on edge, waiting for the next blow. At least this way there's no one near me who could deliver that blow.

I can't have Steph sleeping next to me. Not now, when in

the middle of the night, in my half-sleep state, there's a fleeting moment when I think the warm body against me is Blake.

I'm so very uninterested in experiencing that despicable moment of calm and sleepy happiness followed by cold, harsh reality every damn night, over and over again.

It's unfair what he did to me. When my parents were arrested most of my energy went into figuring out how to survive amid the chaos. And that's exactly what I did. Day by day. Year by year. Maybe it wasn't much of a life. More like an existence. But it was enough.

Blake... Blake showed me a vision of what my future might be like if I wanted it. He gave me hope.

He made me love him.

He turned himself into my home.

Now he's gone.

And I'm homeless.

But life doesn't stop for a broken heart.

So somehow, I keep going.

It takes a bit of time for Steph to rat me out to Blair. All things considered, I think I've done a pretty good job pretending everything's fine, so I'm not the least bit suspicious when Blair asks me to babysit Hazel to have a date night with Nora.

Instead, I put on a smile and, like an idiot, walk straight into an ambush.

"I'm here," I call once I'm inside the apartment.

"In the living room," Blair yells.

I toe off my shoes and go in search of Hazel. Out of all the people in the world, she's my absolute favorite. There's no contest. There's a chance that without her I might've done something dumb like bail. Again. Like I do. But I made a promise to her in that hospital room, and I intend to keep it. People are assholes. It's something Hazel will find out eventually, whether I like it or not. But I'm really not keen on teaching her that lesson by making myself an example.

I walk into Blair and Nora's open plan living room and look around. Instead of Hazel, I find Blair. Alone.

I look around. "Where's Hazel?"

"Nora took her to visit her parents."

"So, I'm not babysitting," I surmise.

"No," Blair confirms. "And I didn't even let you know."

"Uh-huh," I mutter. "I guess I'll take off if you don't need me."

She puts her hands on her hips. "I don't think you get it. You had to give up gigs to be here."

"It's fine," I say.

"And since you're family, I won't pay you for babysitting."

"I don't expect you to?" I look around slowly. Is this some kind of prank?

"And you had to fight through rush hour traffic," Blair says, and raises her brows like she's prompting me to do something, only I have no clue what it is. And I have no energy to solve the puzzle.

I give a tired shrug. "It's not like I'm driving."

"No," she says, shaking her head. "Your night's pretty much ruined. To think it could've all been avoided if I had just texted you and told you you didn't need to come."

"Well." I rub my palm over my face. "Next time."

Blair slams her foot down. "What the fuck is wrong with you?"

"Nothing," I say.

"Don't 'nothing' me. You should be annoyed. You should be all sarcastic and insufferable and you're supposed to give me so much shit for this. So, I repeat, what the fuck is wrong with you?"

"Well, jeez. Sorry for trying to be a nice person. Fine. Yes, my night is ruined. I'm so lucky to have such a thoughtless person in my life."

She rolls her eyes. "Pathetic. It's like your heart isn't even in it." Her expression morphs from angry to worried. That's so much worse. "Seriously, what's wrong?"

"Nothi—"

"You look like shit," Blair interrupts and waves her hand toward my face. "The shadows under your eyes have shadows."

"I haven't been sleeping well. I'm working on it. Look, if you don't need me, I'm gonna get going."

"Fat chance of that happening. We're going out." She's already moving. Pulling on one of her oversized sweaters and throwing her phone, keys and wallet into her bag.

"I'm really not in the mood," I say to her back, but I already know she won't listen, and I'll end up going wherever it is she wants to go. It's just easier to not argue and do what she says.

"Come on," she says. "Or we'll be late."

"Late for what?" I call after her.

She doesn't answer, so in the end, I just follow her.

"What is this?" I ask once we've stepped out of the cab and are standing in front of a red brick building. I'd be lying if I said the lack of windows isn't disconcerting.

"Only the best place in New York City. You can thank me after."

She opens the door and pushes me inside, where a very tall dude hands us boiler suits, safety goggles, and hard hats.

I look at Blair. "If this is some weird sex thing, I'm not interested."

She rolls her eyes. "Oh, no. And after all the trouble I went through to find you a dominatrix."

Once we have the gear on, a guy appears in the doorway and nods toward the hallway behind him. "The deluxe room is ready for you. Have fun."

So we head to the back and end up in a room at the end of the hallway. The thing's filled with the most random junk. A bunch of old computer monitors and TVs. Some seriously ugly plates and glasses. A toaster and a microwave. More random crap.

Blair walks to the table set up in the middle of the room and places a wine glass on top. She wordlessly hands me a baseball bat.

I look at it and the glass, and my tired brain finally catches on.

"Break it?" I ask. Just in case.

"Go to town," she says.

So I smash the glass, and it breaks, showering the floor with shards. It feels... good. Cathartic. So I take a plate and fling it at a wall. I swing the bat at one of the computer monitors, over and over until it's in pieces.

I destroy more plates and more glasses and the toaster and the fucking microwave. I swing the bat at everything I can reach until there's only debris left, and my arm aches, and my heart thunders in my chest from exhaustion.

When it's all said and done, I drop to the floor and look at the chaos around me and feel very small and pathetic and lost.

And when Blair puts her arms around me and hugs me, I cry.

THIRTY-TWO

Sometimes in life, there are moments when people do things that are so inexplicably stupid that no matter how hard you try, it's impossible to figure out the leap of logic that led to them thinking that was a good idea.

And this time the person doing something inexplicably stupid isn't even me.

I spend the rest of my weekend at Blair and Nora's. I sleep in their guest room. Play with Hazel. Take a break from life until I'm ready to face everything again. Until I'm ready to go and pick up the pieces.

My determination lasts for a whole twenty-five minutes because when I trudge up the stairs of my apartment on Monday morning, I find Blake sitting next to my door with a book on his lap and his legs stretched out in front of him, one crossed over the other.

I stop in front of him.

He has the nerve to look good. Maybe a bit tired. Maybe a bit sad. But good. So good I need to stuff my hands into my pockets to prevent myself from doing something stupid.

"Hey," he says like it's normal that he's here.

"What are you doing here?" I ask, and I'm actually impressed by how level my voice sounds, even if inside I'm completely baffled about this turn of events.

He looks at me thoughtfully.

"Difficult to say. I don't really have a plan. Other than fighting for you, I mean. But I haven't a hundred percent figured out how to go about this yet, so I guess for now the plan is to just wear you down. I'll see what happens with that and go from there."

My mouth has fallen open by the end of that little speech.

"Seriously, what do you want?" I ask once I've gathered myself a bit.

He tilts his head to the side and lets his eyes wander over me —up, down, and back up until he meets my gaze again.

"You," he says simply. "Just you. All of you. Forever."

I ignore the way my stomach somersaults at those words. "You can't be serious."

"I'm very serious."

I stand there like an idiot, mouth opening and closing, but there's absolutely nothing I can think of to say to that, so in the end, I go inside and slam the door behind me.

"Good talk," Blake calls through the door.

Since I can't seem to think of anything more productive to do, I flip off the door.

I've got nothing planned for the day since my weekend at Blair's didn't leave me much chance to book jobs, so I just hide in my apartment, a prisoner in my own home. I think I deserve to be dramatic.

I take the world's longest shower before I dig out the remnants of the takeout Thai food I ordered a few days ago and flop down on the couch. It's really quiet, and my ears are starting to ring from how hard I'm straining them to hear something, anything, from the other side of the door. I turn on the

TV to stop this damn self-sabotage. I watch ten episodes of *How It's Made* and, gun to my head, I can't recall a single thing that was made on that show.

I try to read, but I can't concentrate, so eventually I shove my earphones in and turn the music up loud on my phone. It helps a bit. My insides are still twisting themselves into knots and shapes, but at least I can't hear anything. Doesn't stop me from being aware he's out there, though.

And maybe it's the fact that he *is* out there, but once it starts to get dark outside, I fall asleep on the couch, and I only wake up once it's morning again.

I stare at the ceiling and slowly wake up. My phone died sometime in the middle of the night, so the only thing I can hear is the distant sound of traffic from outside.

I get up and go to the hallway. Press my ear against the door and listen. Nothing. Take a look through the peephole. Nothing. Slowly open the door. Nothing.

So this is how it ends.

Not with a bang, but with silence.

This is not how it ends.

Blake's back in the afternoon. And the next day. And the next. Sometimes he's there the whole day. Sometimes only a few hours. Sometimes he works on something on his laptop. Sometimes he reads one of his battered paperbacks. Sometimes he listens to music.

But he's there.

Just outside my door.

Just out of reach.

Every. God. Damn. Fucking. Day.

I ignore him. Pretend he's not there when I walk past him

on my way out or when I'm coming home from work. I can feel his eyes on me, but he doesn't try and talk to me, just watches me. His gaze holds everything—regret, need, hope. It's all there. I don't know what to do with it. What to do with him.

Sunday is the first time in seven days I hear his voice. He pulls his earbuds out of his ears when he sees me come up the stairs and lowers his iPad.

"I like your hair," he says.

My palm moves over the top of my freshly cut hair.

"It was getting long," I say.

"It looks good."

"Thanks," I say before I escape inside.

This stilted conversation is somehow even worse than silence.

"I tried to watch *Battlefield Earth* yesterday," he says while I push the key into the lock.

I raise my brows at him. "Why?"

He shrugs. "You said it was so bad you couldn't get through it. I got curious."

I lean my shoulder against the wall next to my door. "And?"

"I feel like I need an exorcism. Know any priests?"

My lips twitch involuntarily.

"Besides," he continues, "it's not the same without you."

How do I stop missing somebody who's parked right outside my door every day?

How do I stop loving him?

I don't have an answer.

It's raining.

It's raining so much no sane person would go outside.

But Blake is here again.

Sopping wet, but his smile is as bright as ever.

"You're gonna get pneumonia," I say.

"Rain doesn't cause pneumonia. That's old wives' tale."

"I bet the cold does the trick."

He shrugs. "Maybe. Guess we'll see."

I hover in the doorway. It's none of my business. It's not. It's not. It's not.

But even though it's not, I still push the door open and hold it for him.

He sends me a quizzical look.

"I'd hurry if I were you," I say.

He gets up and follows me inside. I get him dry clothes.

He takes the clothes silently.

"This doesn't mean anything," I mumble when he comes out of the bathroom dressed in my clothes, making my heart do weird things in my chest.

"I'll get a Lyft," he says.

My head snaps up in surprise. "You're not staying?"

He tilts his head to the side. "Do you want me to stay?"

I don't know what to say because I don't know what I want.

He sends me a small smile. "I'll get a ride," he repeats. "Because when you let me inside, it's going to be because you choose to do it. Not because of rain or because you feel sorry for me. I want you to want me here. And I want you to be sure."

"You can't sit here forever," I grit out through my teeth once I reach my door.

In the interests of being completely honest with myself, I'm way more pissed with myself right now than with him.

I'd walked in the front door and everything had been extremely quiet. So the whole way upstairs I'd had an uncomfortable squeezing feeling in my chest. Until I saw him sitting there, and then it got worse because I was relieved.

I hate myself.

"Can't I?" he asks.

"No," I snap.

"Guess we'll see about that one," he says lightly.

My door really isn't equipped for all the slamming it's had to endure lately.

I'm just unlocking the door when Blake asks, "How was your week?"

"Fine," I say before I can think better of it.

My hand falls away from the key, and I shift my weight from one foot to the other.

"Cookie?" he asks and extends a bag toward me.

"No, thank you."

He's still holding the bag out. "You sure? They're not homemade, but they're still pretty good."

"I already ate."

He shrugs and puts the bag down next to himself before he sends me a speculative look as if gauging how willing I am to continue this conversation. "You don't work at the sandwich shop anymore."

"It was always a temporary position."

He nods. "How's the piano going?"

I look away. It's stupid to feel guilty about this. It's not like I'm letting him down by not playing.

But the guilt is there. And the absolute best part of this mess is that I'm not sure if it's aimed at me or him.

"Did you finish your application to Berklee?" Blake tilts his head to the side and looks at me expectantly, and the anger I've been wishing for ever since he knelt in front of me on my kitchen floor slowly crawls forward. It takes a look at Blake's easy smile and it takes in the hopeful look in his eyes. It spreads its tentacles through my insides and squeezes my lungs into a vise.

I want to crawl into his lap and let him kiss me and let him make everything better again. I want the life I had before he barged into it and made it pointless.

Fuck him.

Fuck him.

Fuck him.

I used to be fine.

And what am I now?

Unhappy.

That's the word that nicely summarizes everything I am.

I'm unhappy.

And lonely.

And sad.

And pathetic.

And my life? Turns out my life—the life I was so completely fine with—is also sad, and lonely, and pathetic.

And I wouldn't fucking know that if it weren't for him!

I slam the door behind me.

Fuck. Him.

I walk into the living room. In the apartment that's supposed to be my home, albeit temporary, but it's supposed to be my home! The hotel room air has never been stronger. Especially now I've spent so much goddamn time feeling at home with Blake.

In five seconds, I'm out the door again.

Blake snaps his head up, a surprised look on his face.

"Another job?" he asks with a frown.

I don't bother to answer.

"Going out?" he calls after my retreating back.

I turn around and look at his stupid, beautiful face and his stupid, hopeful expression.

He wouldn't have to stand behind my door if he hadn't broken us.

"Yeah," I say. "Clearly you and I didn't work out, so I guess I'll go and see what else is out there."

I storm out my building, down the street, until I stop and realize I have fucking nowhere to go. After a short debate, I call Steph.

This is the worst party I've ever been to. Even getting drunk doesn't help. It's still too loud and too boring, and I'd rather be anywhere else.

"Stop scowling," Steph chides.

"I'm not."

"Please. Even the bartender's avoiding our corner. How exactly are you planning to find a rebound if you look like you're contemplating murder?"

I give him an exaggerated, toothy grin. "Better?"

"Somehow even creepier." He sighs. "Come on. Let me take you home. You know as well as I do you don't really want to be here."

"I do want to be here. I'm not going to let *him* ruin fucking sex for me."

"You're supposed to get over him first, not just jump into bad decisions."

I gape at the extremely unwelcome voice of reason sitting next to me. "That's exactly the opposite of what I'm supposed to do. Jesus Christ, you're not supposed to be the voice of reason here. Do what you do best and convince me to do stupid shit."

"I would if I thought that was what you really wanted." He sighs and rubs his palm over his face. "People make mistakes," he says quietly, barely audible over the noise of the bar.

My jaw clenches. "You don't know anything about this situation."

There's a wholly un-Steph-like seriousness in his eyes as he quirks his brow at me. "Babe, I know all about fucking up."

I'm pissed off and stupid, but at least I have enough brain cells left to flinch at my own idiocy.

I stare at my glass and the remnants of the amber liquid at the bottom.

"Sorry," I mumble.

Steph just shrugs. "Don't worry about it." He empties his own glass and makes a face. "He's still sitting behind your door?"

I nod and try to motion for the bartender, but he ignores me. Figures. My shoulders slump, and I stare moodily at the rows of bottles behind the counter.

"How am I supposed to trust him again after everything?" I ask.

He sends me a contemplative look. "I don't think you can hope for one single moment of clarity where you just suddenly trust him again. It's more that you have to decide whether you're giving him the chance to gain the trust back or not. Forgiving him doesn't mean you'll forget what happened. It's you accepting that it *did* happen and then moving on."

I stare at him before I thump my head against the bar. "I hate it when you make sense."

"Believe me, I'm not enjoying it that much either." He claps me on the back, gets up, and throws some money on the bar. "Come on. Let's get going."

We trudge back to my place. When we round the corner, I stop.

He's still here. Standing now. Leaning against the wall next to my door. And when he hears us coming, his gaze snaps up, and then his eyes narrow at Steph.

I know what he's thinking. I'd be an idiot not to.

I also realize that if I want to really hurt him back, this is the way to do it.

I'd like to say I'm a decent person.

I'd like to say I'm not vindictive.

I'd like to say I'm not cruel.

But I'd be lying.

So, I take Steph's hand and pull him forward.

"Come on," I say.

I unlock the door.

Open it.

Push Steph inside.

Stop in the doorway.

Meet Blake's gaze.

"I'd get out of hearing range if I were you."

And then I close the door in his face and slump against it.

When I look up, I find Steph's eyes on me. For the first time ever, when he looks at me, all I can see is disappointment.

He shakes his head.

"You fucking asshole," he says.

I have no way to disagree.

THIRTY-THREE

Being angry is easy. It's when you run out of anger that you're screwed.

And I have. Run out of anger.

It's back to emptiness.

It's already late morning when I hear something outside my door. I stand in the middle of my living room and strain my ears, trying to detect a sound. A scrape. Anything.

Eventually, with the rattle of my heartbeat as my soundtrack, I slowly walk to my door and open it.

My stomach gives a jolt. I don't know if it's relief or disbelief. Maybe both.

Because he's here again.

We take each other in. Everything I saw on my face when I looked in the mirror this morning is echoed back to me in Blake's. He looks like me. Tired and beaten down and regretful.

He's breaking me, and I'm breaking him.

He's hurting me, and I'm hurting him.

I flop down next to him and stare at the wall.

"You're back."

"I am." He sends me a level look.

"Even after last night?"

His jaw tenses for a moment before he very purposefully relaxes it. The jealous fire in his gaze burns brightly, though.

"You didn't do it," he says flatly.

I sigh and drop my head back, staring at the tired white ceiling.

"What do you think's going to happen if you keep sitting out here?" I finally ask when the silence gets so loud my ears start to hurt.

"I don't know," he says. "I don't know," he repeats, and clutches the back of his neck. "Best-case scenario... You'll give me another chance. You'll let me be in your life. You'll let me cook for you because you're not that great at it, and we need to eat. And you'll move into my place, and we'll make a home. We'll make each other laugh, and we'll build blanket forts together and watch shitty movies in them. You'll let me love you, and you'll love me back."

I let the words wash through me. I let myself imagine and wish and want.

"And the worst-case scenario?" I ask after a little bit.

I can feel his eyes on the side of my face as he considers the question.

"Worst case," he says slowly. "I'll sit out here until I'm old and gray and one day keel over of a heart attack because I've been eating junk food for decades, and my dead body traumatizes all your neighbors, so they'll hate you forever."

A snort escapes, and I rub my palm over my face.

"I'll be moving out soon. This is Blair's friend's apartment. He'll be coming back from his tour and will want his place back."

"Then I'll die in some other hallway, somewhere else in the city," Blake says with a shrug. "And some other neighbors will hate you."

"What if I don't tell you where I'm going?"

"I'm not sure it helps my case, but finding your location is the least of my worries," he says. It sounds like a joke, but I know it's not.

His eyes are on me again.

"Needless to say, I'd prefer the first option," he adds. "Less death."

His hand is next to mine. So close I can feel the heat of his skin. I'd only have to move mine an inch and we'd be touching, but that last inch might as well be an insurmountable chasm.

"I won't hurt you again," Blake says.

"You can't promise that."

"I'm sorry," he says.

"I know," I whisper. And it's startling to realize that I do.

I believe him. I believe he's sorry. I believe he wouldn't lie again. I do.

"If I could do anything, go back in time and do it differently, I would," he says.

"I know," I repeat.

We're both silent for the longest time before I find the words I need to say.

"I'm a coward," I say.

He whips his head toward me. "No, you're not."

"I am. Everything you said? Blanket forts and cooking and love? I want it."

He turns his body toward me, clothes shuffling in the otherwise quiet hallway. "Then take it. You can have it. *We* can have it."

I shake my head and choke out the words. "Can't." I lift up my hand, and it's fucking shaking. "Too afraid." I stare at the wall. "Do you know what the worst part about being happy is?"

He shakes his head.

"When it ends. When you're left with nothing. I've had nothing twice now. I don't think I can do it a third time."

"So you'd rather be alone?" he blurts. I don't think he means to say it. I don't think he means to sound so frustrated with me.

"I'd rather be numb than in pain." I shrug. "Told you I was a coward."

He chews on nothing for a little while, hands still balling into fists and then releasing.

"Well," he finally says, "I won't accept that." He flops back against the wall and crosses his arms over his chest like a petulant child.

"That's not for you to decide," I say tiredly.

"Watch me," he says.

Christ's sake!

"What's the plan, then? You'll just pointlessly sit here and wait for me to change my mind? I won't."

"You will. One day." He sounds so ridiculously confident in himself. In me. That one day I'll get my head out of my ass and stop being afraid.

So what are my options here? Be selfish on top of being a coward? Isn't that a great prospect.

Have him just sit here and wait for the what if? Wait for something that might never come?

"What will make you stop?" I ask.

He closes his eyes and shakes his head. "Don't do this."

"What will make you stop?" I repeat.

I have to wait an eternity for the answer.

"If you ask me to stop," he eventually says.

Another eternity passes.

"Then I'm asking you to stop."

THIRTY-FOUR

I WANTED NUMB, and that's what I got, so I can't really complain.

Ever since Blake got up and walked away, things have gone back to normal.

Just like I wanted.

Weeks and weeks of my new normal without Blake.

Just like I wanted.

I go to work.

I find a new apartment with Steph. In Brooklyn Heights. Apparently he's not planning to go back to LA, so it seems like as good a plan as any. I have a decent size room. We'll move in soon.

I hang out with Blair, Nora, and Hazel.

I go out with Steph. Watch him flirt. Go home alone.

I find a new steady gig at a bar. Add temp jobs to the rotation as I go.

I go see Dad and pretend everything's fine.

Because I am.

I'm fine.

This is what I wanted.

I have a quiet life and no chance of getting hurt.

It's great.

I'm fine.

I'm so fine I don't even blink an eye when I get home and find Sarah waiting behind my door.

She looks nervous standing here in front of me in a pair of loose, dark gray pants and a powder-pink blouse. Her chestnut hair is in a bun at the nape of her neck, a pair of sunglasses is pushed on the top of her head, and her coat is hanging over her arm. She looks like the picture of sophistication and elegance. A stark contrast to my dusty jeans, worn boots, and leather jacket.

She sends me a cautious smile and clutches her coat. "Hello, Jude."

I nod in response.

My name comes out almost naturally.

We stand there for a while before I remember this is my hallway, in front of my apartment.

"Do you want to come in?" I ask.

"If you don't mind?"

I open the door and let her inside. She hangs her coat on the hook and wipes her palms on the sides of her pants. I motion her into the living room.

"It's a nice place," she says as she looks around.

"Thank you," I say. "I'm moving soon."

"Oh?"

"This place belongs to a friend of a friend."

She nods. "Well, I hope the new place is just as nice," she says brightly.

As far as small talk goes, this is not the best. We've had worse, though.

The silence that follows now that we've covered my living

arrangements is much more awkward, but I have no idea what to say, so I just wait.

Sarah goes to the window and glances outside. Then slowly walks around the apartment, taking it all in.

"Would you like something to drink?" I ask before I remember I don't have much of anything to offer since I've put off going grocery shopping for a week now.

"Water would be nice," she says.

I take a glass and fill it. When I turn around, she's studying the photos on the shelf.

"Here you go," I say. Louder than I was planning. She snaps her head toward me, a guilty look on her face, and comes to the kitchen table. She sits and takes a sip. I sit down as well.

"I don't come to New York that often," Sarah says.

I go full-on asshole with my, "Oh? How come?"

I'm not sure if she winces or if I'm imagining it.

"Not a lot of good memories," she says. "I made my worst mistakes here."

What am I supposed to say to that? I'm sorry? Yes, you did?

She clears her throat. "It's a bit of a clichéd story. I never really got along with my parents," she says and looks at me. "They were always more interested in their respective careers than in me. So I looked for love elsewhere. Tried to find somewhere I belonged. Needless to say, the crowd I picked for myself wasn't the best. We were all the same. Upper middle-class upbringing. Kids with too much money and too little common sense. We partied a lot. Made a lot of bad decisions. And then you happened. And I thought... I was elated. Excited. You were going to be that one person who was completely mine. Unconditionally mine. My own little family. We were going to be perfect." She looks down at her hands. "I had a lot of good intentions, but none of the strength to see them through."

Her eyes move back to the photos. I have a feeling she isn't really seeing them anymore, though.

"My parents rented me an apartment and gave me an allowance, but otherwise they washed their hands of me. Of us." She stares at the wall, unseeing, transported back in time. "My grandmother used to say that when a parent loves their child, it's unconditional. It'll always be there, no matter the mistakes the child makes or the trouble they get into, you'll still love them." She toys with the edge of her water glass, a manicured nail circling the rim absently. "But it's different for the child. Take a child's love for granted and abuse it long enough, and it'll run out." She lifts her gaze and faces me. "I wasn't a good mother."

I can't agree or disagree.

Because I don't remember.

It's probably a good thing I don't.

"I wish I could say I would've gotten sober and made a good life for you, but the truth is, I don't know if I would've." She glances at the photos yet again. The long-ago life in San Diego. "Maybe you were always meant to be theirs."

"Is that supposed to make it all okay?" I ask.

She shakes her head. "I'm not making excuses."

"Why are you here then?"

"To see if you're okay. I'm leaving tomorrow morning, so it was now or... I don't want to say never, but I suppose it's now or God-knows-when." She quirks her brow at me. "I don't suppose you were planning to visit?"

"You didn't trust what Blake had to say?" The words should sound bitter, but they come out pretty tonelessly.

She sends me a confused frown. "I... Well, certainly, but he wasn't exactly a well of information."

It's my turn to frown. "What do you mean?"

"I mean... Well, it's not as if he told me much of anything about you. Just that you were living in New York, and he found me your address, phone number, and email. But that was months ago."

I blink and try to process what she's saying.

"You never contacted me," I say to buy myself some time before I have to really think about what I just learned.

"No," she says. "I messed up the first time so badly I just kept putting it off, telling myself I'd think of the perfect thing to say, but that perfect thing never came to me *today*, so I always needed just a bit more time."

"Then why did he look me up if you didn't ask him to?"

Sarah considers me for a bit. "How much did Blake tell you about his past?"

I blink at the question.

"Uh, that he was abandoned by his mother. Brought up in foster care. Then he got into trouble for hacking. Juvie. He tried to steal your car."

She nods, and for some reason she's now looking at me with a wholly different kind of curiosity. "He actually told you all of that?"

I roll my eyes. "No, I made it up just now."

Her lips twitch, but then she turns serious again. "I don't know if he's ever told anybody about any of it."

"You seem to know," I point out.

"I know because I read his file. Otherwise he'd be a complete mystery." She sends me another long, level look. "It's not an easy thing. To be abandoned. Never really wanted by anybody. To know your parents didn't want you. And then foster care... There are wonderful families who make a huge difference, but there's always the side that's not so pretty. Blake got to experience his fair share of the not-so-pretty. Getting through that... It makes one a survivor. Do you know what characterizes all survivors, Jude?"

I shake my head.

"They put themselves first," she says. "They put themselves first because they have to. Do that long enough, it becomes a habit."

"That's not Blake," I argue.

"That's the Blake I know," she counters and raises her hands at whatever she sees on my face. "I'm not saying he's a bad person. Quite the opposite, actually. But for as long as I've known him, when push comes to shove, he puts his own interests first." She gives me a long, level look. "Not so much when it comes to you, it seems."

I narrow my eyes at her. "I don't understand what you're doing. Are you warning me to stay away or..."

She laughs and shakes her head. "God, no. I lost the right to do anything when it comes to you a long time ago. I'm not saying it right. Blake's loyal to himself before anyone. Or at least he used to be. Seems things have changed a bit there." She takes her glass and finishes her water, then nods. "Well, I came here to see if you're okay, and I suppose I've done that." She sends me another smile and a look that's a mix of melancholy and longing. "It was good to see you," she says quietly.

She goes to the hallway, and I sit and stare at her water glass. When the door closes behind her, I jump up and hurry to the front door. I pull it open and call out, "Sarah?"

She turns around on the landing, surprise coloring her features.

"We should do this again," I say. "If you're ever in New York. Or maybe if I happen to find myself in Seattle. We can do lunch, maybe?"

She nods and sends me a tentative smile. "I'd... I'd like that. David has business here from time to time. Maybe I'll tag along the next time he comes here."

I nod too. "Well... you know my number."

She smiles once more before she turns to leave.
I go back inside.
Close the door.
And now I don't have any idea what to do with myself anymore.

THIRTY-FIVE

I tap my fingers against the tabletop as I wait. The guard by the door keeps sending me annoyed looks, but I can't seem to stop, even with his death glare aimed at my head every few seconds.

I only stop when they escort Dad in. He looks at me with a quizzical expression on his face. It's not our usual meeting day, and he's trying to gauge if something's wrong. Figure out why I'm here.

"Hey, kiddo," he says. He hasn't called me that in ages. I don't know what it is he sees on my face that makes him call me that now.

"Hey, Dad," I say.

Strong arms wrap around me and let me go, and we take our seats.

He waits while I try to figure out what I want to say. He's always been good at that.

In the end I go with the one thing I've never had the guts to ask him.

"Do you regret it?"

He doesn't look stumped. More like he's been waiting for that question for years now.

"I assume by 'it' you mean you? Do I regret you?"

I nod.

"No," he says. Simple as that. No hesitation.

"You're in prison," I point out.

He just shrugs. "I always knew there was a chance this is where I'd end up. I made my peace with it a long time ago. Did I hope it wouldn't happen? Of course. I'm human. We do bad things and hope we won't get caught. It's in our nature."

"You got caught because of me," I say.

He shakes his head and reaches forward. Grabs my hand and covers it with his palm. "No. Abby and I got caught because of what we did. You have absolutely no part in this."

"Hands!" the guard yells, and Dad backs away. He leans back and tilts his head to the side.

"You don't look so good," he says.

"I'm—"

"Yes, yes, you're fine," he says. "You were fine the last time you were here too, and you looked even worse then."

"I..." I lean my elbows on the table and my head falls forward until I'm hiding my face in my hands. And then I tell him.

About Blake.

About how he lied.

About how I don't know how to trust people.

About how lonely I am.

About how screwed up I feel.

About Blake.

About how I miss him.

About how I don't know what to do anymore.

Once I'm done, there's a long, long silence on Dad's end. Until I finally look up and face him. He looks very contemplative before he sighs.

"Well, that was certainly a lot."

I give a miserable nod.

"You know, Abby once broke up with me," he says then.

I gape at him. I did not see that one coming.

He gets that faraway look in his eyes that appears every time he thinks or talks about Mom. "We'd just found out we couldn't have kids."

"I always wondered why you guys never had more than me."

"Yes, well. It was a difficult thing to cope with. We went through a real rough patch, and somehow ended up at a point where in her mind, she loved me so much she dumped me, because then I could have kids with someone else."

"That... doesn't sound like the best logic," I say.

"Sometimes people say and do things that don't seem like the best choices. It's easy to get on your high horse when you've never been in their shoes. Life's messy. People are messy."

"But you made up."

"We did. I was always happier with her than without her, so I took a risk, and it paid off," he says and fixes his gaze at me. "You've never had much of a choice in any of the pivotal moments of your life. Here you have one."

"What if I don't want it? You choose for me." I'm only half-joking.

"Son, I love you, but your love life is entirely your business."

I slump back in my chair and let out a deep sigh.

"Some parent you are."

He laughs before he smiles, and that smile holds all the love in the world. A love I wouldn't have in my life if I'd decided to be stubborn and had stayed away and not forgiven him.

"For what it's worth," Dad says, "whatever you choose to do —with this, or in life in general—I will always have your back." He smiles at me. "It'll get better. One way or another."

THIRTY-SIX

Things only get more confusing.

I drag my ass home a few days later and find an envelope taped to my door. I stare at it for a bit.

"That nice boy brought it over earlier."

I jump and whip my head around at my neighbor's voice. Mrs. Connolly is standing in her doorway and looking at me with the excited expression of a person who's finally been included in something interesting.

"A nice boy?" I ask.

"The one who's always waiting behind your door for you. You should really give him a key. Such a nice young man. So polite."

"Uh-huh," I say and pull the envelope off.

"I kept my eye on that. So nobody would mess with it," Mrs. Connolly says with a firm nod. "Youth these days. You never know."

"Yeah, the world's all ruined," I say distractedly, turning the envelope over in my hands. There's nothing written on it anywhere.

"I worry about this generation." Mrs. Connolly is on a roll

now, and since youth is ruined anyway, I don't think she minds that I'm giving her more to complain about when I go inside my apartment in the middle of her rant and shut the door on her.

I spend a good twenty minutes having a stare-off with the envelope at my kitchen table before I give up and tear the envelope open.

It's an address. Just three lines. Not far from here. I can make it in fifteen minutes.

But do I want to make it?

Yeah, who am I kidding? There's no way my curiosity will let me sit this one out, so I get up with a sigh, grab my stuff, and head out.

I end up in front of a completely nondescript building. I look at the people milling around in the afternoon sunshine, bundled up in coats and hats. Since staring at the door doesn't seem to give me any answers, I eventually get my ass in gear and go inside. There, at the reception desk, is an older gentleman who greets me with a friendly smile. He's wearing suspenders over a checkered shirt and looks pretty much how I'd imagine a grandfather looks.

"Welcome, welcome," he says. "How may I help you on this fine day?"

I look down at the paper with the address and then at the man. "I was given this address?" I say uncertainly. "I mean, I think this is the right place."

He motions for the paper, and I slide it over.

"Ah," he says. "You must be Jude."

"Yes?" I say.

"Roy," he says. "Pleased to meet you. You and I are gonna be seeing a lot of each other."

I... don't know what to say to that, so I just nod.

Roy takes a pen and writes a few numbers underneath the address on the paper I handed to him a moment ago, then he slides it over again.

"Room 216. There's an electronic keypad. Just use the code. I'll be here if you run into any problems."

I take the paper and read the numbers before I look at Roy. "Thank you?"

He nods and smiles, and since I still have no clue what's going on, I turn around and head down the hallway he's pointing out to me.

At the end of the corridor, I find room 216 and put in the code. The door opens with a quiet beep.

I push it open and go inside.

It's a small room. One window in the back wall with a view of some type of courtyard. Black ceiling with spotlights in it.

And another fucking piano in the middle of the room.

My feet carry me forward until I'm sitting on the bench and staring at another envelope.

I debate opening it before my cowardly side strikes again. So I do the less intimidating thing first.

I play.

It's easy once I start.

Less scary than I built it up to be in my head.

And once I'm done, I open the envelope.

Jude,

I told you once you've given me two firsts. Well, I was lying even back then. See, there are a few more I failed to mention. I'm going to fix that now.

I have never been caught off guard. Until you.

I have never been selfless. Until you.

I have never met an unforgettable person. Until you.
I have never seen a smile stop the world. Until you.
I have never wanted to belong with anybody. Until you.
I have never wanted a home. Until you.
I have never wanted forever. Until you.
I have never had my heart so shamelessly stolen. Until you.
I have never understood what people mean when they say it's better to have loved and lost.

Until you.

Because it's been worth it. Because I get to love you. And maybe it won't be blanket forts and home and growing old together for us. Maybe that's not the road ahead for you and me. But the highs have been well fucking worth the lowest of lows. At least for me.

Since you're reading this love letter—also my first, by the way —I assume you've found the piano. It's yours. And so is the room. For as long as you want it. And I hope you want it for a long, long time. Because you're talented, and someone who gets as much joy out of playing as you do should have a piano and a place to play it. Plus, you're fucking hot when you play.

I guess that's it. You asked me to stop, and I obviously didn't, but I promise, I will now.

I stare at Blake's words for the longest time.
 A love letter.
 My first.
 My only.
 It holds all the promises between the lines.
 Love and home and forever.
 All mine for the taking.
 If I'm brave enough.

THIRTY-SEVEN

The lock rattles and the key turns.

Footsteps sound in the hallway.

A thump and a shuffle.

Something rustles.

My heartbeat thunders in my ears, louder and louder with each passing second.

And then he's here.

He doesn't see me at first. His head is down, looking at something in the paper bag he's carrying.

I open my mouth, but no sound comes out.

He puts the bag on the counter.

I clear my throat.

"Shit!" Blake whirls around and somehow swipes at the bag so it smashes to the floor.

His eyes widen when they land on me, and he stills.

"Hi," I say.

He seems lost for words for a moment.

"I realized I never gave you back your key," I say.

His tongue peeks out as he licks his lips.

"So you figured you'd hand deliver it?" he asks.

"More like, I had a key, so I didn't have to pick the lock. It's very convenient."

"It's a good thing you have it then."

I take a step closer.

"I got your note. The one with the address."

He eyes me carefully. "I was worried somebody would steal it."

"I have nosy neighbors, so they kept an eye on it."

"Good," he says.

Another step closer.

"I also got the letter."

He swallows.

There's twenty feet between us.

"That was a lot of firsts."

Ten feet.

He nods, seemingly unable to make words.

Five feet.

"You realized you've kind of screwed yourself, right?"

Three feet.

"Oh?" he breathes out.

Two feet.

"You're supposed to start with small gifts so you have something to work up to."

One foot.

"Now, if you happen to fuck up, what're you gonna do? Get me a fucking helicopter?"

"Lucky for me, hacking pays pretty well," he says.

"Helicopter-well?"

He snorts and shakes his head. "I don't plan to fuck up that badly anytime in the near future, so I figure I can start saving now for the helicopter fund. Just in case."

"Smart," I say.

I erase that last foot. Now there's nothing between us.

Only lips on lips and bodies pressed together as close as humanly possible. Blake hides his face in my neck and clutches me so tightly I can barely breathe, but I don't mind.

How can I? I'm finally home.

And then Blake's kissing me again, and we end up on the floor, him underneath me, his back against the couch, me on top of him, straddling his lap. His lips never leave mine.

The two of us, we shouldn't work this perfectly.

We started with a lie, but somehow, we never ended. Even if I asked him to stop, we never truly did.

I cup Blake's cheek and kiss him. Kiss him until I can't breathe or think and can only feel. The rightness of us. No matter what.

Somewhere between the kisses, we stumble to the bed and lose the clothes, and then it's truly just us. Bodies moving and hearts beating. Blake's hands in my hair, pulling and tugging. His lips on my chest and my solar plexus and my abdomen and my right thigh. His voice in my ear telling me words I never knew I needed to hear. All variations of "love" and "beautiful" and "forever," and I take them and echo them right back.

His fingers lace with mine, and he's inside me, forehead against mine, breath whispering over my lips.

I let myself be carried away into that inconceivable closeness I've only ever shared with him.

Afterward, we lie on the bed, my head on his chest, my thigh thrown over his, sticky and tired and calm. Blake's fingers are combing through my hair, an occasional kiss landing anywhere he can reach.

"Thank you," he says softly.

"For sex?" I mumble into his chest. "Impeccable manners as always."

He laughs and pinches my side until I squirm and lift my head to glare at him.

"Do you mind? I'm trying to bask in the afterglow here."

"Thank you for coming back. For giving me another chance."

I put my arms on his chest, rest my chin on them, and look at him. "You know how it's always considered super romantic when people are all, 'I can't live without you!'"

Blake's lips twitch, and he nods. "I have a feeling you have thoughts."

"Naturally. Really, which part of that is supposed to be romantic? Saying 'I can't live without you' is pretty much equivalent to saying 'I'm with you because I don't have any other choice.' And that's fucking stupid. And we're not gonna do that. I *can* live without you. I just choose not to. And I'm terrified as fuck, still, by the way. But... I also love you more than I'm afraid."

Blake sends me one of those wide smiles that is so quintessentially him.

"That's the most romantic thing anybody's ever said to me."

"I have a way with words."

"That you do." He gently pulls at my earlobe. "And I love you too."

"I know," I say, because whatever else I'm uncertain about, this is the one thing I know.

"I'm scared, too. You know that, right?" Blake asks.

"We'll figure it out."

And with Blake that's all I need.

I don't want big promises or even bigger vows.

I want the journey.

With him.

Together.

And when he wraps himself around me and hugs me tightly, it feels like my heart is going to burst.

I've never felt like this before.

Until him.

BLAKE

10 years later

The sunrise is still a good fifteen minutes away, but the sky already has streaks of gold in it. The last of the morning fog is coiling around the pilings of the fishing pier, clinging to dear life while fighting an already lost battle with the day. The waves crash and a soft breeze moves through my hair and swipes over my bare forearms.

The air in my lungs is ocean and salt, and my bare toes dig into the soft sand.

I smile when I hear the glass door behind me slide open. Bare feet pad across the deck, and then the love of my life wraps himself around me from behind.

"Shit, it's cold," Jude grumbles as he loops his arms around my chest and maneuvers his legs over mine. He puts his chin on my shoulder and gives a small, contented sigh as he slumps against me.

"You're up early," he mutters into the side of my neck.

I turn my head and quirk my brow at him.

"I'm up early because *you're* up early," he says. "You insist we sleep with the window open, so our bedroom turns into the North Pole."

"We're in North Carolina, and it's July," I point out.

"And then you have the audacity to sneak out of the bed and leave me freezing," he continues like I haven't even spoken.

"It's just me here, so you're allowed to admit you missed me," I say.

He hums and kisses my neck. "I feel like I should file a complaint. When you first forced me to like you, I wasn't that worried. I figured the feelings would cool down eventually, I'd start hating the way you chew or breathe, and everything would go back to normal. But it's only getting worse."

"You poor thing." I laugh and wrap my arms around his where they're hugging me from behind.

"Happy birthday, love," he murmurs, and kisses my neck again.

I close my eyes and smile. Every time he does that, calls me love, my stomach jolts. Even now, all these years later. It's the same jolt I got when I first saw him on that roof, all windswept hair and guarded looks disguised with jokes and flirting. He was impossible not to fall for.

The sun peeks out from below the horizon and paints everything golden.

"Beautiful," Jude murmurs, and I nod.

Jude has taught me to appreciate the little things in life. Those small moments in time that leave you feeling completely alive. Sunrises and thunderstorms. Stargazing and roaming around the city streets with no real purpose. I didn't know those were things to appreciate before. Not until Jude. He showed me how.

"Can't believe we have to go back home tomorrow," he says through a yawn.

"We can always come back."

"Yeah," he says. "Guess it's time to get back to real life anyway. Dad asked if we wanted to come to dinner on Friday."

Grant had been released from prison eight years ago. The first few years had been tough. It was quite a wake-up call to see how little anybody cares about helping people integrate back into society. Grant had Jude and me, and it still wasn't easy with all the setbacks and preconceived notions people had about him. I don't have any idea how people do it without a support network.

Jude and I moved into our own apartment a few years ago, so Grant is living in my old place now, and he seems at peace. Happy, even. At least when Jude is around.

"Sure," I say belatedly. "Dinner sounds great." I hesitate, but while we're already on the topic... "Sarah's coming to town in August."

Jude nods. "Okay." There's no real emotion in his tone. Things with Sarah are and will always be tense for Jude. It's just how it is, and I've learned to accept it. I've never been able to figure out exactly why, but the two of them? They don't really click. Oh, they're both polite. Painfully so. But Jude rarely volunteers things about his life to her. She calls from time to time to catch up, but those conversations remain surface level. Snippets about the hospital where Jude works as a music therapist. Snippets about whatever Jude and I are up to. Snippets about Blair, Nora, Steph, Hazel, and her little brother, Nicky. There are very few details and very little depth to those conversations.

Sarah will always remain an outsider in Jude's life. She's there, somewhere on the periphery, but never fully invited in. I suppose sometimes there's just too much water under the bridge.

"I got you a present," Jude says, and presses his cheek against mine.

BLAKE

"I should hope so," I say. "Seeing as it's my birthday."

That makes him chuckle. "I've never seen a person who gets so excited about birthday presents. And I have no idea why. My presents suck."

"No, they don't."

"Seriously? I can't think of one decent gift I've given you so far. In a decade."

"There've been plenty of good ones," I say loyally.

"Yeah, which ones, exactly, were the good ones?"

"The sexy coupons with dirty stuff you were going to do to me."

"You didn't use a single one of those," he protests.

"I would've, but you did all those dirty things to me for free. Next time play hard to get, and I'll whip them out in a snap."

"One failed, somewhat decent, although embarrassingly cheesy, gift in a decade," he amends. "Go me."

"There was also the happy ending massage parlor role play."

"You had an allergic reaction to the oil I was using!"

"It's the thought that counts. Besides, I had a lot of fun at the ER listening to you try to explain to the nurse how my dick turned that color."

"Fuck off." He groans and hides his face in my neck.

"I love your gifts," I say. "So come on. Show me what you got me."

"No. I'm now thinking this one might be my worst present yet, so you know what? We'll forget it and... I'll extend the validity of the sexy coupons, *and* I'll be less slutty this time, so you'll actually get to use them. Happy birthday! And no sex for you tonight, mister. Unless you come at me with a coupon."

This definitely has me curious now. I extricate myself from Jude's arms and turn around so I'm facing him.

"What did you get me?"

"I just told you, didn't I? Coupons," he says stubbornly, avoiding my gaze.

I hold out my hand toward him, palm up, and crook my finger. "Lay it on me."

He glowers at me for a little while, but eventually, after muttering under his breath, he pulls something out of his pocket and puts it in my palm. That something turns out to be a small wooden box.

My eyes dart back to Jude.

"This looks suspiciously like a—" I start.

"I'm not proposing," Jude says loudly before he rubs his palm over his face. "See, I told you I'm terrible at it."

"Can I open it?" I ask.

"Might as well," Jude mutters.

I flick the lid of the box open. Inside, there's a ring.

I glance up at Jude. "Are you a hundred percent sure you're not proposing?"

He winces and nods.

"Then you have to explain the ring with a few more words."

"I'd rather not because it makes me sound like an asshole."

"Lucky for you, I love you even if you *are* an asshole."

"You sweet talker, you." He sighs. "Fine. I don't care about marriage. Like... at all. And, correct me if I've completely misunderstood you over the last ten years, but you don't give a crap about getting married either."

"I mean, I'd do it if that was what you wanted," I say.

"Right. Well, I don't."

"Then what's with the ring?"

"It'll remind you of me when I'm not around?" he says, not looking that sure himself.

"Uh-huh. Why do you think I need the reminder all of a sudden?"

BLAKE

He chews on it for the longest time before he says, "It'll also remind other assholes that you're taken."

"Other assholes?" I ask.

He mutters something that sounds like *Ethan*.

I stare at him in total confusion. "Ethan?"

Do I know an Ethan? Because I can't—

"Nora's assistant, Ethan?" I ask, even more confused now.

"Fucking Ethan," Jude mutters. "It's not even specifically about Ethan. It's all those other idiots, too."

"I'm sure somewhere there's a logical explanation, but I'm just not seeing it."

"He wants into your pants," Jude grumbles.

"I'm pretty sure he doesn't."

"Oh, please," he scoffs, and then his voice goes weirdly breathy, and he widens his eyes until he looks like he's a Disney character. *"Oh, Mr. McAdams, you're so brilliant. I didn't even realize the reason my laptop wasn't working was because the battery was empty. How can I ever thank you? Maybe a drink after work? Or I can blow you in the bathroom?"* He glowers at me. "Sound familiar?"

"Not even a little bit. Are you... are you jealous?" I ask, and I can't hide my smile any longer, which only earns me a thoroughly disgusted look.

"No," he says before he shakes his head, takes out the ring and holds it out to me. "Just put on the damn ring. And next time you stop by Nora's office, don't wear gloves."

Instead of taking the ring he's still holding out to me, I grab the back of his neck and pull him forward until he's in my lap and I'm kissing him.

When I'm done with him and pull away, he looks deliciously disheveled.

"So this ring is just a really fancy way of pissing on me," I conclude with a grin.

"No," he says indignantly. "It's a nice present."

"You're totally marking your territory."

"I'm appreciating you on your birthday."

"Want me to tattoo 'Jude's Property' on my ass?" I ask.

"This isn't—" He tilts his head to the side. "Actually, would you?"

"I'm warming up to the idea." I kiss him again. "You know you've got nothing to worry about, right? You're the only person I've ever loved. It's not going to change. Ever."

His eyes soften, and his forehead falls against mine. "It's not about you. I know you. I trust you. I just want to punch everyone who flirts with you in the face, and I'm afraid one day I'm actually going to do it. This ring will weed out the decent people who'll honor the sanctity of our fake marriage, so if I do end up punching somebody, I won't have to feel bad because they're a shitty human being to begin with."

I laugh and take his hand in mine. I gently unwrap his fingers from where he's rolled them into a fist around the ring.

"Well, in that case, put a ring on it."

"You don't have to," he says with a sigh. "It's stupid."

"No. It's actually hot as fuck."

He throws me a skeptical look. "Which part?"

"The one where you want to make your ownership clear to everybody."

He presses another hard kiss to my mouth. "Shut up."

"Jealousy also looks hot on you."

He rolls his eyes. "You think everything looks hot on me."

"I know. I'm a gentleman of great taste. Can I get you a ring, too?"

He scrunches his nose and makes a face. "I mean, I appreciate the gesture, but I happen to like when people hit on me." I snort out a laugh, and he smiles and nods. "Yeah, go ahead. Buy me a ring if you want to. Brand me like cattle."

BLAKE

"You're so romantic," I say with a mock-exasperated sigh.

His gaze turns serious, and he studies me for a few seconds. "Does it ever bother you?"

"Does what ever bother me?"

"That I'm not romantic."

I tilt my head curiously. "Where's this coming from?"

He shrugs. "I don't know. The other day at work when I was finishing up, one of the nurses was serenaded and there were a lot of flowers and chocolate hearts and everything involved. And the other nurses were all, 'they've been together for fifteen years, and he still does things like this for her.'"

"Good for them. Sounds like my personal nightmare."

He sends me a tentative grin. "Right?"

I twine my fingers through his hair and tug him forward. "I don't want that. That's their love. Their version. I want yours. I want you to love me just the way you love me. Just make it forever. That's all I need."

His smile widens. "Done."

Simple as that.

Because that's how life is with Jude. Simple and happy. Everything I never knew I wanted. Until Jude.

And I get to have him.

Forever.

ALSO BY BRIAR PRESCOTT

Standalones
Project Hero
Rare
Inevitable
Better With You series
The Happy List
The Dating Experiment
The Underdog
The Inconvenient Love

ACKNOWLEDGMENTS

I would like to thank all my alpha readers. As stated before, without you, this book would still only have two chapters.

Thank you, Kate and Heather for helping me fool people into believing I can write English.

And last but not least, thank you to all the ARC readers, bloggers, bookfluencers, and readers for taking a chance on this book. Without you, writing would be pointless.

ABOUT THE AUTHOR

Briar Prescott is a work in progress. She swears too much, doesn't eat enough leafy greens and binge watches too much television. It's okay, though. One of these days she'll get a hang of that adulting thing.
    Probably.
    Maybe.
    She hopes.
    Want to check in occasionally to hear what's up? Sign up to her newsletter.

Printed in Great Britain
by Amazon